SAGA INTO
THE TWENTIETH
CENTURY

0973-HAEG

SAGA INTO THE TWENTIETH CENTURY

Louise Haeger

Louise Haeger

To order additional copies of this book, contact:
Xlibris Corporation
1-888-7-XLIBRIS
www.Xlibris.com
Orders@Xlibris.com

Contents

To my children, grandchildren,
great grandchildren and great great grandchildren.
To Steve who kept the computer running
and Asenath who taught me.
To my devoted husband, Ray,
whose love and support
has carried me through the century.

0973-HAEG

1

Chuck and Anna

The night air was crisp and clear. The smell of dust and clean night air mingled with the smell of the horses made him think of the fields. He could hear the clip clop of the horses' hooves on the road. It made another kind of music in his head and gradually transformed his thinking from farmer to musician.

As he rode he thought of his two little daughters, Clare and Onna, who were staying with his brother Fritz and his wife Helga, a short, stout-built women with a loving nature. Chuck knew his little girls would have lots of liebe (love) from this aunt. He had lost their mother at the birth of their youngest daughter Onna, a tiny little girl with a sweet little laugh. No doubt she would be delicate like her mother he thought. By the time he arrived at the hall, he was mentally ready to play.

Chuck loved to play the violin, especially the one he had made. The violin had taken a year to make, cutting and fitting each piece was a labor of love. He played at all the area dances. This was the one highlight of his busy life as a farmer. Chuck found it strange that he could hear the music. He was born hearing impaired, making conversation difficult to understand. The music from his violin thrilled the people and he was in high demand.

Tying the horses to the hitching post, he went into the big barn, and climbed the wide steps to the hay loft where the dance was held. Across the floor he noticed a handsome, strapping young German boy. "Ha'lau," Chuck called to the boy who was dressed in long sleeved,bright red plaid flannel shirt

and bib overhauls. His blonde hair was slicked back, giving
him a pleasant, friendly appearance.

"Are you here with your parents?" Chuck asked.

"Naw," said the young man, "My schwester (sister) is here
with me. I came because she likes the m"alisch (music) and there
was no one to be with her."

Just then the band began to warm up and Chuck had to ex-
cuse himself. "I had better get up there," he said with a nod of his
head toward the bandstand. As Chuck and the rest of the musicians began to play, he noticed a beautiful, robust young woman
sitting beside the boy. Her dark hair, pulled back in a ribbon,was
further flattered by the high bodice and handmade lace collar of
her soft light brown dress. As they played, he noticed that she
appeared to enjoy the music and did not get up to dance with any
of the young men who stopped to converse with her.

Chuck could hardly wait for their first break. He was afraid
they would leave before he could meet the sister. Finally, the break
came. As he approached their table, the young man stood up. "I
don't believe you gave me your name," He said with a shy smile. "I
would like to introduce you to my schwester."

"Oh, ah, ah." Chuck stuttered in his excitement. "It's
Falhaugen. Chuck Falhaugen."

Just then the girl stood, "This is Anna, my schwester, and my
name is Paul." Anna looked up into Chuck's face. Her brown eyes
sparkling and a beguiling smile on her mouth. Chuck's mouth
went dry and his hands began to perspire. He could feel his heart
beat a little faster and a warmth spread from his neck to his ears.

"I am so pleased to meet you." Chuck responded warmly.
"Would you care to sit by me for our lunch break."

"I would love to," replied Anna as she extended her hand.
Chuck thought that she had a strong hand that seemed use to
hard work and no pampering.

During the lunch break, Anna learned about Chuck's daughters and the wife he had lost. Anna told Chuck about her brothers
and that she had no schwesters.

"I have a few acres about a mile from here." Chuck explained. "I could use a little help. Perhaps your brother here would like to come and give me a hand." he said with a nod in Paul's direction.

"Ja," Paul responded excitedly.

"Do you have a horse?" Chuck asked as he took a bite of cookie.

"Ja," Paul said.

"Just where do you live from here," questioned Chuck?

"About ein meile Norden," explained Paul pointing in the direction they lived.

"Well that won't be too far to travel," Chuck decided aloud as he got up from the table and nodded a good-bye toward Anna.

Going back up to the band platform with a satisfied smile on his face, Chuck picked up his violin. He played better that he had in a long time. Chuck had had little enthusiasm for anything since his wife died. Anna seemed to have given him a lift in his spirit.

After the dance was over, Chuck hurried down to give Paul the directions to his farm. Paul was out of his chair and heading towards him as well, his sister right behind. "Anna, would you like to come along with your brother. I have a big house, and you could prepare us lunch if you like." Chuck cajoled looking from Anna to Paul and then back to Anna.

Anna, looking at him with secret interest, agreed to come.

"It is simple to find your way to my place. Just follow the stand of trees along the river. When you see a break in the trees, that is my place." directed Chuck.

"That seems easy enough," Paul said shyly smoothing his hand back through his hair in a nervous gesture.

"Okay then, shall we say Monday," Chuck suggested reaching out to shake his hand.

"That will be gutt (good)," Paul replied returning the handshake.

Early Monday morning as Chuck was standing in his window drinking a cup of coffee and meditating about the weekend, he saw two riders coming up the draw. He could see the dust trail clouding behind them. Setting his cup down and walking out on the porch, he watched Anna and Paul get down from their horses. Chuck went out to meet them taking Anna by the arm and leading her into the house, while Paul tied the two horses at the hitching post by the barn before following them inside. "How about a cup of coffee." Chuck coaxed as he reached for the pot and began pouring not waiting for Anna's reply.

As they sat down, Chuck began to explain his plan for the day, "Paul and I will be out mending fences. You won't need to do much for lunch. There are summer sausages in the root cellar below the basement. Please feel free to look around and use whatever you find."

After their coffee and a quick tour of the house, Chuck and Paul went out in the field. Coming in from the fencing project several hours later, the men could smell a wonderful aroma. They stopped to wash in the basin on the stand just outside the kitchen. Anna had baked fresh bread and made stew and dumplings from the canned meat she found in the root cellar.

"Whoa!" exclaimed Chuck with a hearty laugh. "I didn't expect you to do all this much." He looked around the kitchen and noticed a women's touch. He was a tidy house keeper himself, but she had added a sprig of this and a touch of that to bring a new fresh smell to the house.

"I had plenty of time," Anna chuckled with a shrug of her shoulders. "It will give you enough extra for another meal." They sat enjoying the meal and each other's company for a long time. Finally, Paul pushed back his chair reminding Anna that they should be going.

As they prepared to leave, Chuck asked them if they would ride in the buggy with him to the next dance.

"That would be very nice," Anna responded for both of them. "It sure is better than riding in the saddle."

Chuck returned to the house whistling as Paul and Anna rode off toward home. He sat at the kitchen table mulling over all that had taken place since the dance last week. This young girl was causing him to have sleepless nights. He wanted her to become someone special in his life. For such a short time of knowing Anna, he thought as he began cleaning up the few things left from dinner, she had a way of causing his heart to race at the sight of her. I think perhaps this Anna could fill the void in my life. She has a beautiful smile and a soft voice like music to my ears. Strange, he mused, how I can even hear her speak.

During the next few months, several dances had been attended and Chuck had taken Anna to church a few times. They were beginning to develop a serious relationship. During the lunch break at the next dance they attended, Chuck asked Anna to step outside with him for a bit. "Anna," he began shyly smoothing the hair back from his forehead. "We have spent a lot of time together the past few months, and I have grown very fond of you. Do you think . . . , I mean, well, what I want to say is . . . , That is ah . . . would you consider being my wife?" Chuck asked hesitantly. Then putting his hand up to silence any possible protest, "I know you are a bit younger that I am, but six years is not all that much. I am only thirty-one." He looked at her gently. "However," he said with a tender note, "There might be one problem. I'm not sure how you would feel about becoming an immediate mother. You see I would want to bring my girls home to live with us."

Anna reached up and touched his cheek. "I would be honored to be your wife," she sighed softly. "And I can't think of anything more wonderful than being a mother to your little girls."

"Great," he said with an audible sigh, "We can set the date later," Chuck finished breathlessly. As they returned to the dance, Chuck went up to the band members and asked them to play a waltz.

He took Anna in his arms, waltzing her among the other young women. The other girls, dressed in their frilly long gowns with their full skirts flaring, whispered excitedly as they watched the couple dancing. Chuck couldn't resist comparing the girls in their frilly dresses and giggling immaturity. In his mind, he thought how much more beautiful Anna was in her plain brown dress, her hair tied back in a ribbon. She had a smile that radiated her kind gentle spirit. Chuck felt his heart race when he thought of the depth of character Anna showed. He knew that his two daughters would be in good hands. When the music ended, Chuck took her back to her chair and smiled shyly before returning to the band and his violin.

Chuck took Paul and Anna home after the dance. Paul excused himself and went inside as Chuck took Anna by both hands. Looking into her eyes, he said, "Anna, I would like to ride over tomorrow and discuss further what we talked about tonight."

She smiled and nodded a yes, not trusting her voice.

Slowly he turned to go. Then waving, he mounted the wagon and rode away whistling loudly.

Saturday morning, Chuck rose early, finishing his chores in record time. He headed for Anna's, arriving just as the milking was finished. As Chuck dismounted and led the horse to the barn, Paul was coming out of the barn. "Here, let me help you," he said taking the horse and settling him to eat in the barn. Then they went into the house.

"Kam in. Kam in," welcomed Anna's mother. "Sit and have a cup of coffee and some Kuchen. Anna has just taken it from the oven."

"Thank you. I will," Chuck said dipping his head toward Anna's mother in respect.

Anna's father, coming in from outside, dusted the dirt from his pants, washed his hands in the wash bowl that stood by the door, and poured himself a cup of coffee. Then he sat down at the table with Chuck, Anna, and her mother. "Du mude werden heiraten," questioned her father?

"That's right," responded Chuck mentally translating Anna's father's question. "That is if she will have me."

Anna spoke up quickly, "I already said I would be pleased to be your wife."

"Then I guess all that's left is to set the date." Anna's mother interjected.

"Perhaps after the harvesting," she said smoothing the folds of her apron.

"That's fine with me," Chuck said smiling at Anna's mother in agreement and then to Anna for approval.

Glancing at Anna first, then at Chuck, mother asked, "What kind of wedding are you considering?"

"It is up to Anna," Chuck said with a smile.

"If you don't mind," Anna hesitantly replied timidly touching Chuck on the arm. "I would like a simple wedding with our families and a few of our friends."

"Good," Chuck agreed. "Then why not make it November thirtieth." That settled, Chuck stood to leave saying his thank you to Anna's mother and father. Anna followed him outside to wave good-bye.

October had arrived, and Anna spent a busy month getting her dress sewn, making the baked goods for the reception, and planning the decorations. She and her mother had been to the local store and had picked up soft white cotton for her wedding dress, white lace for the bodice, and fifty tiny pearl buttons. It had taken a good week of late nights to sew her dress. She was finally satisfied. The long flowing skirt and puffed sleeves at the shoulders billowing out to the elbow flattered her robust figure. The tight fitting arms buttoned with pearl buttons to close at the wrist. The back which opened all the way to her hip had been a real challenge to complete. Now, she was content with her accomplishment. The dress finished, she busied herself tightly with making a variety of cookies, mouth watering Springale', fruit bars, ginger snaps, and the old time favorite of everyone—sugar cookies.

Finally, the day had arrived. Standing in the nursery of the church where she and her ladies had been getting ready, she surveyed the finished product of the weeks of preparation. Anna felt pleased with herself. The groom's family seated on the right and the bride's family seated on the left as was the custom. She could hear the excited voices of the many guests. The deep round voice of a young man followed by the lilting laughter of a young woman

drifted back to her. She could hear the whispers of mothers settling their little ones. Her stomach felt like butterflies had taken
up residence and her legs felt a bit like rubber bands, first tighten-
ing and then loose. To distract her fears, she looked again through
the window of the nursery which looked out into the sanctuary.
She was happy with the decorations, an assortment of house plants
from various families, on loan for the day. Angelwing Begonias
with bright pink, their heart-shaped flowers drooping from strong
branches, Split-leaf Philodendra vining over trellises, tall Benjamin
Ficas standing near the altar while white winter house mums and
purple African Violets lined the window sills adding just the home-
spun touch she had wanted to achieve.

Just then the tall serene pastor dressed in his black robe with
its high banded collar came in and stood behind the pulpit waiting for the wedding music to start. Chuck came in and stood next
to the pastor. She thought Chuck an extremely handsome man in
his gray tailored suit and his blonde hair slicked down so carefully.
She knew before the wedding ceremony was over that one tuft of
his hair would be sticking up and she would love it. Fritz, his
brother and best man, came in next and stood beside him. She
thought how much she had grown to love this new soon to be
family of hers.

As the wedding music started, Anna lifted her head and
looked into the soft tender eyes of her father looking down at
her. He thought she looked blissful and content and perhaps a
little nervous, but he tucked her arm in his with a determind
pat. As they moved into the annex then down the isle and
toward her new life. Anna noticed her father's square German
chin set in a firm way he had of saying don't cross me. I think
his message is to Chuck, thought Anna. After all she was his
only daughter. Perhaps that look was meant to send a message.
Be good to her or else.

Chuck looked up to see Anna, her dark hair pinned up in a
neat bun and a white shoulder length veil cascading down in filmy
folds complimenting her dress. His heart leaped to his chest be-

fore settling on his face with a smile and then drumming a soft tap tap tap to the music.

Reaching Chuck and his best man, Anna's father brought her up beside them. The pastor moving out from the pulpit to stand before them and asked in an audience size voice, "Who gives this woman in marriage?"

Anna's father spoke up in a clear confident voice, " Ihr mutter und ich du." Having said this, he turned and walked to the bench to sit by his wife. He reached over to pat the hand of his wife who had just wiped an escaping tear from her eye.

As the pastor quoted the wedding vows, Anna's heart began to pound and the room began to swim. How am I going to be a good mother to two little girls who really don't know me she thought. Will they like me? She took a deep breath and mentally sent up a little prayer for help. While deep in her thoughts, the pastor had finish reading the marriage service. She looked up just in time to hear the pastor say, "Anna and Chuck face each other." Then he said, "Do you, Chuck, take this woman to be your lawfully wedded wife?"

"I do," said Chuck solemnly.

"You may place the ring on Anna's finger?" requested the pastor.

Chuck, smiling lovingly at Anna, placed the ring on her finger.

Pastor now looking at Anna said, "Do you, Anna, take Chuck to be your lawfully wedded husband?"

"I do," Anna said looking up at Chuck, her brown eyes sparkling with her love for him.

"Then with the power vested in me," the pastor concluded, "I now pronounce you man and wife." After a short pause and a twinkle he added, "You may kiss the bride."

Chuck took Anna in his arms. Holding her gently, he gave her a tender kiss. The young children giggled and the young men whistled. The pastor then took the couple by the shoulders and turned them toward the guest, "Ladies and gentlemen," he announced. "I would like you to meet the new couple, Mr. and Mrs. Falhaugen. As the wedding music began to play, they walked quickly up the isle, smiling and nodding their heads to their guests intermittently acknowledging their presence.

The guests slowly found their way out of the church. Some were milling around catching up on the latest gossip while some waited to throw rice at the bride and groom. As Anna and Chuck ran to their buggy which Paul had brought to the front of the church, they were pelted with rice. Then Anna, looking over her shoulder and still running, threw the bouquet of pink and white Geraniums she had kept flowering in the house for her wedding day for just this purpose. Her best friend, Pansy, caught it. Anna smiled. Good she thought, maybe Pansy would have the next wedding. Pansy had been keeping company with a fine young man that she had known all her life. They had become visibly quite fond of each other. Perhaps Roger would finally pop the question, then Pansy would be as happy as she was at this moment.

The women, going back into the church to retrieve their plants, came out shouting to each other that they would meet at the bride and groom's place for the charivari. The sleds crunched and scritched in the crisp snow as they all headed to their respective homes. The snow had come a little early this year making it a crisp memorable day for her wedding.

Milking needed to be done and the animals cared for before they could go to the charivari which often lasted into the wee hours of the morning, if not two and three days.

Chores done, the sleds were packed with the food and blankets. They all piled in including the children. Everyone arrived at Chuck's place with horns blowing, pans and kettles rattling, and the children screeching with delight. Jumping out of the sleigh in high spirits, the adults began carrying the food and other items they would need during the long celebration. The older children tumbled out of the sleigh and headed toward the river with their skates slung over their shoulders. They could be heard singing and laughing all the way to the river.

The men carried the food baskets into the house while the women helped each other gather the babies out of the sleds and into the house, settling them in dresser drawers or large wooden boxes and covering them with the warm blankets they had brought.

Next, the men unhitched the horses from the sleds and turned them loose in the corral knowing this night would be long since it was the men's intent to keep the bride and groom separated from each other and otherwise occupied. However, it was much more entertaining than spiriting the bride away and hiding her from the groom all night which was usually the type of charivari that took place at weddings where there were young unattached fellows who enjoyed frustrating the groom. The men gathered in the largest room, each with a bottle of homebrew. The ladies, in their long wool dresses busied themselves setting out the sausages and homemade breads with each ladies prize preserves. Each had brought a special treat from their own cellar. The sweet chunk pickles, as well as the very spicy dill were the hit of the men. There was an array of sausages such as blood sausage, a specialty found mostly in this area of North Dakota where there was a large settlement of German people who had brought their recipes from the old country. Also they brought the more common sausage such as liverwurst, summer sausage and head cheese. This homemade sausage can still be found commercially in Carson, North Dakota where it is still processed to have the same taste. People from all over the country stop to purchase this sausage on their way through or going out of their way just to find it.

The cookies Anna had baked for her guests were brought out and put at the end of the long lace-covered table. Large pots of coffee and a big pot of hot chocolate, made from fresh milk, sat at the back of the woodstove to keep warm for all to help themselves. Finally tired, cold, wet and hungry, the older children came piling into the house. The women helped them get out of their wet clothes and sat them down to sandwiches heaped with various sausages, homemade butter and pickles on homemade bread. They ate ravenously and then dipping a cup of hot chocolate and picking up a handful of cookies headed upstairs to the big bedrooms, empty except for a bed. No pictures decorated the walls. No dresser to hold clothes nor the many collectible items which clutter the floors, shelves, and closets of the current generation. A bed and a circular rug on the floor were the only items in either of the two big bedrooms at the top of the stairs. The girls picked one of the rooms and the boys the other. This is the way it had always been. Once the rooms were chosen, they remained off limits to the other gender throughout the party. Soon the children went in search of entertainment. Finding some board games in the downstairs' living room, the children carried them up to their perspective rooms. All of a sudden, the adults could hear the boys quibble over the games saying that the girls had taken the best and left the least fun ones for them. The adults left them to their squabbles, knowing the oldest and more sensible of the children would sort it out in a quiet fashion quickly not wanting a father to dish out discipline and ruin their fun.

Once the children were fed and occupied, the women called, "Fill your plates, boys." The men stopped their conversations and followed their noses to where the table was laden with food. The smell of hot bread, sausage, apple pie, and coffee filled the air. Piling their plates with food and picking up another home-brew, they circled Chuck and gave him a hearty slap on the back, joking and teasing, and attempting to make him lose his balance. He successfully outmaneuvered their jolting and managed to acquire a full plate of food.

As the men sat laughing and teasing the groom, the women surrounded the bride giving her a plate of food. As they ate, the women told various old wive's tales. Stories such as what to expect on a wedding night were threaded among stories of putting a dirty dish cloth under a child's pillow to get rid of warts or holding a threaded needle over a pregnant woman's belly to tell the sex of a child. Anna thought it silly to believe that a boy could be detected if the needle went back and forth whereas a girl was predicted if the needle made a circle. Such silliness indeed. "Would you like some more coffee or home-brew?" Interrupted Pansy. She was afraid that Anna was about to voice her doubts of these old wives' tales and ruin the fun. She and Anna had had many discussions about the silliness of these beliefs, but tonight was not the night to discourage the well wishers. Anna looked up to see her friend holding a steaming pot of coffee in her pot holder covered right hand and a home-brew in the other. Sensible Anna, she thought smiling down at her.

"Perhaps home-brew." Anna accepted shyly looking up at Pansy. "It might steady my nerves."

The charivari having lasted three days gave the children time to enjoy each other's company while ice skating and playing the many games popular in those days. One of the popular games and of course most available was kick the can. The farm children who managed to get together could always find an old can. This game was played outside and the object was to see who could kick the can farthest. During the three days, the men left only to do chores and then returned again for the festivities. Everyone took turns sleeping as they became tired. The older children took turns minding the babies while the women prepared food and played cards with the men. At times the chairs were moved to the side, and they all danced into the wee hours of the morning while Chuck played his violin.

Finally, the women having spun the last of their old wives' tales, and the men having exhausted their endless arguments about which crops grew best, gathered their families, hitched up their sleds, wished the couple everlasting happiness and started for their own homes. A light snow falling sent the children into a wild happy state and they began to sing songs. Anna and Chuck could still hear the children's excited voices singing Jingle Bells miles away as they stood on their front porch. The children were rushing it since Christmas was a few weeks away.

"Oh Anna, we are finally alone," remarked Chuck taking Anna in his arms, "I love our friends, but they sure do like to aggravate the newly weds, do they not?"

"Ja, but they left us plenty of food so we will not have much to do for a day or two," Anna said as she looked lovingly up at Chuck. "Guess I can give all my attention to you." Chuck smiled and moved into the house.

"Speaking of being alone," said Anna reaching to brush back a lock of Chuck's hair as he prepared to sit at the table. "When will we be bringing the girls home?"

Chuck reaching for two bottles of home-brew motioned for Anna to sit, he moved to sit beside her they sat sipping the beer slowly. Both thinking their own thoughts.

Finally, Chuck put his arm over Anna's shoulder, "Liebeshin," he said nuzzling her neck, "Let's wait to bring the girls home. We must get used to each other first. Children of their age can be difficult. I think some short weekend visits first might help break the ice. The girls have grown to love their aunt and uncle having been with them for so long." reflected Chuck.

"Whatever you wish," Anna conceded. "But I am willing to work with them. I am aware that it will be difficult."

As Anna went to the stove to heat their evening meal, Chuck sat in the old rocker that had been his Mother's and reminisced about things his parents had talked of when they had first started out. He told Anna about his Grandparents and their children who had come over from Germany and along with other families. They had rented railroad boxcars and come to North Dakota with all their earthly goods. When they arrived in North Dakota the box-cars were put on siding tracks and that is where all the immigrants lived until they each received the plots of ground they were to homestead.

Finally, Chuck guided Anna to the bedroom. Anna bashfully prepared for bed behind the dressing divider.

The next few months were wonderful, happy times for Anna and Chuck. When their work was done they spent time skating, dancing, visiting with neighbors and always Chuck playing the violin.

Over the first few months, the two little girls had come home on visits and finally to live. Onna a tiny girl with a beautiful, happy spirit always smiling, laughing, and trying to be helpful. Clare, just the opposite, was a sullen girl. Anna just couldn't find a way to reach her. Clare seemed to want to be by herself not wanting to be in the kitchen with Anna, but out in the barns or fields with her father. Anna had done her best to make the girls feel happy and part of a family. She wanted them both to love her as mama before their own child arrived. She wanted them to know they were special and much loved. It was easy with Onna, but Clare didn't seem to trust.

It had been three years since that wonderful day of their wedding. As Anna set the table for the evening meal tiny little Onna tried to toddle around and help.

"Come Onna," called Anna. "Crawl up in your chair." Chuck had made the chair, sturdy but more the height of a highchair. Because of her age and not wanting to make her feel bad, he had made it to look like an adult chair.

Onna crawled up in the chair as Clare and Chuck came in from the barn.

"Take off your wraps," Chuck directed Clare. "Wash up and sit at the table."

Chuck finished washing up and sat down at the head of the table by Clare as Anna drew her chair up by Onna.

Trying to draw Clare into a conversation, Anna said, "What have you and Father been doing Clare?"

Clare remained silent sullenly looking up at her father for him to respond. Anna did not push for an answer but continued to pass the food. She held the heavy bowl while Onna dished herself a spoon of vegetables.

Once the meal was finished, Chuck took the two little girls in to a big chair and sitting each one on his knee, he read them a story as Anna finished up the kitchen.

Finally he sent the girls of to bed, giving them both a big hug and kiss with a loving swat on their backside.

The girls were quiet and apparently asleep when Anna finished the kitchen. She came in holding a set of cards to challenge

Chuck to a game. As they finished the last hand, Anna chided Chuck on her having won most of the games. "That's all right there will be another day and you will not be so lucky," Chuck said as he let out a chuckle. "How about some chocolate and cookies to soothe my injured ego."

"Ya, you deserve something special, and . . ." she paused. "and I made special sugar cookies just for tonight," she teased.

They finished their snack. Anna banked the kitchen stove while Chuck banked the heater. Then he came up behind Anna and putting his arms around her shoulders, he led her off to bed.

As they lay talking over the days events, Anna turned to Chuck and said, "I just can't seem to sich verstandigen (reach) Clare."

"Daunt machen (don't fret)," Chuck replied giving her a little peck on the cheek. "She is difficult and hard to reach for me too."

Anna, giving a little sigh, turned to snuggle spoon fashion, but sleep would not come. Her thoughts went over these first few years. They had enjoyed a variety of weekly outings. Chuck played his violin at the dances. They played cards with their neighbors on occasions between harvesting and planting. Anna had spent many hours with neighbor ladies at quilting parties. She thought of the quilting parties. The ladies took turns gathering in different houses, tying quilts, exchanging special recipes, and sharing desserts prepared especially for that day. Each lady had prepared her quilt ready to tie by sewing together blocks made from worn out clothes. Patterns varied, some in rings or stars or even just blocks. The finished top was placed face down on a large surface, the quilt filler was placed next, and then a plain piece went over the top. These two pieces with the filler in the middle were basted together and rolled up awaiting the ladies to help tie. When tying a quilt, each lady brought her big darning needle. They layed the quilt out on a big table around which sat all the ladies. Each lady took one section and ran her needle with yarn from the top down through the two pieces and back up to the top again; then cutting the thread, they tied it in a loop at the top. This helped keep the batting in place. Quilts were not the only sewing done at these social gatherings. When a new baby was expected, the neighbors sewed all the baby clothes that would be needed.

Anna knew why she couldn't sleep. Tomorrow's party was for her. She was about to have their first baby. The baby moved within her, soothing her thoughts and soon she was asleep.

The ladies were in a festive mood, all were trying to guess what the sex of the baby would be.

"Well they already have two girls. It would be nice if this one were a boy."

"Anna, what do you want?" The ladies chimed in at once.

"I really just want a strong baby," She said with a smile of contentment rubbing the round little foot-shape that seemed to be doing a tap dance on the inside of her belly.

Since Chuck already had two girls when they married, they had decided not to have more children right away. They wanted to make the girls feel comfortable and become a family with just them first.

The party was a success and Anna had plenty of clothes and advise by the time the ladies left.

Finally, the day arrived when Chuck and Anna had a beautiful baby girl. Her strong legs dimpled with rolls of fat. Her dark hair framed a round face.

"We now have a full family," said Chuck. "My girls and our little girl will be special for all."

Onna looked down at her new little sister. "Oh Mama she is so cute. Can I pleeeease hold her?" she begged.

"Chuck, please pull up a chair for her and put little June in her arms," said Anna. "She wants to get acquainted with her new sister."

Onna sat holding the new baby singing a song and touching her smooth cheek. Her eyes shined and twinkled as she sang.

After awhile Anna called to Clare, "Would you like to come see your new sister?"

"No," she snapped. "I need to help father," with that she slammed out the door.

Anna picked up the baby and lay back on the bed. "Would you like to come sit beside us Onna?" invited Anna. Tears of frustration slipped from Anna's eyes, but she thought to herself. I know I just need to give her time.

2

Children arrive

Standing at the wood stove, Anna thought of her family and their different personalities as she prepared the dumplings for the beef stew which would be the noon meal. Nine years had passed since Chuck's two little girls had come to live with them. Anna thought of Clare, Chuck's oldest daughter by his first marriage. She was a thin unhappy girl with pale complexion and blonde wispy hair. She had remained sad from the first and had a tendency to be sharp-tongued with everyone except her horse which she could usually be found riding when she could escape. Anna had not been able to soften Clare's anger nor earn her love. On the other hand, Chuck's youngest daughter Onna, was a petite little girl, full of fun and mischief. Tiny at birth, she had never put on the round body of a farm child. However, her sweet, ready smile and tiny stature gave her a charismatic quality that charmed them all. She had welcomed Anna as a mother, and they had been close from the beginning.

Swiftly and with a practiced hand Anna banked the fire though it was the end of April it was still very cold outside. The older children were at school. Jeff, his blonde hair falling over his eyes, tugged at her skirt. She knew she must hurry and get him fed as well as his younger sister Sue. Anna felt an urgency to get them down for a nap soon. As she worked she thought of her children.

Anna had now birthed five of their own. Three boys and two girls. June was the first of her brood. She looked much like Anna

with her dark hair and chunky build. Her smile showed the gener-
osity of her character. She was always her mother's willing helper.

Chris, their first son, was a willful child. However, his snappy
blue eyes and black curly hair like Fritz, Chuck's brother, tended
to win him his way with the girls, and often his mother she thought
with a chuckle. Chris was a big help to his father. Chuck had
remarked often how much of the milking chore Chris did, but
Chris was inclined to be a bit selfish, and unlike June who thought
of the younger ones before herself, Chris made sure he got his
share first.

Their third child, a son, lived only two months. Anna's thoughts
rested for a moment on the difficult time they had had over that
loss. Then she remembered how they were able to finally give it to
the Lord and move on.

Jeff, another son, was born fourth. He was short like his pater-
nal grandmother. His blonde hair was slightly curly and had a
tendency to stick up in the back. His blue-gray eyes and bewitching smile betrayed the mischief and enjoyment he made of life.

Their fifth child was a cupid-mouthed little girl named Sue.
Her dark curls and slim body charmed almost everyone in the
house—even Chris at times. The fact that she was the baby added
to her charm. All she needed to do it seemed was look at them
with her spicy brown eyes and everyone melted to her demands.
Everyone except Clare who found her only a charming nuisance.

Anna was pulled back to the present when Chuck came in for
lunch. "How are you doing?" He asked, concern in his voice. Pouring a cup of coffee and laddling some of the stew and dumplings
into bowls for Jeff and Sue before dishing some for himself.

"I'm alright for now," she said reassuring him with a touch.
Anna helped Jeff and Sue up to the table. She didn't feel like eating but didn't want to worry Chuck so she nibbled as they talked
of the work needing to be done and the work already accomplished.
Chuck helped Anna put Jeff and Sue down for their naps.

"Do you need help with anything more before I go back out
to finish the chores?" Chuck asked.

"No. You go ahead," she said but she knew she would be needing his help before long. She hoped the birth would be finished by the time Jeff and Sue woke from their naps and before the other children arrived home from school.

As Anna cleaned up the kitchen and began preparations for the coming event, she thought of their life on the farm. She loved the large farmhouse that Chuck had inherited from his Grandparents. They had a half section of their own land and rented some of the surrounding ground. Their house was a two-story wood frame with a deep rock-lined basement, a second level hole was dug and framed to provide a root cellar for storing vegetables. Since families were often snowed in for several days at a time in Almont, North Dakota where they lived, shelves had been erected to store the large quantity of food that had been canned ready for the long winter. Very little prepared food was ever purchased. She was kept busy from morning till night preparing meals for her family as were most of the farmers they knew. People from other farms often helped each other put up crops. This was a neighborly way of getting the work done without hiring outside help.

Anna felt another contraction and stood still breathing steadily. Not much longer she thought. Anna was thankful she had canned and preserved enought to hold them through the winter and into the summer. Fruits, vegetables and meats had been put in canning jars and placed in huge boilers (water bath) to process. This had taken many hours, starting early in the morning and going well past midnight. The older girls helped with both the canning and the baking of breads. Fruits were scarce, but they had gotten some apples and had made them into apple sauce and apple butter. The children had gathered wild berries which had been cooked, juiced and made into jelly.

During the fall when the butchering was done, a large barrel was filled with water and enough salt to make a heavy brine. Then hams and bacons were placed in this barrel and kept there until they were well cured. A light fire was kept for a long period of time to smoke the ham and bacon in a building designed for that purpose. The pork chops that had been saved were cut up and fried well done. They were put in forty gallon crocks one layer at a time, and the grease which was rendered lard from the pork, was poured hot over them to seal them. These huge crocks were now stored in a cold area of the cellar. Chuck had brought up one of these crocks for her earlier. Anna removed some of the pork chops for dinner. Then she reheated the lard and poured it over the crock to make sure the remaining pork was kept sealed. Chris could return the crock to the cellar when he came home. She started the pork chops frying. She hoped they would be done in time and waiting on the back of the woodstove for her family's dinner tonight. She went to the ice box for milk to make biscuits. Just then another contraction seized her and she steadied herself holding onto the icebox.

Keeping food from spoiling was always a chore. She was grateful for the icehouse Chuck's family had built. Ice was gathered in the winter and buried in flax straw which had been saved in this house. Unless it was an unusually hot summer, the ice was kept from melting for most of the year.

3

Fredrick in North Dakota

When Chuck returned to the house a short while later, he anxiously looked towards Anna who was still standing very still. "I believe it is time," She said through short breaths. "The water is heated and the clothes and blankets are already laid out. Can you help me?" She headed for the bedroom not waiting for an answer.

Chuck went to the wash basin beside the door and poured hot water in the pan. He picked up the brown lie soap and scrubbed his hands with a brush like a doctor scrubbing for surgery. Rinsing his hands in clear water from a second pan, he dried them on a clean towel before going to Anna.

Searching Anna's eyes for strength and assurance, Chuck bit his lip with apprehension. He had lost his first wife when Onna had been born, and every time he helped Anna with the birthing of their children, this old fear came upon him. It was during these times that Chuck remembered the loss of their third son only two short months after his birth.

Anna tried desperately to keep from crying out with the pain as she knew Chuck was frightened, but finally a cry escaped. "I believe it is time," she moaned. The pain was steady and she could feel the pressure. She pushed and Chuck could see the baby's head, and he cupped his hands. With the next cry from Anna, he held his new son in the palm of his big hand. "Oh Anna, what a beautiful little fellow we have gotten." Chuck exclaimed! He laid the boy on his mother's belly while he cut the cord. Then he took the boy and cleaned him with the warm water Anna had readied. He marveled again at God's wonderful plan. He noted the boy's strong legs all wrinkled with fat before tightly wrapping him in a blanket returning him to his mother. He went to get more warm water. He knew he must clean Anna so she would not get the birthing fever that so many women got after having a baby. Once he had finished cleaning Anna, he cleaned the surrounding area. He needed to hurry as he knew Sue and Jeff would soon wake from their nap.

Chris, Onna, June and Clare had not yet returned from school. Chuck felt pleased with the day, things had gone well and all were safe. He whispered a prayer of thanksgiving as he finished his cleaning.

As Anna sat in the rocker nursing the new baby, Jeff woke and wondered into their bedroom. He was upset to find someone taking his place in his mother's lap. "Come," said Anna coaxing him with her finger. "Meet your new little brother, Fredrick."

Jeff, pushed his blonde wayward hair back from his eyes and peaked into the folds of the blanket. He tried to crawl up on his mother's knee, but Chuck picking him up and putting him on his shoulders said, "We will go outside to the barn, and you will help me milk the cows. Yah?" As they went through the house Anna could here Chuck talking to the boy and the boy bouncing on his shoulders in squeals of laughter. "Soon you will have a cow of your own to milk." The door clicked shut.

Chris, coming in from school poked his head into the bedroom. When he saw his mother holding a new little bundle in her arms, he knew it was another baby. Like rabbits he thought and without a word he headed into the kitchen to get himself a sandwich. He checked the ice box for ice before picking up his sandwich and heading outside the back way. There he met Clare on the steps just coming in the house. "When you go in there," he said pointing his head back past the kitchen toward the bedroom, "You will see we have another squalling baby in the house." Clare turned and headed for the barn where she picked up a brush and began to groom her horse. She too had had enough of babies.

Wandering from her bedroom and not finding her mother, Sue began to cry just as June and Onna came into the house. Soothing her with a snack, June picked her up and put her in the chair. Then she joined Onna at her mother's side to see the new little baby. "Oh Mama," June cooed, "What a sweet little face."

Onna and June looked at each other and then at the baby in their mother's arms. Both knew they would need to take over the supper preparation, put Jeff and Sue to bed, and make sure the rest of the children did their chores. Chris and Clare were not inclined to be much help in the house. They seemed to resent each new additions to the family.

Having finished the milking, Chuck came in with Jeff on his shoulders. June reached up and took the little fellow down and sat him at the table with a snack. As she worked, she told him little stories about how important a job it was to be a big brother to little Fredrick.

Chuck, called Chris in from outside. "I believe it is time for you to get your chores done," he said firmly. "The barn needs to be cleaned and the separator washed before the cream dries on it and becomes a problem to clean. The girls are preparing dinner and you can see Mother has her hands full. Take the crock with you and return it to the cellar, and don't forget to fill the ice box."

Scraping his feet in rebellion as he walked out the door, Chris muttered under his breath, "Well, I certainly didn't ask for more babies."

Clare too had been sulking and staying out of doors. Unlike Chris however, she knew how to stay busy and had not drawn attention to herself. But like Chris she was not happy to see a new baby arrive. After returning the crock to the cellar, Chris went to the barn. He took the cows out of the stanchion, a place where cows are restrained to keep them still while milking. There was a feed trough of grain and silage in front of the stanchion and he checked to make sure it was clean and filled for the next milking. He took the cows out to the corral, and then hurried to clean the barn, hoping supper would be ready soon he could feel the hunger pains or was it frustration. He was just finishing when Onna stepped out on the porch. He could hear her shrill tiny voice that seemed to penetrate and carry a great distance, "Dinn er er!"

That tiny little girl and that excruciating voice. Even I can hear her, thought her dad. When she wants to call attention to something it is amazing how far that voice will carry.

Everyone came and sat quietly at the table enjoying the good dinner the girls had finshed preparing. Aside from father telling the children the baby had been named Fredrick, there was not much conversation. Once dinner was finished, the girls cleaned up the dishes and put the little ones to bed while Chris and his father finished the barn chores.

4

Lisa in Idaho

John and Rena were finally settled into their newly rented house near Sandpoint, Idaho in a little town called Kootanai. It was by the railroad tracks and walking distance to the beautiful Pend Oreille Lake. Many farms with lush fertile soil surrounded the area. In the distance, not more than seven or eight miles, loomed the mountainous area with a heavy growth of beautiful evergreen and pine trees.

The small town was not more than a fourth mile from the new house they had rented. John's sister Helen and her husband Jacob, lived a short distance from their place with her three children. Helen had powder blue eyes and a stocky build. She tended to be sharp with her speech. Some said it was because she was next to the oldest of several brothers, and being the only girl, perhaps she had developed her sharp tongue in order to stick up for herself. Jacob was a towering man, heavy boned, tall and broad at the shoulders, but he was as lovable as a teddy bear. John was a slight built man, just the opposite of Jacob in stature. But John, like Jacob, also had a gentle nature. John worked as the night watchman at the lumber yard in town. Jacob was relief conductor and sometimes brakeman on the train that went through town heading back east.

Rena's mother, Anna, lived in the house next door with Rena's father Amos. Anna was a small woman with a great hump on her back between her shoulders, possibly due to heavy work and a loss of calcium in the bone. These were hard times. Although Amos

was a carpenter by trade, he had become so crippled from camp-
ing on the damp ground near the site where he built houses and
barns that he was unable to work.

Rena and John had three children living. A twin to the eldest
son died a few weeks after birth. Gus, the eldest, had dark hair,
blue-green eyes and a gentle, loving spirit. He had long legs and
was tall for his age. Phil, born eleven months after Gus, was a
cocky spirited boy with snappy blue eyes, blonde hair that showed
signs of darkening. He seemed able to command his will upon all
around him. Mercy, a chunky little three year old, with a cupid
mouth, brown hair, and green eyes was a quiet child who seemed
to be in her own little world most of the time.

Today Mercy is asleep in her bed. The boys are at school. John
was still in bed since he worked nights and slept days. Anna, Helen,
and Amos were in the house. Anna had filled the boiler on the
stove with water and built the fire up to get it hot. Helen and
Amos were sitting at the table drinking coffee. This room was the
center of everything from dining to sewing to canning. Today this
room was going to be a birthing room.

"When Mercy wakes, send her out to the woodshed. She can
stay with me," said Amos tucking his crutches under his arm and
headed for the door with a click—clack, click—clack, cli—

"Thank you Amos," Anna smiled to her husband. "Things
will be busy in here before too long. Rena seems to be in a great
deal of pain."

Helen looked up to see little Mercy standing by the stove
rubbing the sleep from her eyes "Mama," she whimpered.

"Oh Mercy, Mama doesn't feel well. She is resting," soothed
Helen. "Come, let's have a cup of oatmeal, and then Grandpa
Amos said you could help him in the woodshed."

"What Grandpa do?" quizzed Mercy.

"Maybe he will cut you some blocks to play with," said
Grandma Anna folding more towels and setting out the tools she
would need.

Helen hurried Mercy to finish her cereal and headed her out to find Grandpa. She had just left the house when Anna heard a shrill cry from the cot where Rena lay. She hurried back to her daughter's side just in time to hear another pain filled cry.

"Helen, come quick and help me," she called. Helen came bringing with her towels and some of the hot water Anna had prepared ahead of time. "I have the table cleared and readied to tend the baby when it arrives," Helen commented firmly.

"It is so cold today," Anna declared. "Why did she have to pick February to do this."

"I don't think she planned to do it at all," retorted Helen with a chuckle.

"I guess you're right Helen. Though I do envy her. I never had the choice to have more than her brother and her," sighed Anna. "I just lost all the rest," They worked companionably talking Rena through the pain.

Another cry from Rena and then Anna held her newest grand-child in both hands. Cutting the cord, she held the baby up and gave her a quick pop on the bottom which brought a loud protest-ing cry. Placing her in the thin wrapper, she handed Rena's newest daughter to Helen to bathe while she went back to attending her daughter.

Having finished with Rena and getting her settled, she re-turned to the table to see the new grandchild.

"Look at that!" exclaimed Helen. "She has gotten up on her knees like she is ready to take off."

Going to the door, Anna called. "AaaaaaaMos, come see your new grandchild and let Mercy see her new sister."

Mercy and Grandpa Amos came as fast as Grandpa could come on his crutches. Mercy running circles around him.

"Mommy sick," declared Mercy. "Aunty said so, Baby can't lay with her. She wake her up."

"I think Mother is already awake," said Grandma Anna. "She wants to say hi to you."

Grandpa helped Mercy along as he went on his crutches giving Mercy a nudge with the tip of his crutch to keep her going ahead of him. Mercy always thought it was a little game that she and Grandpa played.

"Why she so little?" asked Mercy looking at Grandpa with her green eyes wide and questioning?

"Well, because she is brand new. Do you remember how little your calf was when it was born."

"Oh! then she'll grow too, huh, Grandpa?" whispered Mercy.

"You don't have to whisper," said Grandpa. "Right now baby will go to sleep even when it is noisy."

Amos looked at his daughter. She seemed so tired and spent. A great feeling of helplessness came over him because he was unable to bend over and give her the hug she so much needed.

"Rena, you have a beautiful new baby. I am happy for you," he said with a smile tenderly touching her forehead with his hand. "Mercy is here beside you to give you a kiss and then I will take her with me."

"Thank you daddy. I am so happy you can be here," Rena said in a weak voice.

Around four o'clock John came in rubbing his eyes and dressed in his bib overhalls ready for his barn chores. "What is going on in here?" he yawned his eyes twinkling with knowing. Walking over to where Rena lay with the new baby beside her, he touched her hand tenderly. "How are you Rena? I see we have another baby."

"It's a girl John," said Rena proudly.

With two fingers, he stroked the little girl's cheeks, then leaning over, he kissed her sweetly on the mouth. "I am going to do the chores. Before I head for work I'll come see how you are doing. Thank you," he said after a emotional pause, and then he wiggled his ears which always made her giggle just a little.

5

Fredrick in North Dakota

Fredrick, now nine months old, was able to sit on the floor and play with his brother Jeff. He had a strong body and was able to hold himself up very early. He was a bubbly, happy baby, and Jeff found him a fun playmate. Jeff would build things with the wood blocks that his father had cut out for him. Fredrick would knock them over then tip over with peels of baby laughter.

Every morning Mother washed and dressed Sue and the two little boys before feeding them their breakfast. It was Jeff's chore to watch over Fredrick and Sue while Mother prepared the lunch for all the helpers working in the fields. The rest of the children made their own breakfast, packed their lunches, and saddled their horses for the long trip to school. Once at school they put the horses in the barn with the feed and water for the long day at school.

Anna and Chuck usually ate their breakfast around five in the morning enjoying the calm and each other's company before the rest of the family were up, and before Chuck had to go out into the field.

This morning as Anna and Chuck sat having their quiet breakfast, they talked about the children and their different personalities. "Clare is so distant Chuck, I can't seem to reach her. You would have thought by now that she could have blended in with the rest of the family," Anna murmured, the pain of rejection evident in her voice.

"I guess she has an anger inside her because her mother died. Perhaps she thinks it was Onna's fault," Chuck gently reminded Anna as he had throughout the years.

"Onna is such a little treasure. Always a smile no matter what any one does to hurt her feelings. I really don't know how I would manage without her," Anna commented, "and those witty little stories she tells the little ones are so entertaining they even keep me interested."

"Thank you Anna for loving my girls and being such a good mother to them," Chuck soothed. "I know it isn't easy with Clare."

"Well, they are my girls too now, and our Chris is a good match for Clare as to temperament. He sees to it that he gets the pick of everything and the rest just seem to back away and let him get by with it," reflected Anna with a little chuckle.

The only one that seems able to handle Chris is little Sue, considered Anna lapsing into her own thoughts. She seems to charm him out of his moods, and with her bewitching little smile she even gets him to laugh a little. "Chuck we really have a jewel in June," Anna said aloud. "She seems able to keep things level, and what a help. She doesn't have to be told what needs to be done; she just seems to appear when I need her."

"Oh then there is Jeff," Chuck said with a twinkle in his eye as he began to tell Anna how Jeff always seemed to hide his mischief until it was too late, once it was found out, to punish him. He was able somehow to make it look like some one else had done the bad deed. I think the little fellow is going to be a bit like my mother and perhaps even be small like she was."

"Little Fredrick is a piece of all of them don't you think," put in Anna. "I think he might even out do Jeff in mischief. His little mind seems to be working overtime. Just watch what he does with the blocks you cut out for him. Young as he is, you wouldn't think he could figure out how to stack them in a way to make it look like a building. He must copy Jeff or Sue, but even that," Anna said pointing to Fredrick's newest building, "is not the same as others."

Anna's eye's sparkled as she looked up at Chuck showing her great love and pride in little Fredrick.

Chuck got up from the table and bent over Anna giving her a little kiss. "Quess I'd better get those cows milked so you will have time to separate the cream before the children pile down here. I'll need to head out to the creamery this morning," he said. "When I get back, I need to get things ready to do the butchering so make sure Chris stays around."

It was fall. This was the time of year when all the sausage was made. The meat was canned and the pork put in the barrels of salt brine to prepare for the last finishing touches in the smokehouse for smoking the hams and bacon. The sausage meat was ground up and seasoned and packed in cleaned out casings gotten from the animal entrails. They were then put in big vats of hot water to cook for several hours to be sure all the meat was done. After this the sausage was hung in the cellar. This was a form of preservation. The sausages were similar to those called summer sausage which you see in the markets today, however commercial casings are used today on sausages, not the animal entrails.

6

Lisa in Idaho

Almost three years had past since Lisa was born. Amos and Anna now lived with John and Rena and their four children. There small farm had a big red barn, a machinery building and a two-story house. The large machinery building also had a loft spacious enough to hold the years ice harvested from Pend Oreille Lake. Sawdust was hauled each year from the big sawmill where John worked to the loft in order to bury the ice which helped it stay frozen for most of the year. Because this part of Idaho did not get very warm, the saw dust along with the insulation served well. This was a blessing since money was short and, other than canning or drying, this was the only means of preserving foods.

Since Amos was badly crippled with arthritis and could no longer work, he watched over Mercy and Lisa while Anna helped her daughter pick berries from the wild bushes surrounding the area farms. Mercy would be going to school next year and Amos would only have little Lisa to follow him around. He enjoyed these two little girls. Mercy had a soft loving nature, yet when she wanted her own way, she proved to be a very stubborn child not budging an inch once she made up her mind. Lisa was a very happy baby inclined to laugh at very simple things making her easy to enter-tain. She very seldom cried even if hurt as was the case today when Mercy dumped her buggy over spilling her on the ground. Lisa's blankets were in a heap burying her which made it difficult for grandpa Amos since the use of his crutches prevented him from bending over very far. But utilizing his handicap, he took the tip of his crutch and removed the blankets just enough to uncover Lisa so that Mercy could help Lisa get up.

Anna and Rena came back from berry picking just in time to see the process. They remained out of sight holding their breath, not wanting to make Amos feel incompetent. Once the situation was under control, they revealed themself to Amos then climbed the steps to the back of the house and went in both giggling with relief. As Rena began to prepare the evening meal, Anna washed and prepared the berries ready to preserve in jams and jellies saving some for the evening meal.

Gus and Phil came in from the school with Phil poking and jabbing at Gus trying to get him mad. Gus simply moved away from him and gave him a disgusted look. "Look, if you two get your father's attention," Mother said hearing the commotion before actually seeing the boys, "you'll get a trip out to the barn, and it won't be to finish your chores. It'll be a leather strap applied generously to your back sides." Both boys quieted down a bit while they each grabbed a hunk of bread spread with salted lard before heading out to feed the animals. As they headed out the door, however, both were pushing and shoving and laughing noisily.

Rena realized that it was time for John to get up in order to get the milking done and eat supper before reporting to work at the mill as a night watchman.

The next morning the sun was out and Rena and her mother were out planting the garden while Amos entertained the girls at the side of the woodshed. He stood propped up with one crutch under his left arm to balance himself while he whittled with a jack knife on a board. Mercy squinted up at her grandpa. "What you doin'?"

"Oh, just working on a surprise for the your mother," Grandpa answered his knife slowly carving chips of wood flying here and there. The girls were making mud pies at his feet and Amos thought how the women were going to howl at him for letting them get so messed up. Oh well, thought Amos with a shrug, they are happy and it keeps them near me. It would be harder to get them if they wandered off. The wind was still a little crisp this spring day, but the sun shining on him warmed his hands enough to limber them up so he could get the knife to do what he wanted. Amos' thoughts made him wonder if his life would be long enough to finish these dressers for Rena.

7

Christmas in North Dakota

Time moved swiftly with all the work that needed to be done. Christmas was again upon them. This was the time of year when all the cookies, candies, and popcorn balls needed to be made. Anna looked out of the window and saw a sled with two of the neighbor ladies coming to help with the candies and cookies which all would share when they were finished. It was a time when neighbors enjoyed each other's company yet still managed to get the things done for the holiday season.

Helga and Pansy rapped twice then came into the kitchen, "YOOHOO! Anna?" Pansy sang. "Oh, there you are?" she said in a lower voice upon seeing Anna already setting up in the kitchen. They all began to chatter at once filling each other in on the news since they had last been together. Finally, Helga and Anna settled their younger children down for a nap while Pansy busied herself setting out the ingredients each lady had brought. They planned their free time for baking, gardening, and deep cleaning around school and the younger children's nap time. Once the children were settled, they set to work deciding on the best plan for getting the most done in a day.

"Let's make the candies first," Helga suggested. "I thought perhaps Divinity, Fudge, Penuche, Toffee, and Caramel Popcorn.

"That is a real good idea," Anna agreed, "Then we can use the egg yolks left over for cookies."

"Why don't we divide up the jobs," proposed Pansy taking charge. "Why don't you make the Divinity, Anna. Yours is always smooth and its melts in the mouth. And Helga, you make the best Toffee. I can make the Caramel Popcorn. Whoever has time can work on the Fudge and Penuche"

Finally the candies and cookies are done, the kitchen cleaned and the ladies exhausted, but they have spent a wonderful day together. They gather up their children and head out to the sleigh giving Anna a hug and a promise to get together soon. The air is crisp, and the sleighs make a crunching noise on the crisp snow as each makes its way down the lane. Both ladies hoping to get home before it gets dark.

Anna smiles to herself as she closes the door. She is pleased with their accomplishment. All the Christmas candy and cookies are done for the holiday. She can now concentrate on finishing the special gifts she has been making for each child.

Things are going to be hectic starting tomorrow what with the children out of school for the long Christmas vacation she thought. The house will be alive with all their comings and goings along with the need for bigger noon meals and the continuous battles. Chris and Clare always seemed to cause some turmoil. Clare seemed to feel that since she was the oldest, she should have first choice of everything and she made sure she voiced her opinion loudly. Chris being a bit bullish didn't accept it.

*   *   *

Christmas vacation started peacefully. With the help of June and Onna, Jeff and Sue were dressed and being fed breakfast while Anna bathed and dressed Fredrick. Fredrick was in a happy bubbly mood this morning and Anna's heart lifted with joy watching him. He is so much like my brother Paul thought Anna smiling to herself with thoughts of childhood memories.

When Chuck came in, they all sat down to a big breakfast of sausage, fried potatoes, boiled eggs and toast made from the delicious homemade bread. Today Anna had put apple butter on the table for a treat. They usually didn't eat together or have time for such a big breakfast when the children were in school. Usually they each grabbed a bowl of cereal that had been in a double boiler at the back of the wood stove cooking slowly all night then they went out to do their chores before heading to school. Since the only heat in the house was wood stoves the big heater as well as the cook stoves fires were banked so they would keep a slow even fire through the night.

It being Saturday, the children had gotten up early to finish their chores. It was a clear day, though crisp, the sun was shining. It was a beautiful day for ice skating. "Hurry!" shouted Chris throwing the end of his scarf around his neck, "I'll race you girls to the tree at the end of the pasture."

June laughed softly, "I don't think you will make it ahead of any of the girls."

"Oh yeah," shouted Chris as he started off down the steps and through the path toward the lake at break neck speed.

Catching up to Chris, the girls stopped and starred. "Watch out!" they yelled, a chorus of imminent danger in their voices just as Chris hit a heavy twig sticking up in the ice. Chris's skate hit the twig full force sending him end over end landing heavily on his arm.

"Oh No!" June exclaimed as all the girls skated to where he was laying very still.

"Chris, Chris, talk to us. Are you all right," they yelled. "Oh no!" cried June. "We will have to drag him back. Onna quick!" directed June. "Skate back ahead of us. Get Dad and the sled. We will have to pull him back to the house."

Onna found her father in the barn. While she dashed around the barn finding the sled and pulling it out of its storage place she excitedly explained what had happened to Chris.

As Chuck headed for the house to prepare Anna, Onna returned to the lake with the sled. Turning he hollored, "Where is Clare?"

"I don't know," Onna hollored back. "She didn't go skating with us. I don't know where she is."

"What is all the excitement," asked Anna as Chuck came into the house.

"Chris has had a skating accident," Chuck yelled. Then in a calmer voice. "The girls are bringing him back from the River We need to take him to the doctor so prepare things so the girls can handle the little ones while we are gone."

By the time the girls had Chris loaded on their little sled back to the barn, Chuck had the big sled hitched to the team of horses. Anna was already there with a few warm bricks under the blanket to keep Chris warm.

In one easy motion, Chuck reached down, picked up his son, and settled him in the blanket being careful of the arm that was poking out at the strangest angle. "Why are you putting me in the sled?" questioning Chris. I want to go in the house."

"We are taking you in to the doctor," Mother informed him softly.

"Why," said Chris in a agitated voice.

"Because you may have broken your arm Chris, and we don't have any way to fix it out here." Anna said speaking in a tone he knew not to question. Mother was soft and loving, but Chris knew not to argue further.

Finding Jeff sledding on the hillside, the girls called him and they all went in the house. Taking off their coats and boots, they set them beside the door on a rug so that the snow could drip off. Onna asked Jeff to play with the little ones while June and Onna fixed them a little lunch to keep them happy. They made a special bread pudding with fresh whip cream.

Onna had Fredrick in her lap. She was feeding him hot soup blowing on each spoonful so that it wouldn't burn his mouth.

Clare, coming in from outside, threw her coat on the floor and swaggered to the stove to see what might be there to eat. "I though you went skating," she said looking around. And where is Mom and Dad?" she quizzed haughtily.

"Well, if you hadn't been so uppity," Onna said. "You would have been skating with us and you would know."

"So what's the big secret." Clare said expressively. "Did Chris get his way and talk Mom and Dad into buying that gun he has been wanting?".

"No!" sighed June softly. "He was hurt skating. They have taken him to the doctor."

"Oh boy, that's a good one," raved Clare sarcastically. "No one else gets a doctor."

"Oh don't be so bitter about everything Clare," June consoled.

"Well it's true," Clare said as she headed for her coat on the floor. Putting it on she went out and slammed the door behind her.

"Come Sue you're a big girl. Fredrick is tired. Lay him down and put him to sleep," Onna said hugging Sue as she led her to the bed and laid Fredrick down.

Sue crawled up beside him and began to hum a little tune that she had heard her father play on the violin. Fredrick was soon fast asleep. Sue's eye became heavy before long and she too was asleep.

"Jeff, why don't you fill the woodbox," June coaxed handing him his jacket and lightly guiding him toward the door. "Mom and Dad may be late, and we all have to pitch in and get the chores done."

"I think I will use the canned meat and make some stew. We have plenty of turnips, parsnips, carrots and potatoes," Onna said as she put the kettle further to the back of the stove so it would simmer. She began to peel the vegetables as June finished clearing the dishes from the children's lunch.

It was growing dark, and the snow had begun to fall. I do hope the wind don't kick up and drift so they have a hard time getting back June thought to herself.

Jeff finished filling the woodbox and sat down on the floor near the door to take off his boots rubbing his hands together to get them warm.

"Come on Onna," said June as she headed for her coat and boots. "Let's get out there and get the milking and feeding done before the weather gets any worse. Jeff can stay in here and watch the little ones. If Sue and Fredrick wake up before we finish Jeff," Onna directed. "Set them down with blocks and play with them."

Back from the milking and other chores, the two girls set dinner on the table and Jeff brought the baby in and put him in the high chair directing Sue to crawl up on a chair herself.

After dinner and chores, Jeff sat playing a game by himself pretending he had a partner. June's thoughts turned to past Christmases. I do hope we don't have a big problem to ruin the Christmas spirit. No matter what is troubling her, thought June, Mom always seems to keep things happy through the holidays.

Rubbing his eyes, Jeff finally put his games away. Putting on his coat and boots, he headed out of the door to the outhouse before climbing the stairs to bed. He held on to the rope that connected the house to the outhouse. This was a habit for this time of year. It was snowing and blowing badly but he could still see fairly well. The rope protected one from getting lost when the wind and snow blew enough that there was no visibility. Sometimes there was ice under the snow and one could lose their footing. If it was windy one could be blown into the fields.

In the house, each dressing room alongside their bedrooms had a chamber pot which required dumping and cleaning each morning. It was a job that each attended without being told. Not doing the job lost your privilege to have a chamber pot requiring you to get up and go to the outhouse in the middle of the night or before getting dressed in the morning.

"I will put Fredrick to bed while you take care of Sue," suggested June. "Then we can wait together for mom and dad." The babies were tucked in on the day bed downstairs since they wanted to be able to hear them if they woke up and began to cry.

June brought out the cards and began to shuffle them. "You want to play a game or two with me, Onna? I really don't want to go to bed until Mom and Dad get back."

"Sure that will help pass the time," Onna said sitting in the big chair by the stove. She was so tiny that the big chair made her look much younger than she was.

After several hands, they both began to get a little edgy wondering what was happening with their parents and Chris.

June got up and banked the heater as she had so often watched her mother do. Onna fed the kitchen stove again so it would stay a little warmer knowing they would not be going to bed soon.

"Have you seen Clare?" June quizzed Onna.

"Ya, she stomped upstairs while we were cleaning up after dinner. Guess she would rather starve than do a little work," Onna chuckled.

It was now almost day light. June stretched her shoulders and yawned widely. What could have happened to their parents. She was beginning to really worry, but she didn't dare let on..

"Perhaps we should put a double boiler on with cereal. It won't be long and Jeff and the little ones will be hungry," said June as she began to prepare the cereal for the back of the stove.

Onna went to the window. "It is getting light out, but the snow has stopped falling."

"I guess while they are all still asleep, we better go see if we can get the milking done," June said looking at Onna.

"We better hurry up if we are to be done before Fredrick cries. We can't count on Clare. She'll just yell at him," Onna commented with a frown as she dressed to go out.

They were just in the process of separating the milk just as they heard Jeff come down the stairs.

"Where's Mom?" questioned Jeff as he sat down at the table.

"They haven't returned yet so you will need to be a big boy and help out. You can start by dishing up your own cereal. It's at the back of the stove," June comforted gently. "When you have finished eating, get washed up and be ready to entertain Sue and Fredrick."

Clare came stomping down the stairs and sat at the table expecting to be waited on.

After waiting a short while Onna said sharply, "If you want something to eat Clare, you'll have to get it yourself. You haven't done anything else to help. You can at least help yourself.

"Who made you boss?" Clare retorted.

"I don't need to be boss," Onna replied in a frustrated tone, "but if you want anything guess it's up to you."

Fredrick began to cry. June went in to the day bed to get him while Sue came bouncing out on her own. Crawling up into the closest chair, she began to eat the bowl of cereal Onna put before her.

Clare finished what she had fixed herself. She put her bowl in the dish pan with no move to wash it herself. Then going into the front room, she flopped in the big chair where she began to read a book.

Looking out of the window, Jeff spotted a sled in the distance. "I bet that's Mom and Dad," he said jumping down and running to the door excitedly.

"Get back in here," June commanded. "You don't have a coat on and besides you need to be useful and help with the two little ones until we get the kitchen work done."

Jeff stomped back in, "Ah Gee! Why me? What's wrong with Clare? She isn't doing anything."

"That's a good question," Onna mused more to herself then Jeff. Then louder, "I think you will have to ask Dad that question when he has time to answer it."

Hearing the crunch of a sled on the crisp snow, the girls ran to the door. There was Chris getting out of the sled, his arm held with something that looked like a dish towel hung around his neck. Chuck was putting the team away, and Anna came toward the house stumbling some as though she had something wrong with her.

While Onna ran to help their mother, June put on her coat and boots and ran out to see if Father needed her help. "What kept you?" she asked as she reached him. "Was it the storm?"

"No, though it was pretty bad. It was your mother. She is not feeling well so we had to stop in town to rest. The excitement of Chris being hurt was trying for her," explained Father. "You had better go back in and do what you can to help her. Send Clare out to help me."

She ran into the house with her thoughts on her mother. She hoped there was not something seriously wrong with her. Getting in the house she called Clare, "Go help Father."

"Why can't you go?" Clare yelled back.

"Father said to tell you to come," June shot back. "If that's not what you are going to do, you go tell him yourself."

June turned to Mother and saw frustration along with something else she couldn't quite understand. "I'm sorry. Mother you look tired out. You need to lie down and rest. Jeff has been a real big boy and helped with the babies."

Chuck came in to check on Anna. Finding her asleep, he sat down to a cup of hot coffee to warm himself while the girls busied themselves fixing him some fried potatoes, eggs, toast and summer sausage.

"Thank you, June and Onna. I see you have things in hand."

Sitting on the floor Sue and Frederick were playing with a spool that was empty of thread. Jeff was entertaining them with a stack of blocks built like a barn. Clare was back with her book.

Chris, coming to the table in apparent pain, he asked if he could have something to eat. "We all had cereal so I guess you can do with that too," Onna said. "Can't say any of us feels too sorry for you since you were being your usual show off, big shot."

"That's enough," said Father. He is suffering enough. I'm sure it will be lesson enough to think before being so rambunctious."

It would take more than this to change Chris, thought June. In fact he probably was enjoying all the special attention.

Mother woke and came into the kitchen. Dipping herself some oatmeal and pouring a cup of coffee, she sat down at the table. "Thank you girls for handling everything while we were gone."

"It wasn't that bad," June said waving her hand back in a gesture to indicate that it was trouble. "It's just that we were so scared. We thought you might have gotten caught in a storm since it was snowing so hard and blowing too."

"Well perhaps we were blessed it was not that bad in town," Mother related. "I'm sorry we caused you so much worry."

"Your mother was feeling quite bad," Chuck put in, "so I thought it best to have her rest. I knew you girls could be counted on to take care of everything. I also want to thank you for not getting into problems with Clare. I know she can be difficult at times."

Onna and June looked at each other remembering there angry words with Clare and felt ashamed. Then they both began to share how much help Jeff had helped.

"Whoa!" said Chuck, "One at a time. I can't understand you."

, "Jeff brought in all the wood for the fires," Onna exclaimed!

"He watched the little ones while we did the milking," put in June.

8

Christmas in Idaho

Lisa laughed and bounced happily as Mercy pulled her around the yard on the little sled. At the speed Mercy was pulling her, Amos feared she might dump her over. He started to stop her then changed his mind, shrugging his shoulders. I guess it won't hurt her, Amos thought as he stood propped against the sunnyside of the house steadily working on a long piece of wood with his whittling knife.

Finishing the project he was working on and beginning to feel a chill, Amos called, "Come on girls. I think you have had enough for today."

"No, Grandpa!" Mercy argued, "Can't we please stay more longer, Pleeease?"

"No!" Grandpa said firmly, "I am cold and tired. It is time for these bones to sit and drink a warm cup of coffee."

"Oh! Hot chocolate for us too, huh Grandpa?" exclaimed Mercy as she pulled the sled up to the back door and helped Lisa get out.

Amos carefully sought his way through the snow following the girls to the back of the house and dragging the board on which he had been whittling. Placing the board carefully against the far wall so it would not get damaged, he herded the girls into the house using the tip of his crutch to tap them gently on their backsides.

Grandma Anna took charge of unwrapping Lisa while Mercy sat in the corner tugging off her own boots. Once they were stripped of their wet wraps, Anna sat Lisa in her high chair while Mercy climbed up on the stool beside her. Rena had poured her father a cup of coffee and gave him a hot bowl of rich and creamy potato soup. She had made it this morning while he watched the girls play outside. Since it had looked so cold outside this morning, she had peeled and cubed six big potatoes and put them on to boil in a little water. While they boiled she had sautéed a half onion until it was tender adding a pinch of salt and a little pepper to the potatoes while they cooked so the flavor would penetrate the potatoes. This sat simmering on the back of the wood kitchen stove while she melted a scoop of homemade butter (about quarter of pound) and added enough flour to make a soft paste. Adding this to the potato mixture, she let it all come to a light boil stirring as it thickened. Finally, she added cream which she had skimmed off the pan of milk from this mornings milking. Her father was already enjoying his bowl and her mother had dipped enough for the two girls.

"Would you like a bowl of soup," Rena called to her mother who was tidying ap the area around the cot at the end of this big family area so she could put Lisa down for her nap.

"I sure would." Anna hollored back so Rena could hear since the room was long and the ceiling high making it hard to hear on the opposite side of the room.

When Lisa and Mercy had finished their soup, Anna washed Lisa and put her on the cot for a nap at the same time encouraging Mercy to crawl up with her making her think she was being the big girl helper to put the baby to sleep.

"Well that's done," Anna said as she plopped down to the bowl of soup her daughter had dipped for her. "And what have you been up to this morning," she question snappily as she looked at her husband?

"I've been a whittling," he shot back in a hurt tone.

"What are you wasting your time on now," Anna taunted nastily.

"I don't call it waste Anna, and you will see in time," Amos replied. His eyes met Anna's with mischief in them.

Anna got up and stomped away carrying the dirty dishes to the dish pan. Amos, she thought always seemed to get enjoyment out of getting her riled.

"I have you a tree drug up at the back door of the woodshed Anna. When the boys get home they can do what is needed to help you women set it up," Amos directed.

Later in the afternoon, Phil sauntered in the door in apparent glee having done something to upset Gus.

"Okay Phil. What are you up to?" Mother questioned?

"Nothing," Phil chimed. "Gus's mad because I took the pencil that he got in trade for his old one. I don't see what's so special about this ole' pencil anyway," he said turning the pencil around in his fingers with both hands in front of him.

"Perhaps it has special meaning only to him," Mother defended reminding him, "You know how he is always trading things. It is a special part of him. He thinks he has a better deal so why must you continually antagonize him this way? I think you can better use up all that energy by getting that tree into the living room and help me get it and decorated for Christmas.

Gus played with Lisa and Mercy in Mother's bedroom downstairs while Anna prepared supper and Phil and mother put up and decorated the Christmas tree.

The projects done and dinner on the table everyone sat down to eat dinner even John who was awake pleased to find things moving along well ready for Christmas. As he put on his heavy work coat and pulled on his heavy rubber boots for work each of the children circled him begging to have the leftovers from his lunch box in the morning when he arrived home from work.

"Well now, it seems you expect me to go hungry just so you can find something left in my lunch box am I right," Father teased ruffling the boys hair.

"Oh no!" said soft hearted Gus. "We don't want you to be hungry, Papa."

*   *   *

Christmas eve found John driving the family to the local Christian Church down the road. He was off from work until after midnight tonight. He would have to go in for awhile but not the whole night.

Arriving at the church in their Model T Ford, Rena and the four children piled out and found their seats in the church while Father went home to get Grandpa Amos and Grandma Anna.

The church had its own Christmas tree on the riser behind the pulpit and a cradle representing baby Jesus sat to one side. The program started with the singing of *Silent Night*. Phil and Gus followed the teacher to the front of the church and into the back room because they were going to be wise men in the play. When the play was over, the organ began to play *Come All Ye Faithful* and Phil and Gus came back to stand beside Mother. The lights were turned up and the children were invited to come up to the altar one at a time to receive their sack. Lisa figeted nervously, she wanted to go right NOW. Grandma Anna held tightly to her hand, but Lisa wiggled all the more. Gus had told her all about the sacks filled with oranges, candy and nuts. Gus had also told her that oranges and nuts were expensive in Idaho. Oh what a treat she thought! Mother did not let the children have much sugar. Rena had been a teacher before her family so she was well versed on what was nutritious and good for growing bodies and teeth. That made the Christmas sacks the children got at church and after the school play an exciting and wonderful experience.

9

Back in North Dakota Christmas Eve

"Because it is Christmas Eve all of the family will go to church," said Mother to June, "even the babies. Please heat the rocks and bricks in the oven so we can put them under the blankets to keep the children warm." Mother could hear Chuck in the other room with the little ones telling the story he had been told as a child. Every Christmas Eve before church he repeated the story to his children.

> "Twas the night before Christmas.
> And I was only four.
> I thought I'd catch old Santa
> So I hid behind the door.
> I got so very sleepy
> That I just lay down my head
> And when I awoke
> It was morning
> And I was fast in bed.
> My Daddy said he found me
> With my stockings full of toys.
> I didn't catch ole' Santa
> But I guess he sure caught me.

The children chattering excited and happy after hearing the familiar Christmas story went to the kitchen where mother had poured cups of chocolate and set out a plate of cookies for them.

As the children finished, they got up taking their cups with them and putting them by the dish pan to be washed later.

Finally bundled in their warm clothes, the children scrambled to get their places in the sleigh. Anna tucked the little ones under the blanket near her with the warmed bricks.

They arrived at the church just as many of their neighbors were arriving. The candlelight service was so moving that even the babies were quiet and watched in wonder. The service ended and there was a great feeling of joy. The happy voices of children sharing with friends and the well wishes from adults filled the air.

Arriving home they all piled out of the sleigh. Chuck put the team away as the rest stomped and jostled their way into the house removing snow and wraps and laughing with excitement.

June and Onna herded the young ones up to bed while Anna settled Fredrick. Clare and Chris had already gone up to bed.

Anna sat down in the rocker to rest a bit before ending the special Christmas Eve, Chuck bent down and gave her a loving kiss on the forehead. "Would you like a cup of coffee or chocolate Anna?"

"Oh that would be so nice," Anna replied. "I think I would like chocolate please."

Chuck came back with two cups of chocolate. He handed one to Anna as well as a sprinale he had picked up from the cookie plate and then settled down in the chair beside her rocker with his own cup and cookie.

"I think we had better get busy with the tree," Anna said after awhile. "The children should be asleep by now, don't you think?"

"I have it ready in the barn," Chuck replied getting up and heading for his coat and boots.

"Good," Anna said pushing her heavy bulk out of the chair and heading to the space under the stairs. "And I will get out of my hiding place the things I have wrapped."

"Well, what do you think?" Chuck said holding the tree with both hands and looking to the top of the tree that almost touched the ceiling.

"It is beautiful!" Anna smiled with satisfaction taking up a strand of popcorn rope which she and the children had made this morning, she began to drape it around tree. They both hung the special decorations that the children had made throughout the years.

Once the tree was decorated, Anna put the wrapped presents around the back as Chuck placed the special unwrapped gifts for the children towards the front. Then Chuck went to the basement and came back with several bags that held various nuts, opening the bags he laid them under the tree and spread a few of the nuts out from the opening. Anna set out the big fruit jars that held the colorful ribbon candy she had made.

Chuck and Anna, wrapped in each others arms, looked at the tree and decided the tree was ready for morning.

Anna sat down and began to rock slowly, "Chuck would you please play me some Christmas music?"

"I would love to play for you," Chuck said as he reached for his violin. "What would you have me play?"

"How about *Tunenbaun* and *Silent Night* to start with." she said closing her eyes and drifting to the smooth sound of his bow.

Chuck played for some time. Finally he noticed Anna's head begin to droop so he put down the violin and took her by the arms leding her to bed. As they lay side by side, Chuck reached over patting her hand. "You have been such a wonderful wife and mother Anna. Thank you," he whispered tenderly.

The children all got up very early Christmas morning. Seeing popcorn balls and bags of nuts under the tree along with the jars of ribbon candy, the children all whooped with glee. There were handmade toys for the little ones and clothes and shoes for the older ones. Their excitement soon brought Anna and Chuck from their bed.

"Can I wear the new dress and shoes today Father?" asked Onna her blonde hair bouncing up and down as she jumped with excitement.

"Me too?" chimed in Sue running to Mother with her present.

"Ja," said Mother with a smile. "You may all go dress in your new clothes, then come down to the table for breakfast."

Anna was pleased with her girl's excitement. She had secretly made all of the clothes throughout the year, being careful to make them a little larger so they would fit them by Christmas. The dress for Sue was made out of wool which she had saved. She had added handcrochet lace at the neck.

Clare and June's dresses were made of soft flannel in a flower design and decorated with embroidered pockets. The dresses were ankle length. The bonnets were made from the same material and gathered in a little cup-like affair to fit the shape of the head. A ribbon tied the neck closed and ruffles accented the face. In the summer the ruffle was made stiff enough to stand up and become shade from the sun. Then it was called a sun bonnet. The dress sleeves had enough material to make a little puff at the shoulder. The sleeves came down to the wrist complimenting the arm from elbow down. Onna was so tiny that Anna had made her a dress with a shirred top which hung loose from the shoulders with the hem coming just below her knees. Shirred means the material is finely gathered and falls from that point into a full skirt—usually there are between four and six rows of shirr making a complete top to a dress down to the bottom of the arm holes.

Chris and Jeff both had new wool knee pants and crisp white cotton shirts.

The peaceful sound of the church bells ringing had been interrupted by the children's excited voices as they came to the breakfast table. Chuck could not remember a Christmas morning without the church bells. They could be heard for long distances and most local farmers enjoyed them. Chuck sat at the head of the table. Mother sat near him. Jeff and Sue on either side of her and Fredrick in her lap. On the table she had placed the family's favorite hot cross rolls, boiled eggs, fried potatoes, apple sauce and wild berry jelly to put on toast made from homemade bread. Hot chocolate made with deep dark cocoa and fresh creamy milk was poured for the children and rye coffee for Anna and Chuck. The older girls were amazed that Mother had put such a big breakfast together while they were upstairs getting dressed. They knew all the work that had gone into decorating the tree and laying out the gifts. June and Onna both kissed their mother and thanked her quietly before sitting down.

"Children, now that you have tried on your new clothes, I think you had better change into clothes you can play in before you get started with the rest of the gifts under the tree," directed Mother. The children laughing and playful hurried up the stairs to change returning quickly to see what else might be under the tree for them.

Chris grabbed the BB gun. "This mine." he called to Father.

"Ya you betcha," his father said pleased to see that the boy was impressed.

Under the tree were little wood pull toys for Fredrick and a specially made wagon for Jeff. Onna found a carved box with threads and needles that she could have all to herself. There was even a knitting needle so she could learn to knit like Anna. Her favorite, however was the crochet needle because she had already learned to crochet.

June unwrapped a jar of beads and the needle and threads to string them. Now she would be able to make herself a necklace she thought.

Clare opened a paint set and quickly took it to the barn to begin painting a picture of her horse. Sue squealed with delight as she unwrapped the little rag doll with the button eyes and yellow hair.

Jeff, blowing a shrill sound on the new whistle said, "Is this mine? Do you think I can call the cows with it?"

"Ja, it tis yours; but I doubt twill help you call the cows," explained Father. "Cows are not trained by a whistle. Usually they must be brought in by someone."

The children played with their toys while Mother cleaned the kitchen and started dinner preparations. The turkey was already in the oven as it had been since late Christmas eve. She hummed

Silent Night as she worked and thought of the many wonderful Christmases the family had shared in this house. *"All is calm.. All is bright.,"* she sang aloud. God had given us so much for which to be thankful, Anna thought. As Anna prepared the dinner, her thoughts drifted back to happy times that she and Chuck had enjoyed before all the family began to arrive. She did so enjoy his music, but now she did not often get to many of the dances. She would go to the special holiday one she decided and take the children. One day, she thought, when all the children are grown then I will again go with Chuck to every dance. It wasn't that she felt bitter or upset because she had a big family, in fact she knew she was blessed. Her friend Sheila couldn't seemed to have children. Yes, Anna thought, I have been blessed. There would be plenty of time later.

If dinner is to be eaten before the milking is to be done, Anna thought, I will need to get it on the table soon. "Come girls," Mother called sharply shaking herself from her memories. "Help me set dinner on the table."

The girls worked easily with their mother. Finally dinner was on the table. "Come on everyone," coaxed June in her soft gentle voice brushing back a stray of dark brown hair with the back of her hand. She smoothed the apron over her somewhat stocky build and wished she could be a little more like Onna. I am built just like Mother but look how Father loves her, she thought shrugging her shoulders and smiling. She watched as Father herded the little ones to the table. Her thoughts were interrupted with the clammer of the older children jostling each other to find their places.

The family bowed their head while Father prayed, "Come hi Jazus ziunza gust unsagna vasdue uns beshared hust." Come Lord Jesus be our guest and let our daily food be blest, June mentally translated.

They all finished with, "Amen."

Father and Mother spoke German much of the time. Mother said it was easier for Father to understand German with his limited hearing. However, when the children or others were around, Chuck spoke English as his grandparents had insisted saying, "We are in America. We speak American." As for Anna she had a much better command of the English having been a teacher when she was young.

The children spoke mostly English. They were forbidden to speak German in school since the teacher was Norwegian. However, she spoke Norwegian back and forth with the Norwegian children which didn't seem fair to the German children.

The table was filled with the wonderful foods that had been canned and prepared throughout the summer and fall. Crisp pickles, home churned butter, homemade rolls, turkey and dressing, giblet gravy, mashed potatoes, beet pickles, and creamed carrots made by adding cream thickened with flour and water paste and a touch of butter.

When they finished, everyone was so stuffed that they had to wait to eat the apple and mincemeat pie that was waiting for them. The mincemeat was made with real meat. The steaming hot pumpkin pie was made from pumpkin picked ripe from the vine, baked and cleaned from its rind, then put through a sieve to make it clear of the little threads which run through squash or pumpkin pulp. There was fresh rich whip cream to compliment the pie. Father had separated the cream the day before because he knew that cream must be at least one day old or it will not whip.

After dinner Chris went outside to play with his gun. Standing at the edge of the barn pretending to see a cattle rustler, he took imaginary aim. Jeff, blowing his whistle, went out into the yard as the family in the house clapped their hands to their ears in agony; some wondering how long they would be able to endure the noise and Chris lost his imaginary aim momentarily.

The girls, even Clara, helped Mother clean up the kitchen before sitting down to enjoy their own gifts. Chuck and Anna spent the rest of the afternoon playing cards. Coming in one at a time, the older children helped themselves to a piece of pie before drifting off to bed.

Chuck and Anna sat awhile in the quiet kerosene lamp light to enjoy their rye coffee and pumpkin pie with whip cream.

"Tell me about your family again Chuck," Anna coaxed. She loved hearing the story.

"My parents arrived in Chicago from Germany with my grandparents," said Chuck. I was born soon after they arrived. Along with several other families that had arrived from Germany, they each paid the railroad for a boxcar in which to put all their belongings. Each box car had a wood stove for heating and cooking since all the families rode in the box as they traveled. Once they arrived in North Dakota, the boxcar was put on a side track and the families lived in it until they had put in a claim for a piece of ground to homestead. After receiving a piece of land, the men helped each other build their first small cabins. This house was built by my grandparents. My sisters and brother were out on their own when my grandparents died so the farm was left to me and my first wife."

School was on vacation until after New Years. This morning the children all got up early thinking to get in some extra play time. Anna could hear them coming down the narrow steps two at a time.

"Oh good! Breakfast is ready!" Chris praised skidding to a halt and dishing up the scrambled eggs, ham and potatoes, eating a bit as he headed to the table. "Yum! these potatoes are nice and crisp Mother."

"Well, you better hurry up and eat," urged Mother. "Your father expects you to help with the milking. And I think he also wants your help in the shop today since he is working on the machinery for spring. He said the plows need to be sharpened and the planters need some work as well."

"But I was going skating," pouted Chris.

"Well, I'm sure there will be time enough for that later today," Mother scolded softly. Besides you might think about the fact that your arm is not yet well from your last skating exhibition. "Your father said to send you out to the shed as soon as you finished your breakfast."

Anna tried to ignore the disappointment on her eldest son's face. It is too bad children on the farm need to grow up so soon she thought.

Looking up Mother saw June slowly walking down the stairs to breakfast. Here was another one of her children having to take on responsibility early. She knew, however, that this was how families survived on the farm. "Guten Morgan Mother," June greeted cheerfully as she helped herself to the food being kept warm on the back of the stove.

"Whaaa! Whaaa!" June hearing little Fredrick put her food down and went to get him. She changed his diaper before bringing him in and setting him in his high chair to eat. "Here Fredrick be a good little boy and eat your oatmeal." June sat back down at the table next to the high chair ready to help Fredrick if necessary. Taking a bit of food she said, "Umm! this is sure good, Mother."

"Well, it's time off from school and you all deserve something special for all the help you are around the farm," said Mother taking in the whole farm and the house with a swoop of the big wooden spoon in her hand.

On her way down to breakfast, Onna found Sue climbing out of bed so she took her by the hand and helped her down the stairs waiting on each step for Sue's tiny little legs to catch up. Entering the kitchen, Onna stopped to wash their hands and faces in the wash pan on the stand near the door before dishing up their breakfast. They both sat at the table in their long flannel gowns enjoying the warmth of the kitchen fire.

Clare had already dressed in warm clothes ready for outside. Bounding down the stairs, she caught up to Jeff who was also on his way down. "Move over," she ordered trying to push past him on the narrow passage.

"I don't have to," Jeff yelled as they scuffled down the steps.

"What are you up to Clare?" Mother quizzed seeing Clare dressed for the out of doors.

"After I eat breakfast," sniffed Clare in defiance, " I am going to saddle old Prince and go for a ride."

"Don't you think you should go help your father and Chris in the shed first," said Anna gently. "They are working on the machines to get them ready for the planting season."

"But it's school vacation," complained Clare sulkily. "I don't think I should have to do anything like that now. I wanted to go riding."

"Good breakfast," Jeff interjected with a mouth full of food listening to the conversation between Mother and Clare. "I think I'll go help them!" said Jeff sticking out his tongue at Clare.

"I think you can be more help to me in the house," countered Mother. "I need you to play with Fredrick as soon as he has been bathed and dressed."

"Oh Mama," whaled Jeff catching the smirk of silent mocking from Clare.

When Chuck came in for lunch later he said, "When the children have had their lunch, I guess they can go play. The seeder can wait until tomorrow. Children need a little time to enjoy their vacation from school. Chris wants to skate awhile and Clare wants to go riding. What do you think, Mother?"

"That sounds fine Chuck, but warn Chris not go showing off. That arm is still not completely healed. I think Onna and June wanted to work on their sewing projects. Sue can play with Fredrick until their nap, and Jeff can go out and play in the snow with his sled and whistle. Perhaps we can play a game or two of cards if you wish?" suggested Anna hopefully.

"Ja sure," agreed Chuck thinking how seldom they had time to themselves these days.

Everyone had moved out to do whatever was their special interest. Anna fixed a pot of hot chocolate and left it warming on the back of the fire for the children when they came in from the cold and had set out the pie for all to help themselves. Finally, she poured them each a cup of coffe and they sat down to play cards. Anna was reminded of those first calm days and months after their wedding. But peaceful as those days were, Anna would not trade the voices and clammer of today for those quiet days. She especially felt blessed that Chuck had not had to go off to war . This was probably because of his hearing problem and that they had so many children. Thank heavens the war had ended. Germany had signed the armistice November 11th at 6 am, that was 11 a m Paris time in 1918. Some of the young men had come home badly crippled but still had to do their farming if they were to survive. Anna's thoughts wandered to the fact that if Chuck's parents had not come to the United States, he might have been in Germany—A German!

Cold and wet, the children stomped in a couple of hours later arguing noisily.

Chuck and Anna finished their game. Seeing that it was late afternoon and time for the cows to be brought in for milking, Chuck picked up his hat and headed to the barn. Anna checked on the little ones. Seeing that June had already taken care of the baby, she took Sue and headed for the kitchen to start dinner.

All the children had dipped a cup of hot chocolate and were sitting by the fire drinking it. After they finished, Chris, Clare, and Onna put on their jackets and went out to help their father milk the cows. With all of them helping, it didn't take long. Chris stayed behind to clean the barn. One thing Chris couldn't stand was for animals to have to stand in their own manure. Besides, he wanted to know that the milk he drank was clean. Also Chris liked to do things once in awhile to get his father's attention over Clare.

Chuck put most of the milk in the big ten gallon cans ready for the trip to town in the morning. When he took some of the milk into the house to be separated, he noticed how tired Anna looked. June started the separator and turned it to separate the cream from the milk. Mother would need to make more butter tomorrow since they had used so much in the baking. As soon as all the children came in from the milking and chores, dinner was on the table. "Sit down children. We need to hurry and get done eating so Mother can get the little ones to bed. She needs to have a little rest," Father said with concern in his voice.

When the meal was finished, Clare and Onna cleaned the kitchen while June set up the domino game. Father had made the 28 piece set for Christmas. Each block of wood was divided in the

middle. Each section of 21 of the 28 dominoes was marked with
from one to six dots. Both sections on one domino was blank, and
six of them have one blank section and one with dots. To begin
with all the blocks are face down on the table. Each of the four
players chose 5 blocks. Chris won the first play by having a six-
four combination. June was to his left so she went next and matched
with a double four setting it down at right angle to the four. Clara
next could not play so choose 2 blocks before being able to lay
down a six-three block. Onna played her three and the game continued with much laughing and loud but good natured disagree-
ments regarding rules of the block with blanks. Mother sat in the
rocking chair with Fredrick against her shoulder and sang him to
sleep before she put him down in the crib for the night.

While the older children played dominoes, Father took turns
riding Jeff and Sue on his shoe and chanting an old German riding
song. "Huppa, Huppa, Ritta Gusey ganey neick visa . . ."

After their game was finished, June and Onna took Sue and
Jeff upstairs and put them to bed before getting ready for bed
themselves. Suddenly they heard Clare and Chris arguing their
way up the stairs. June and Onna quickly crawled into bed before
a fracas could develop over something she didn't like in their room.
June really did not like dissension and it seemed Clare was always
good at stirring something up.

Now that he children were finally upstairs for the night, Chuck
and Anna sat down for their last relaxing cup of coffee and a piece
of mincemeat pie. They spent a quiet hour going over the news of
the neighbors which they had gathered from the party telephone
line. The only telephones were the kind you had to crank and then
nothing was private. Usually there were ten parties on one line.
Needless to say one got most of the area's gossip from listening in
on other peoples conversations. The rest of the gossip came from
friends stopping by.

"Tom stopped by on his way back from town," Chuck said.
"They were all talking in town about the improved econcomy in

the cities. Perhaps our grain will bring a fair price next year," Chuck repeated in an optomistic tone.

"That is good news. I heard a conversation on the phone that young Koontz boy and his wife are expecting their fourth child," Anna related in quiet thoughtful comment. "Maybe they will not have to worry so much after all?"

"Even if the economy was not getting better, they would get by just as we did through the war years," Chuck said getting up and giving Anna a loving peck on the cheek.

Anna checked on Fredrick one last time while Chuck went in to bed. Then Anna banked the fires for the night to keep the house warm before she too went in to bed.

The next morning Anna was up earlier than usual making breakfast while Chuck was out milking the cows. Anna had decided that she had better get some baking done. With such a large family bread did not last long. The big house was gradually coming to life as the children began the routine of the day. Anna thought how grateful she was that her older girls were so good with the little ones. June had given little Fredrick his bath, dressed him, and was now putting him in the high chair ready for breakfast. Onna had gotten Sue ready and had encouraged Jeff to get himself washed up and down to breakfast. By the time Chuck came in from milking, they were all ready to sit down for breakfast.

The older girls could see their Mother's plans for the day so they cleaned up the breakfast dishes and made the kitchen ready for baking while Anna gave Fredrick a bottle, rocking him in the chair by the kitchen fire. He soon fell asleep in her arms, and she held him close for awhile enjoying the chance to cuddle the little one before putting him down for the nap. Sue and Jeff seemed content playing a game on the floor in the living room. She could hear their little voices. "Stop Sue," shouted Jeff , "that piece don't go there." Sue, having scattered all the blocks ran in to be by her mother. Jeff ran after her and explained to Mother that he was trying to build a barn and corral with blocks but Sue kept knocking them down.

"Come now." Mother soothed in her soft voice reaching out to ruffle Jeff's hair. She picked up Sue and sat her in the chair near where she was rolling out cookies. "Jeff would you like a cookie and some milk before you finish building that barn?"

"Naw, I'm going out with Father," he said disgustedly as he pulled on his boots.

Hoping to escape before his father called for help, Chris grabbed his skates and headed to the river. Clare wanting no part of the baking scene welcomed another chance to ride her horse.

Clare and Chris going out the door at the same time heading to their separate activities while sending sarcastic barbs to each other as they parted.

Clare having saddled her horse, headed out along the river with the intent to heckel Chris as he skated down river. Just as she reached the area, a jack rabbit suddenly appeared out of the trees frightening her horse who reared and threw her into the trees. The horse took off on a dead run back to the area of the barn. She had landed on a pile of leave under the trees so she was not hurt badly, but her pride was a little bruised. Now she would have to walk all the way back. Chris saw her and took the opportunity tantalize her. Clare stomping down the path toward the house with her shoulders back and her nose in the air. As she rounded the corner, she saw that her father had caught the horse and was already unsaddling her.

"What happened Clare?" Father questioned.

"A rabbit scared her and she threw me off," Clare replied.

"What were you doing riding near the trees? You know I have told you before not to do that. Animals take shelter there and jump out when something comes into view. Go in and help your mother. I'm sure she has things that need to be done. That's what you should have been doing anyway," Father scolded.

That's the last thing she wanted to do. Maybe no one would notice her if she came in quietly, she thought. Taking off her coat and boots, she headed for the stairs as quietly as possible when Onna spotted her.

"Oh there you are, Clare. About time you showed up to help

a little. The rest of us would like to play as well as you and Chris. You always manage to eat your share so come on. Get your hands in a little flour," Onna shrieked in her high pitched voice.

"Come girls," said Anna softly. "Let's not quabble. Perhaps Father settle it when he comes in for lunch."

Clare hearing this moved to the kitchen slowly. She knew full well what Father would do since he had already told her to help. He might even deny her the horse to ride and then she would have to walk to school as well as be stuck in the house all the time. These thoughts running through her mind she began to help.

Onna and June stirred up dough for snickerdoodles while Mother fixed the bread ready to rise. The kitchen was a big roomy place with a long plank table in the middle that could easily sit sixteen people at a time. The benches made it easier to crowd in the young children. The big stone fireplace was at the end of the room. It had been there since the grandparents built the house. In fact it was all that Grandmother had to cook on for the most part of her young life. Now there was a huge cook stove Chuck's parents had set beside the fireplace and only on special occasions was the fireplace used for cooking. There were three homemade cupboards lining the rest of the wall. One had two deep lined bins to hold flour and sugar. On the tops were work shelves that extended the length of the room. The long table was often used to roll out dough. At the entrance to the back door stood a mirror and wash stand with a basin for washing. Next to this stand was a pump in which the water for the house was obtained.

Today the bread would be made with the wheat Chuck had grown last year after harvest. It would have a brown look because it was not refined. The bread was not fluffy and full of air but full bodied and delicious. The pans that baked the bread were made of cast iron. They were heavy to pick up. The pans the cookies were baked in were mostly cast iron as well. Chicken fat saved when chickens were cooked was usually used to make cookies, churned butter for cakes, and rendered lard for pie crust. Chicken fat is very rich so only a small amount was needed.

As June put another batch of cookies in the oven, Onna used a wide bladed knife to take the baked cookies off the iron cookie pan and put them on a corner of the big table on a metal rack that was made for that purpose. The smell of the cookies got Sue's attention. Standing on tip toes, she reached up to capture a cookie, then laughing as she ran back to where she was playing thinking she had not been noticed. June had just turned from the oven and saw her retreat. Smiling to herself, she ignored Sue knowing the little imp thought she had put one over on them.

Clare had managed to do a little work and then while no one seemed to notice had slipped off. Onna knew she had gone but said nothing since Clare's had a habit of pushing her around or elbowing her and pretending it was an accident. Onna knew it was Clare's way of showing she was in charge. Onna felt it was not worth getting unhappy over being scolded by father for fighting. Clare always seemed to make it look like it wasn't her fault.

10

Still in North Dakota

The harsh winter had come and gone. Chuck was in the field planting the grain crops and thinking and planning. He would extend his wheat fields to help feed the bigger family. Since the children were older they would need more bread. Along with this he needed to have barley and corn for cattle feed as well as help get in Anna's garden. But, he thought, for now he needed to concentrate on his part. There needed to be plenty of oats for cattle feed and flax for bedding.

Anna had planted her vegetable and herb gardens and was now planting her annual flower beds. She thought that pink, purple and white petunias would look good among the tulip beds. She would plant marigolds, onions, and nicotina around the dahlia beds to keep the aphid and slugs away. The air was cold and a strong March wind blew making her question whether it might be too early for her to be planting her begonias and dahlia bulbs. She checked the wild garden. The seeds she had colleted and planted in the fall were already sending up tender shoots through the frosty humus soil. She had read about this new type of gardening, letting flowers seed whereever they would. It would be an interesting experiment. After all if Mary Prescott thought it was a beautiful arrangement, she would give it a try. Anna came in from planting the garden. She was very tired. She leaned for a minute against the door post. She felt very heavy. She just wanted to sit for awhile and rest, but she knew she must keep going. The children would soon be home from school, and Fredrick would wake from his nap. She looked out of the door and could still see Jeff and Sue playing at the end of the garden under the tree. "Come," called Anna to the little ones, "I have some cookies and milk for you in the kitchen."

They had just begun eating their snack when the rest of the children came in from school. Gradually the house filled with the sound of children's voices bantering, and for a while Anna forgot her tiredness.

After dinner Chuck noticed that Anna seemed unusually tired. "Girls, you clean up the kitchen and get the little ones to bed. Your mother is tired out." Gratefully, Anna sat rocking little Fredrick by the fire while the girls did as their father asked.

Once they had the little ones in bed, they too went up to their room to read before going to bed. June and Onna enjoyed laying on the straw beds which had a soothing smell and sound. Each year as the straw was harvested and dried, the ticking was washed and then new straw put in the ticking. These sleeping pads were placed on frames which had wire webbing that worked as a spring . The trundle bed was a framed box affair that had casters at the four corners to roll it under the big bed. It was pulled out at night to sleep the younger children. The only beds with regular cotton mattresses were in their parents' room. This was common practice for all families on the farms as they used whatever they could grow as much as possible.

Chris was feeling mean. The house always seemed so crowded these days. There was never any place to be alone. He didn't mind the hard work. In fact he enjoyed the work on the farm, but he didn't like all the noise and clatter of the house. Jeff was now sharing his room since there were more beds for the girls and Fredrick's trundle bed was also in their room.

Chris dished up a piece of pie and took his time eating it before stomping up the stairs to his room. Anna heard his door slam and wondered what was bothering this short tempered son of theirs, but other things were pressing her tonight and she did not feel like dealing with Chris and his moods.

Finally Anna and Chuck were left alone. Chuck could see that Anna did not feel well so he got his own coffee and asked if she would like some.

"No, I think not," she said weakly.

Chuck sat drinking his coffee and thinking about their life together. He wondered what he could do to help ease some of the work for Anna. Finishing his coffee, he got up and banked the fires. "You need to get some rest Anna."

"Ya, perhaps. Thanks for banking the fires," said Anna slowly pushing herself up from the chair.

June heard Fredrick fussing in the middle of the night. Perhaps he too had heard their mother crying or was it screaming. After changing his clothes, she took him to bed with her. Holding him tightly, she sang softly until he went back to sleep. But June lay awake for a long time listening to the night sounds and wondering about her mother.

Morning came and June, knowing there had been a lot of activity in the night, prepared to take over this morning. She got Sue up and told her to wash and get dressed. She called to Onna and asked her to get Jeff washed and dressed before coming to breakfast. "I get Fredrick bathed and dressed," she said holding Fredrick on her left him and holding Sue by the hand. June finished getting Fredrick and Sue cleaned up and then put Fredrick in the high chair. Using her foot to pull out a chair, she directed Sue to climb up. Then she pushed the chair up to the table and dished them both the oatmeal that her father had made before going out to milk the cows. Onna came down shortly with Jeff. June put a bowl of oatmeal in front of him and a plate of toast and wild berry jelly in the center of the table. June left the rest of the children to dish up their own cereal while she got ready for school. When she was ready, she got Fredrick down from his chair and took him, Sue and Jeff in to see Mother who was sitting in the rocker holding something wrapped in a blanket. Smiling tiredly, Mother opened the blanket and said, "Here is your new little sister, Lill."

"Jeff, you and Sue sit here by Mother and play with Fredrick until Father comes in from the barn. I have to go to school," explained June as she peeked into the folds of the blanket. She gave mother a broad smile then hugged each of the little ones before heading off to school. Fredrick began to fuss. He wanted to be in his mother's lap, and he didn't like seeing someone take his place. Jeff picked him up and with Sue's help, they got him interested in a toy that held his attention until Father came in from his chores.

Finally Chuck came in holding a cup of coffee. "Would you like me to fix you some breakfast Anna?" he asked with gentleness.

"No, I don't think so," said Anna quietly. "But could you please hold the baby for awhile. I need to clean up."

After her spit bath and change of clothes, she poured herself a cup of coffee and ate a piece of toast . Then she wandered over to console little Fredrick. Anna watched the three of them play for awhile, then she picked little Fredrick up and sat in the chair rocking until he went to sleep. "Chuck," she asked, "If you will watch Sue and Jeff for a bit, I think I will go lie down and nurse the baby and perhaps take a little nap?"

"Go ahead," Chuck answered giving the baby to Anna. "We will go out to the barn for awhile," and taking Sue and Jeff by the hand he headed for the door.

Anna could not remember being this tired. She had finished nursing the baby and had lain her in the cradle. That part she remembered, but she did not remember lying back down on the bed nor her headhitting the pillow. She awoke when she heard Fredrick crying. Rubbing her eyes, it took a minute for her to remember where she was. Then realizing that it was probably midafternoon, Anna went to get Fredrick and give him something to eat. Soon she could hear Lill's tiny little cry. She let Fredrick out of his chair and took him by the hand. "Come little one. Your sister calls."

Fredrick looked up at his mother. His blue-gray eyes shinning. He let out a little chuckle. He is such a happy, pleasant baby, she thought. He only cries if he is hungry, wet, or hurt. As they walked together, his short legs waddled along beside her until they reached the baby's cradle. She let go of his hand and reached down to pick up the tiny bundle the whole time talking to him about what it was to be a big brother. After she had changed the baby's wet clothes, she took the baby in one arm and with her other hand she led Fredrick over to the rocking chair. There she lifted him up on one knee while holding the baby in the other arm. For a long while she slowly rocked both of them. Fredrick watched his new little sister very carefully then finally reached out and petted her pink cheek. "Nice Kitty," he said.

Mother chuckled, "Not kitty, Fredrick. This is your little sister."

The older children came home from school and changed their clothes. Onna and June rushed to see what Mother might need them to do.

"Will you please put dinner on?" she asked. "You will find some noodles already made. Get a jar of meat from the cellar. You will need to boil it well to make sure it is completely cooked so we won't get sick. Then add the noodles. That should be enough with some vegetables."

Clare and Chris put on warm jackets and went out to find their father. They really didn't want to stay in and have to do anything with the babies. Father saw them coming so he immediately put them to work on the evening chores while he took Sue and Jeff back into the house. In the house he found the girls already busy with dinner so he left the two little ones and went back out to help finish the chores. Anna came to the table just as Chuck, Clare, and Chris came in from the chores. Anna thanked the girls for doing such a nice job with dinner and for feeding the little ones. Once dinner was over and the mess cleaned up, the girls took charge of getting the little ones to bed leaving Mother and Father alone with the new baby.

Anna and Chuck took a cup of coffee and went into the living room to sit awhile and catch up on the news they had heard from the neighbors.

"Did you know that your friend Pansy is having another baby?" Chuck related taking another sip of his coffee. "When I saw Tom at the creamery, he said Pansy's husband was over at his place. He said Pansy was not doing real well this time,"

"Oh that's not good." Anna thought, "I should have gone over before now to see if she needed my help." "I will have to take the wagon and go see about her when the girls are here with the little one," Anna saidaloud.

"Anna, you have too much to do with the new baby. You can not stress yourself right now. You know that you had a bad time with this one." Chuck argued.

"I will be fine. And the girls will feel good that they are allowed to watch Lill by themself for a few hours," Anna explained.

"I guess with your loving nature I can't keep you from doing it. You always look out for everyone else and not yourself," Chuck complained. "Even with your big family, you always seem to have time to knit sweaters for all the new babies and help all the young brides learn to can and take care of their gardens," Chuck said looking at Anna with pride.

11

Near accident in Idaho

Today John and Rena were visiting their friends, the Andersons. Richard, their son was about the same age as Gus and Phil and they had became fast friends. Richard's sister, Mable, who was a few years younger, was a great match for Mercy. The four of them had a great time playing around the big dairy farm with all the special places to play hide and seek. The dairy had a large herd of cows and a carrier system with huge buckets that carried feed and silage into the barn on a continuous pulley system. Lisa was a bit younger and being rather impetuous she made herself quite a pain to keep an eye which was their job. They hit upon an idea. They decided the buckets would be a good place to put Lisain. She couldn't get out, and if they turned on the pulley it would keep her busy.

Lisa sat in the big bucket and rocked it as the pulley moved it along, but she became frightened when it looked like the bucket was going to dump her out at the end so she began to cry and scream for Mercy.

Mercy, busy playing hide and seek, at first did not pay attention, but suddenly froze in her tracts. "Where is Lisa?" She got up from her hiding place and began running to where the buckets had moved.

"One, two, three, four!" yelled Richard as he hit her on the back.

"Forget it!" yelled Mercy back at him. "Stop that thing! Can't you see that Lisa is about to be dumped out!"

Then in a panic Richard looked up knowing what could happen. Seeing Mercy running toward the bucket, he also headed toward the switch off. Running as fast as he could, Richard reached the switch just as the buckets reached the end and was about to dump. He pulled the switch just as Mercy reached the bucket and pulled a screaming Lisa out giving her a big hug and wiping tears from her face with the back of her own sleeve.

"I gonna fall," Lisa sobbed.

"No, I wouldn't let anything happen to you," Mercy soothed as she continued to hug her. But in her mind she scolded herself for being so selfish as to put her little sister in such danger. She could have been killed her mind screamed. She shivered at the thought of how close it had been.

Lisa was very dirty and Mercy wondered how she was going to explain this to mom as she walked her back up to the house.

"Come children," called their mother. "We need to head home. It is time for us to get dinner for your dad, and the Andersons have milking and chores to do.

Oh wow, at least she didn't have to confront the Andersons, Mercy reflected.

12

Accidents in North Dakota

Lill was asleep in the house. Fredrick sat playing in the dirt beside his mother as she worked in the garden, his blonde hair blowing in the wind. Seeing Jeff coming along the path to the garden, Mother directed him to watch Fredrick while she went in the house to check on Lill.

After a while Jeff became sidetracked by a garden snake and didn't notice Fredrick toddled over to the path where he had seen his father disappear earlier. Suddenly Jeff saw Fredrick standing in the center of the path where the gate opened to the corral. Looking beyond him, Jeff saw the horses from the pasture headed straight for Fredrick and the corral beyond. Jeff began to run for the boy, but was unable to reach him before the herd of horses ran through the gate and over the top of Fredrick. In slow motion Jeff heard himself yelling and yelling and running and running, but he was helpless to do anything.

Anna, coming from the house, saw what was happening and she too began to scream, "No! No! He will be killed!"

Chuck hearing the screams, looked over in time to see the last of the horses running over Fredrick's lifeless little body. His heart sank like a rock to the pit of his stomach. His legs became stones and his body went cold. Thirty horses had just run over the top of his son. Chuck temporarily paralyzed, watched as Anna picked up their child's limp form. When he could finally move, he ran to close the corral gate behind the horses so no more damage could be done. Running back to Anna, he took the boy in his arms and ran for the house. Putting him down on the table, he gently brushed the dirt from him. The tears were falling unashamed as he checked, slowly moved his hands over every inch of his son's body. He was amazed to find no broken bones, no cuts or bruises. All of a sudden, Fredrick opened his eyes and looked up with a smile and a little giggle.

"This is a miracle," Anna whispered in disbelief. "Look at him laugh. He thinks it is funny."

Chuck stayed in the house with Anna. After Anna bathed and dressed Fredrick, Chuck took him to the rocker and while Anna tended to Lill he rocked his son. This surely is a miracle he thought.

The children coming in from school, wondered at the tender care of their father toward Fredrick. Chuck gave Fredrick to June, grabbed his hat and headed for the door.

"It's been a tough day for everyone," Father explained. "Fredrick was almost killed when the herd of horses ran over the top of him."

"What!" exclaimed the group as Father went on to explain the accident. "Oh how awful!" June shivered.

"It's been hard on your mother so get the little ones fed and into bed. When I am done with the chores outside, I will be in to help. I don't want your mother having to do anything tonight," Father barked orders to all of them. "Chris and Clare come out and help milk the cows and take them out to the pasture. Onna start supper. Sue you are big enough to help Onna."

"Jeff," said Father, "Come here." Jeff was cowering in the corner. He expected to be punished since he was suppose to be taking care of Fredrick. "What seems to be your problem?"

Sniffling Jeff stuttered, "It's a ah,all my fau fau fault."

"No," comforted Father, "It's hard to keep up with babies. It was an accident. Now you come help me," and draping an arm around Jeff's shoulder, Father walked Jeff out to the barn.

After the chores were done, dinner over, and the babies in bed, Anna and Chuck sat down to read their Bible. Feeling especially blessed that their happy little son had been spared, they gave a special prayer of thanks before going off to bed. The older children finished up the kitchen and went up to bed as well.

The next morning all were up early. The children got themselves fed and off to school. Anna tended to the younger ones before sitting down to her own breakfast. Chuck came in to check on her a few times during the morning. After lunch he offered to help her. "I'm alright," she assured him. "But if you would put Sue and Jeff busy doing something, I could catch up in the garden while baby Lill and Fredrick are asleep."

"Sure thing, Mother," he said as he took the two children by the hand. Donning their coats, they all headed for the barn.

13

Flu season in North Dakota claims lives

Late fall was here and the cold weather was upon them. Chuck and Anna sat drinking their last cup of coffee before going to bed. Anna sighed. She was finding it harder and harder to get all of the gardening, canning, baking, and sewing done. She relied more and more on the older girls for help. She didn't have the same kind of energy she used to have. Baby Lill was getting more active. It was hard to work when she was awake, and Fredrick seemed to be in one crisis after another. She sent up many prayers for him.

The peas and beans were picked and ready can. It was berries picking time and the jelly needed to be made. It would soon be time butcher and process the sausages. Also at this time of year Anna's tulips, irises, gladiolas, daffodils, crocuses and lily bulbs needed to be dug up and stored in the cellar. Everything was ready to harvest.

"It seems that several families are sick with the flu," Chuck said relating to Anna the news he had heard when he took the milk to the creamery that morning. "The Kuntz baby is so sick they are afraid they will loose him."

"How many are sick?" Anna asked.

"It seems that half the farm families have this flu," replied Chuck. "As well as quite a few people in town."

Getting up and gathering their empty coffee cups, Anna took them into the dish pan and stopped by the kitchen stove to bank the fire. Anna opened the heavy frame in front of the fireplace beside the kitchen stove and added two more logs thinking perhaps it would keep the house warmer and keep the chill out since the wind was so strong even though the house was well built the wind came in around the doors.

Chuck finished banking the heater and met Anna as she finished putting rolled rugs against all the outside doors. Putting his arms around her and walking toward the bedroom Chuck said, "I think tomorrow we had better fry up lots of onions to keep on hand. Perhaps they will help keep the children well."

"I will make a big pot of soup too with lots of onions in it then the children who don't eat the fried onions will get them that way," Anna replied.

*   *   *

It had been weeks since Chuck had come home with the news of the spread of flu through the area. The Kuntz baby had died and some of the older people had not been strong enough to fight it off.

It was November and most of the families were beginning to recover, but this morning when Anna came in to the kitchen she missed Chris and Jeff coming down to breakfast. When Chuck came in from milking, she asked him to see why they had not come down.

Chuck set the milk down by the separator and went upstairs thinking the boys had decided to have an early thanksgiving vacation. Opening their bedroom door, he could smell the fever. He felt each of their heads and knew they would have to be helped quickly if they were to get well. He hated to tell Anna.

"Anna, the boys are very hot to the touch." Chuck said going back to the kitchen. "They are both complaining that they ache and their throat hurts. We have to sponge them down and get something down them to break the fever. You boil some onions and make it into a tea while I take them up a little brandy drink. I think a spoon of it in hot water should help." I would go get the doctor, but he hasn't had much luck with his medicine," Chuck complained heading back up to the boys with the brandy drink.

Chuck returned and collected the tea and toast Anna had made for the boys. "I will sponge the boys down and give them the tea to drink. You stay down here so we can try and keep the babies from catching it," Chuck directed grabbing the wash basin filled with warm water and some towels before heading back upstairs to sponge the boys.

By milking time Chuck came down and said he thought the boys could use a bowl of onion soup . Annie heated the soup while he took another brandy water up to them.

With the second dose of brandy water, the boys seemed in better form so he left them eating the soup. "Stay in bed," he said. "I will check, see how you are doing when I come back in from milking."

Once the milking was done and the chores finished, Chuck hurried in to see how the boys were doing. Taking another pan of water, he headed up to sponge the boys down again. When he came back down later, he was able to tell an anxious Anna, "The boys fever seems to be down. They are no longer hot to touch," Chuck commented keeping his distance to prevent any of the germs to pass over to Anna until he had washed in the basin.

Later Chuck found Anna with Fredrick and Lill in the rocking chair with her eyes closed in prayer.

"Did you hear what I said Anna?" Chuck asked.

"Yes dear," Anna returned slowly opening her eyes. "I believe God has answered our prayers."

"It will be a few days before they will be getting up," Chuck said. "Let the girls take their food up to them, and I think they should stay out of school since thanksgiving is not far away."

"As you think best," she said getting up and putting the babies down by the kitchen stove to be near her while she got dinner ready.

The girls had been in their rooms studying ever since coming home from school. Anna hoped they were not getting sick.

June came down from studying interrupting her thoughts, "Mother, I don't feel like going to school tomorrow. I ache all over and I have a bad headache."

"You better crawl into bed. You probably have what the boys have," Mother coaxed.

"But you need me to help with the babies," June argued.

"Father will help me. You rest so you won't get worse," giving her some of the hot drink with brandy Chuck had been giving the boys.

June drug herself back upstairs as Anna went to call Chuck. The babies were both fussing and Anna knew she needed to tend the boys.

"What can I do to help?" Chuck asked as he came in seeing Anna trying to attend two crying babies,

"Chuck please go up and see how the children are. Now June has taken ill and I have not been able to leave the babies to check on the boys or see if the other girls are ill."

Chuck came down and said both boys seem to be recovering, "June said she is feeling better since you gave her the hot drink . Onna and Clare seem to be fine. They at least are well enough to be arguing with each other."

"That is good news, Chuck because both babies are not feeling well. it looks like I will be busy tonight trying to get them settled." Anna had sat down in the rocker and was rocking both babies on her lap. She looked up at Chuck with fear in her eyes. Tears of frustration slowly trickled down her cheeks.

"I know you have reason to have fear since there have been three different farm children who have died. But they were weak children already. The other children in their families came through alright. Our children all seem to be strong and healthy, even our tiny one, Onna, is not sick," Chuck said confidently.

"I know," Anna returned. "I believe . . ." Then in a whisper she said. "Lord, help my unbelief."

"It has only seemed to last a few days in each family," Chuck continued to comfort. "Most of the families around have come through fine," Chuck reminded.

There was a strong wind blowing. It was difficult to keep the house warm. Fredrick cried most of the night because he was cold.

When he woke in the morning, he went to June for comfort. June noticed that his hands were clammy and his little face was really hot. He whimpered and complained that his body hurt. June changed his clothes to make sure he was warm and dry. June was feeling better so she put Fredrick in bed with her knowing Mother was busy taking care of Baby Lill.

Fredrick had developed a high fever, and Mother gave him some of the hot drink Father had made. She put a mustard plaster on his chest to loosen the congestion.

Little Lill's temperature soared even worse than Frederick's and though they continued to sponge her down and keep her warm, nothing seemed to relieve the congestion in the little girl's chest.

By the third day, Lill couldn't make it any further and she succumbed.

Anna and Chuck were terribly grieved to lose this little girl, but they knew they must carry on and try to save Fredrick.

It was a brisk cold morning, when they laid their little Lill to rest in the cemetery where her brother and grandparents lay. The boys had recovered so they along with Clare and Onna stood at the grave to pray over their little lost sister. Even Clare who had never given her much attention seemed to be distressed. Jeff who had been the closest to her hung on his mother. June had stayed with Fredrick since he was still sick. Fredrick remained in bed and was carefully watched day and night. He was given plenty of hot liquids and a thick gruel to sustain him. After several days he began to perk up and after a week he finally was able to get up.

After breakfast Fredrick looked for Lill. He wanted to play but Lill wasn't on the floor. She wasn't in her bed. He wandered from room to room looking and calling her name. Finally he went back to his mother. Lill still wasn't in his mother's arms.

Fredrick called, "Lill, Lill, Lill," making the round of the rooms again. Mother was apprehensive but knew she would have to explain to him. She picked him up and sat down in the rocker by the fire. Slowly she rocked him and in a deep sorrowful voice Mother explained, "Lill went to live with Jesus in heaven." She continued to rock him until he quietened and went to sleep. She laid him down on the couch and covered him with the afghan. Drying her eyes with the bottom corner of her apron, she went into the kitchen to check on Jeff and Sue who were playing a game near the kitchen fire.

14

Poison in the shed in North Dakota

Standing at the kitchen fire, Anna began to think about wash day. Laundry was an all day job. First, the water had to be pumped from the well. The pump in the kitchen had a faucet on one side and an arm-like handle. When this arm was pumped up and down it pulled the water from the well and pushed it out of the faucet. Sometimes, if it had rained, the water was collected in the watering trough outdoors. Then this water was used for washing. After collecting the water, it must be heated in the woodstove reservoir. Two large tubs had to be filled one for washing, one for rinsing. The soap had been made in the fall at butchering time from lye and tallow. Now came the really hard chore. The clothes were rubbed with the soap, then scrub bed up and down against a ribbed board called a washboard until all the grime was removed. The clothes were then wrung out by hand and put in the rinse water. They were rinsed and wrung out again. One had to have strong hands to handle the heavy material. Finally the clothes were hung on a line to dry. In the winter this was a very disagreeable chore since your fingers froze and you had to keep washing to keep them thawed. Some people draped the clothes on racks in the house by the heater. Needless to say everyone was careful about getting school clothes dirty. In the winter, the girls wore a cotton underdresss beneath their wool dresses and a cotton pinafore over the top of their wool dresses so one did not wash the wool dress but perhaps but once a year. It was the work clothes and play clothes that were washed more often as well as the underwear and baby clothes.

Anna moved around the kitchen preparing the evening meal. Her thoughts reminded her that Jeff would be going off to school with the older children next year and she would only have Sue and Fredrick home through the day. No Jeff to help with the younger children. She thought of Fredrick and how very active this three year old son was getting to be. He was built heavier than Jeff and was almost as tall. He had good climbing skills and had already figured out how to open the kitchen door and get himself into the yard. His brother Jeff tried to watch out for him but being young himself Jeff often got side-tracked.

Anna still remembered one particular laundry day when Fredrick found his way into the shed. He climbed to one of the top shelves where he found a bottle of gopher poisoning which he decided to sip. When Jeff discovered him, he grab the poison from Fredrick and raced to show his mother. Anna hurried to the shed, grabbed Fredrick and frantically raced with him to the barn where Chuck was doing the morning milking. She filled a cup with warm milk from the bucket and forced Fredrick to drink. I just can't lose another child. Please God save my child, Anna prayed tears running down her cheeks.

Chuck took Fredrick from her arms and dipped the cup in the warm milk again. He continued to force cup after cup of milk until the little fellow overflowed with milk and began to throw up. Then Chuck took Fredrick into the house and sat rocking him until he had thrown up several times. Finally, he layed him on the couch and Anna sat with him for several more hours. By night Anna was exhausted but happy and thankful that her prayers had been answered. She just couldn't lose this happy spirited baby. Dear Fredrick, with his bubbly laugh and charming ways made a brighter day for everyone. "Once again a miracle has saved his life." Anna mused aloud to no one in particular. "Perhaps a special angel watches over him."

At the dinner table that night, Anna said pleadingly. "Chuck, please remove all the poisons from the shed and lock them up. Fredrick is too inquisitive."

"Ya Anna. I have already started to move those things into the seed shed where there is a lock. I realized today that other children visiting could also get into poisons.

After June and Onna finished the dishes, June asked if she could take Fredrick up to bed and watch out for him .

"That would be nice, June. The rest of you children can go on up to your rooms and study," Mother directed waving her hand towards the stairs directed. "Your father and I needs some time alone."

"Would you like a cup of coffee or a home brew," Anna asked as the children left.

"I think I will have a home brew, Anna. We have had a trying day."

For a time Anna and Chuck sat quietly each in their own thoughts going over the day's events. They each gave thanks to God that they had not lost their special little Fredrick. He was a light in their life. This cheerful little fellow made everyone feel happy when he was around. They talked a little but spent most of the next hours just enjoying the quiet and each other's company. Finally, they finished their home brew, banked the fires and drifted off to bed.

15

Going to town in North Dakota

A week passed and things were getting back to normal so Anna made plans to go to town.. Sugar, flour, salt and some seasonings were all that was needed from town. Anna processed most of the food the family ate. She made coffee from roasted ground rye. Since the water in the area was so alkaline, most families made home brew which the children were allowed to drink. Because they were not denied the beer, they did not seem to abuse drinking it. They treated it as they would water. Most parents believed that beer had nutritional value such as vitamins and minerals.

Today Anna dressed Fredrick in a white crisply ironed shirt and knee pants. Boy's knee pants came down just below the knee with a band around the bottom that buttoned to keep the pants in place. This was the dress for town, school and church until a boy reached his teens. It was a special day when the boys could shed their knee pants for the long pants like their fathers wore.

Anna hooked the team of horses to the buggy which had a canvas cover. This cover was treated with bees wax to make it shed some of the water when it rained. Anna helped Fredrick into the buggy then went around to the other side. As she mounted, her weight tilted the buggy so much that Fredrick thought the buggy would tip completely over. He hung on with both hands and tried to be brave. The buggy had a sturdy frame and soon Mother was in the seat and the buggy leveled out. Fredrick loved going to town with his mother. He always felt that this was his special time with her.

It took quite awhile for the team to pull the buggy down the narrow path to the little town by the railroad track where all the trading was done. In town not only farm supplies were found but tools, mending materials for harnesses, special spices, and foods not grown on the farms. This is where the women found materials to sew the clothes their families wore. Most of the women were very good at sewing and took pride in how well they could sew. Some were especially proud of their new peddle sewing machine that saved them hours of time. They no longer had to sew every-thing by hand stitch by stitch. The buildings were close together. They had low slanting roofs to keep snow off as much as possible. Stables were at the end of the little town where the blacksmith did his work shoeing horses and mending machine. Across the street was the train platform. At the far end of the platform was a big building called a creamery. This is where Anna must stop first and deliver the cans of milk. Next she went to the merchantile store where she hoped there would be some new fabrics.

Anna found a bolt of goods that she had not seen on anyone else at church. She bought enough to make herself a new dress. She also purchased enough material to make each of the girls new dresses and the boys new pants and shirts for Christmas.

Having finished getting threads and materials, she moved to the other side of the store where she was able to replenish the spices she had used up as well as a little stick of candy for Fredrick.

16

Christmas on the farm

Another Christmas season had come and Anna's thought went to the loss of her little girl. She busied herself with the baking for Christmas. The bustle of the seasons activities and the other children helped take up her thoughts and relieve her of the painful loss of her daughter. This was the time the farmers tried to get together if weather permitted. Usually the weather held until after New Years. She had already finished the sewing for each of the children and the presents were tucked away for the big day.

Outside she heard sleigh bells and knew the neighboring farmer was out gathering the farm children for the annual sleigh ride and carole singing. The following day all the neighbor children would be at their place for the skating party on the river which was at the edge of their fields. Anna set aside a bowl of cookies for the children that would be skating. They would be coming in cold and hungry and she always made sure they had plenty of hot chocolate and cookies to warm them up.

"Children get your scarves on and wrap up warm. Be sure your boots are buckled. The sleigh is almost here. I can hear it coming up the lane now," called Anna cupping her hands around her mouth and sticking her head up the stairwell.

The sleigh stopped, but the children in the sleigh continued their singing. ". . . . Their old fa-mil-iar car—ols play, And wild and sweet the words re-peat of peace on earth, good-will to men." Some started the song again while others said hello to Chirs, Onna, Clare, or June. "I heard the bells on Christ-mas

day. Their old fa. . . ." June pulled Jeff up along side of her.
They all joined in the song as the sleigh pulled away, "I thought
how, as the day had come, The belfries of all Chris-ten-dom.
Had rolled a-long th' un-bro-ken song Of peace on earth, good-
will to men." Anna watched out the window until she could
no longer hear the singing. Turning she smiled at Chuck, "What
a wonderful family we have."

"Since the babies are asleep, I guess you and I can have a little
time to ourselves," Chuck said draping his arms around Anna's
shoulder and giving her a little squeeze. "How about a game of
cards and a little brew?"

Making the table ready and getting two home brew, Anna
looked at Chuck with a smile and letting a twinkle of love light her
brown eyes.

As Chuck and Anna were finishing their last game of cards,
they heard the sleigh with its jingling bells and the laughter of the
children coming down their lane.

"Guess we had better fix a bit of hot chocolate to warm them
and lay out a little extra sausage. I am sure they will be hungry
after such an evening," Anna remarked as she gave Chuck a plate
with homemade bread and sausage. "Another brew or hot chocolate?" she asked Chuck as she set his plate down.

"I think a hot cup of your special chocolate would be a good
night cap, Mother," Chuck replied.

The children all rosy cheeked with their eyes sparkling piled
in the door excited and battling each other to be first to get their
wraps off and first to the table where they saw Mother had readied
a snack and hot chocolate.

"Oh Mama," Onna exclaimed in her high pitched voice. "It
was so much fun. Everyone came out of their houses and gave us a
little something as we sang to them."

Clare sat at the end of the table in a somewhat sullen silence.

"What is your problem?" Chuck quizzed as he took another sip of his chocolate. "Didn't the young Hanson boy give
you any attention?"

"Why would I care," Clare retorted as she dumped her chair over by getting up to fast. Picking the chair up, she stomped up the stairs without a backward glance.

Onna chuckled to herself as she watched her sister in her fury leave the room . "Olaf Swensona was giving Hannah Yergeson lots of attention." Onna commented continuing to chuckle.

Jeff yawned and finished the last of his hot chocolate.

June seeing this took him by the arm and led him to the stairs, "Goodnight," she said. "I'll see him tucked in for the night."

Chris gave his father a questioning look before saying, "Can I go ice skating with the other kids in the morning or do you have something special you want me to help with?"

"Naw," Chuck replied. "It is holiday time. You can have your fun."

"Is it not skating party night with the neighbor children?" Anna inquired.

"Ya, it is our turn. We are the last on the schedule for the neighborhood parties," Chuck replied. "Only the dance Saturday remains before we celebrate Christmas at Church Sunday," drinking the last of his chocolate, he moved his chair back and placed his cup in the pan to soak.

Chris followed his father from the table putting his cup in the pan along with his father. "Thanks Father. I will like going skating in the morning by myself."

"Don't skate too long. It won't due for you to be tired out before the guests arrive. I will count on you to be a good neighbor and entertain the young children. Someone needs to help keep them from getting too wild or hurt." Chuck admonished.

"Goodnight Mother. Goodnight Father," Onna yelled over her shoulder as she headed up the stairs with Chris behind her.

Anna had finished banking the fire in the heater as well as the old fireplace as well as the kitchen stove. "It will be cold tonight," Anna said. "I think since Chris will be up early to skate I will put a pot of porridge on the back of the stove for the children to have as they get up."

"You are such a thoughtful, loving mother Anna," Chuck said as he came up beside her. "You always plan for all of us. It makes the holidays seem so very blessed." Putting his strong arms around her shoulders, Chuck gave her a hearty squeeze.

"You go to bed," Anna directed. "I will finish the porridge and check on Fredrick and Sue, then I'll be in."

The next morning Anna was in the kitchen preparing the feast she would have ready for the neighbors as they came to spend the day and evening with them. Chuck was out doing the chores and would soon be in with the milk to separate. Chris had already had a dish of porridge and was on the river skating. Clare was in the living room by the fire with her feet propped up reading a book. June and Onna had Sue and Fredrick in tow making them ready for breakfast as Jeff having helped himself sat at the table finishing his breakfast.

"Do I need to do anything after I get the woodboxes full Mother?" Jeff's charismatic charm was not lost on Anna. His soft blonde curls fell over his blue gray eyes and he wiped them back.

"What are you planning to do when you finish?" his mother quizzed.

"Please, could I go sledding," Jeff pleaded.

"Okay. When you have finished your chore you can go sledding, but be sure to dress warmly and stay close to the barn so we can see you," Anna commanded.

Jeff had just brought his last load to the woodbox when June and Onna sat Sue and Fredrick at the table for breakfast .

After breakfast, Onna took the two little ones to wash them while June dipped water from the boiler at the back of the stove to clean up the breakfast dishes. Onna came back in with a clean Sue and Fredrick, setting them down with some cut out wood blocks to play with, before helping Mother and June prepare for the evening festivities.

Coming in from the outdoor chores, Chuck poured a cup of rye coffee from the pot at the back of the kitchen stove. "What have we here?" he questioned as he lifted a fresh cinnamon roll from where it was cooling. Anna good naturally slapped at his hand as she said, "If you eat it all before our neighbors arrive, what will they think?"

"Knowing what a good cook you are, they will understand it was just too good to leave sitting around," Chuck replied with a chuckle.

June having finished the dishes, began taking the cookies out of the pan and putting more dough in to bake.

Onna began washing up the baking pans as they became empty.

"Anna you have quite a crew of elves here. Did you steal them from Santa's work shop?" Chuck tweaked each girl's ear loving.

"Where is Clare?" quizzed Chuck?

"She is enjoying a good book." Anna said defensively knowing Chuck did not approve of the lack of involvement on Clare's part she added. "It is good for her to read."

"It would be good for her to learn to cook and make some young fellow a nice basket for the next basket social," Chuck admonished.

"Don't be so hard on her, Chuck," Anna pleaded. "She will come around when the time is right."

Onna rattled the dishes to cover her impish giggle over the comments about her sullen sister. Onna knew Clare had an eye for the Hanson boy, but as her father said, he would not like some one who could not cook. He certainly has an eye for good food she thought remembering other box socials and on which baskets he usually bid.

With the baking finished and the cleaning done, Chuck suggested that Anna sit and rest before the neighbors began to arrive.

Chris came in shaking the snow from his clothes as he undressed and hung the outer coats to dry by the door.

"Perhaps you should put those things by the heater his father ordered. You will need them dry later when the rest get here."

Chris pulled out a chair and set it by the heater where he hung his coat and scarf placing his boots behind the heater.

A commotion soon erupted from the area of the living room.

"What seems to be the problem in there?" Father asked heading toward the noise.

"Chris just pushed me," Clare screamed.

"I didn't push her," yelled Chris. "I just moved her feet off the only chair left to sit on in here."

Chuck arrived in the living room in time to see a little more pushing and shoving.

"Can't you two ever do anything without causing a problem?" Father scolded sternly. "Clare, it seems to me that you have had the whole day to yourself. I think it is time you get up out of that chair and set the table for the family. Get some fruit and sausage from the basement and get it sliced. Put the bread and butter on the table along with some milk. Then make some rye coffee for your mother and me. Let's see if you can get it all done before anyone gets here. If you can't, you will have your turn in the kitchen by yourself for the rest of the holiday season.

Finally winding down, Chuck saw Fredrick and Sue peacefully playing with the blocks that he had cut out for them. He wished Chris and Clare could cease this constant battle and get along as peacefully as those two in the corner.

Clare got up and, throwing her book down, headed for the basement.

"Clare," Chuck bellowed.

"Yes Father," answered Clare turning toward him in a gesture of defeat.

"You get back in here and pick up this book. We don't treat books like that. I might add that you had better be quick about lunch. When we have finished eating you will be the one doing the dishes and cleaning the area. Do you have it understood now?"

Clare did as her father directed without further display of displeasure knowing full well she had upset her father enough that she could end up in her room the whole night and she would have no chance to see the Hanson boy if he came.

Chuck left the house to get the evening chores done. He wanted this evening to be special for Anna who seldom had a chance to visit with friends. Anna always made special presents for the children before Christmas arrived and he wanted this day to be special for her.

Chris hearing his father go out, got up and put on his coat and boots. Having heard how upset his father was with Clare, he decided perhaps it would be well to do something to please his father. "I am going out to the barns to help Father," he called to his mother.

"That is good," replied his mother. "He needs a little company, and he could use your help."

Anna went out to help the first family bring in their little ones while Chuck helped get the sleigh unhitched and take care of the team.

"Come in,"Chuck said. "Anna has a hot pot of chocolate and some coffee ready. I'll get the home brew up from the cellar."

The children all began heading for the river with their skates slung over their shoulders. Soon the adults could hear joyous laughter as the children began to skate. In the house the ladies had put the babies down in dresser drawers, and the toddlers were playing with the toy blocks and wooden animals. The women all joining in the excited conversations as each new neighbors arrived.

Gradually the children came in from skating, putting their coats and boots to dry for possible further excursions. They headed for the table stacked with a variety of delicious foods. Taking a plate, Clare directed the Hanson boy to the table setup in the front room. The rest of the young people finished dishing up their plates and floated off to the tables near Clare. Next , the men were invited to load up their plates while the women served them home brew. The teens having finished headed upstairs armed with magazines, and games to play. June and Onna were giggling over a multi-colored bandana worn at the waist of one of the ladies dresses in the magazine. Gertrude, one of the neighbor girls, showed off the new yellow rain slicker she said she would like to have someday.

The furniture in Anna and Chucks room was pushed to the side so the baby's little pads could be lain out. The babies asleep and the older children happily engaged in their games and talking over their magazines the women finally had a chance to dish their food and sit down to eat .

Anna went in to where the men were in deep conversation to check if they were in need of anything before she sat down to enjoy her plate of food. All seemed to be well and Anna returned to the table to enjoy her food and conversation about the latest cookie or bread recipe.

Once the dishes were cleared away, it was decided they would divide up in fours and play cards.

Late in the evening Anna went into the kitchen to see about making a pot of chocolate and a pot of rye coffee. June and Onna had cleared away the dishes and prepared everything for morning. Anna was so overjoyed to see what her girls had done that she could hardly contain herself. She wanted to cry she was so proud of them. "Thank you girls," she shouted up the stairwell.

"Hey, how about some music?" Chuck asked the fellows who usually played with him.

"We don't have our instruments with us," said George. You got any here?"

"Sure do. There's no time this house is empty of instruments. We have enough to get up a little dance music," Chuck said with a twinkle.

Chuck went into the closet and came out with his violin, a set of drums, and a harp.

Soon the music was flowing through the house. The couples were dancing between kitchen, the dinning area where the huge table had been pushed to the corner, and back to the living room.

Babies were beginning to wake up and the young people started looking for snacks. As they piled into the area the couples had less and less room to dance. Finally they decided it was time to make it a night and prepared to go home.

"Don't rush off," Chuck insisted Anna will fix a bite to eat.

Anna had already been in the kitchen slicing sausage and bread, laying out plates of cookies and giving each a cup to have their choice of coffee or hot chocolate. Stomachs full, the cheerful conversation soon came to a close as mothers prepared their babies for the ride home and older children put on their wraps and headed to their sleighs for the ride home.

As the sleighs all lined up joyful goodbyes were heard as well as the songs the young people had begun to sing.

When the crunch of sleighs on crisp snow began to dim, Chuck took his wife in his arms. Under the clear sky with the full moon shining brightly, he gave her a tender kiss. "You make me so proud Anna. I love you very much."

"I truly enjoy this season," Anna said looking up at her husband and returning his kiss. "With the crops harvested and only the outside daily chores to worry about it leaves time to rest and socialize with friends and relatives." Her brown eyes sparkled with love.

"This rest is surely needed," Chuck said. "Once spring arrives work for everyone on the farm men, women and children is from dawn to dusk." Chuch put his arms around Anna's shoulders and led her back into the house.

While they were out, they found that the children had all drifted up to their beds.

They banked the fires and went of to bed. The night would be short as milking time was just three hours away.

*   *   *

As they arrived at the dance the young people began to congregate at the back of the great expanse of the hayloft where the dance was being held.

Around the edges were stacks and stacks of hay bales that were kept for winter feeding. The bales were stacked to the roof at the very back and graduated down so that at the bottom near the floor the bales became benches to sit on. The bales were stacked firmly and evenly lined to prevent any sliding with the movement of dancers. The floor of the hayloft was built sturdy with extra beams to make sure it would be strong enough to handle the weight of the people as they danced.

The happy voices and lively music could be heard for miles around. All the country side could feel the loving spirit of Christmas. The love for neighbors was apparent as everyone chatted and ate with the occassional slap on the back for various acquaintances.

The dance came to an end and greetings of "I'll see you tomorrow at church!" rang throughout the yard as each sleigh moved out on their way home.

Sunday church service had been so wonderful with all the little ones portraying their part in the Christmas play reenacted the birth of the Jesus the Christ Child. This year Fredrick sat on his mother's lap while Chuck held Sue. They watched as the newest baby in the congregation portrayed in calm serenity the baby Jesus. How is it that every year the baby seems so quiet and at peace during this part of the pagent, thought Anna. The older children Chris, June, Onna, Clare, and Jeff sat to the back of the church. They had outgrown their parents' watchful eye and had subtly exert this act of independence. June, however, had a firm hold on Jeff.

Arriving home each changed their clothes and finished their chores before choosing their entertainment for the day. Chris was on the ice. Clare once again curled up with a book. Jeff, without being asked was entertaining Sue and Fredrick. Perhaps the motive was the hope that Santa would remember his good deed. June and Onna had chosen to help mother prepare dinner in the kitchen.

On the back of the stove a huge pot of stew simmered. Onna sifted 3 cups of flour with 4 teaspoons baking powder 1 and 1/2 teaspoons salt. She cut in 6 tablespoons lard. Finally she stirred in 1 and 1/2 cups milk just until blended. Onna pulled the stew pot close to the front so she could see what she was doing. She dropped spoonfuls of the dumpling batter into the bubbling stew making sure the dough was on top of the meat to prevent soggy dumplings. Between each spoonful of dough, she dipped the spoon into the hot broth to make the batter drop easily from the spoon. She pushed the pot to the center of the stove where the stew would continue to bubble uncovered for 10 minutes. Just as Onna put a tight lid on the dumplings, June started another batch knowing Onna's double batch would not be enough for their large family, but a batch any larger than the one Onna made would be too difficult to mix. After 10 minutes of cooking the dumplings covered, Onna began to take her batch out and placing them in the warming oven. Mother began to prepare the rue and would make the gravy once the girls had the dumplings finished.

June rounded up the younger children while Onna finished setting the table. Then Onna went out on the porch to use her special high pitched voice to call those at a distance in to eat.

Once everyone was settled quietly at the table, Chuck bowed his head in prayer.

"The dumplings Gut schmecken, Anna," Chuck praised looking at her, the girls and then Anna in turn.

"Ya das gut," Anna replied. "The girls have become quite the cooks. Ya."

"Since tomorrow is Christmas eve, plan to finish your chores early," Anna directed. "I plan to prepare some of Christmas dinner before Christmas Eve service because it will be midnight by the time we return."

*   *   *

Christmas eve arrived. The family snuggled under the blankets the stones and bricks keeping the children warm under the blankets in the sleigh as they drove the distance to the church for the candle light service. This was always June's favorite service with the candles passed around and the beautiful Christmas carols.

Once the service was over everyone hugged and wished their neighbors a merry Christmas. The young people could be heard making plans to visit each other and scheduling skating parties throughout the Christmas vacation. Then the sleighs were loaded and heading to their homes. The bells jiggling thorugh the crisp night air and the moon bright overhead lighting their way.

June and Onna took charge of getting the younger children to bed as their father ordered the rest to bed.

Anna and Chuck still had a bit of preparation before they could settle down for the night, but at the present they sat with a cup of hot chocolate listening to the sounds of the children overhead preparing for bed.

Finally, the house was quite and time for Anna and Chuck to trim the tree and set out the presents for morning.

Chuck tramped along the shoveled path to the barn to collect the tree he had cut and left there along with the homemade toys he had built through the months for the young children. Anna pulled out of her special hiding place under the stair the carefully wrapped gifts she had made each one of the children.

Chuck placed the little pull toy train that he had made for Fredrick under the decorated tree right in front so the little fellow would see it right away. Then he went down to the cellar to bring up the barrel of nuts and box of oranges and apples that had become a tradition in their family.

Anna reached in the special pot where she had stored the popcorn balls she had prepared for decorating the tree. The stockings hung over the fireplace in the kitchen. In each she placed a candy stick, an orange and an apple along with a special small toy she had purchased at the store.

Finally Chuck and Anna stood arm in arm admiring the tree. Chuck pulled her to him kissing her tenderly, "Thank you for all your labor of love Anna. The children will have a very nice Christmas I think. Ya?"

Chuck banked the fire in the heater while Anna slipped a ham in the oven for breakfast along She had prepared hot cross rolls yesterday and would boil eggs in the morning while the children opened their stockings. It would be an easy breakfast giving them all the time to get their chores done and still enjoy their Christmas morning celebration.

Anna banked the fire in the kitchen stove mindful that it would need to be a bit hotter than usual to bake the ham by morning.

This done they went off to bed and were asleep in no time exhausted from the day's events.

Chuck woke to the sound of the children racing down the stairs. "Merry Christmas Liebe," Chuck said waking Anna with a kiss on her forehead.

Wanting to see the little ones as they came to the tree, they quickly put on their robes and headed down the hall just as they heard Sue discover her rag doll. Anna had made it with black braided hair that had been fashioned from heavy spun thread. The doll had brown button eyes to be most like Sue's and a neatly embroidered red mouth. Fredrick found his pull toy train made from scraps of two-by-fours. Chuck had painted it red so that it resembled the farm hay wagon. It was made with a box and the wheels from spools that had once held thread. The pull strap was made from a piece of worn harness.

Chris found a new pair of skates and was thankful because his had become quite worn. Jeff found a bow and arrow pretended he was an Indian. Each of the older girls found new hair combs to help hold their long tresses in place as well as scarves.

Now it was time to open the wrapped packages and each found a new outfit . Sue had a beautiful pink dress made from crisp material with a bonnet to match. Clare found a special long party dress just right for the next dance. June was happy to find she had a skirt and blouse, and tiny little Onna had the very dress she had always wanted. A grown up dress instead of the little girl dresses that she so often received because of her size.

It was now time for Anna and Chuck to open their presents. Anna moved to Chuck and handed him a specially wrapped present. Opening it he found a beautifully tailored home sewn suit with a new white long sleeved shirt and a very special tie .

"Oh Anna," Chuck exclaimed. "How you must have worked to get this done."

"The difficult part was hiding it from you whenever you popped in from the field unexpectedly," Anna laughed good naturedly.

Anna let out a yell of excitement when she saw what was in the huge package that had so intrigued her all night. It was a Singer treadle sewing machine. "Oh Chuck, this must have cost several cream checks," Anna exclaimed happily.

"You deserve it Anna." Chuck replied. "Besides look at all the sewing you have done by hand. This will save you time."

"There are two more gifts under the tree," Father said with a twinkle looking at June and Onna. "Who do you suppose they belong to?

Onna and June quickly took the hint and grabbed up the presents. They opened them at the same time and soon their excited chatter filled the room.

"Oh Daddy!" June cried holding the homemade violin beneath her chin and began to play the music her father had taught her.

Onna soon joined her in the song as she too unwrapped a similar violin made especially to fit her small frame. "It is beautiful," she squeaked running over to her fathre with a big hug and kiss.

"You must have worked every night on these Father," June praised.

"It took awhile," he said with pride.

"Oh Daddy, thank you," the girls chimed in unison.

Clare sat in the corner in a glum mood feeling she had been by-passed.

"Clare," said father. "Come out to the barn with me and be sure to bundle up. We may be awhile."

Anna knew that it took extra attention for Clare to feel loved. Anna had tried everything to break through her hurt and anger but was never able to reach her. She understood and made allowance more than for the others.

As Chuck and Clare reached the barn it was evident that Clare thought she had been singled out to help with chores. She was stiff and angry. As they entered the barn, however, her mood changed as she saw her horse with a brand new saddle. "Mount her," Chuck directed. "and see how it fits."

"Oh Father, thank you. It is so nice looking. I'm sure it will fit fine. May I go for a ride now," Clare pleaded.

"Of course. That is why I said to bundle up," laughed Chuck.

Chuck returned to the house as Clare rode off following the lane where the snow had been plowed with a scrapper. As he arrived in the house everyone waited to hear what had gone on and where Clare was.

"Look!" Chuck said holding the curtain back from the window.

At this all the children except Sue and Fredrick rushed to the window to see what had happened.

Scraping the frost from the window so they could see, they pushed at each other to get a clearer view.

"Stop the rumpus," said Mother. "You will all be able to see. Be patient and take turns."

17

Another Spring, Summer, Fall,

Winter in North Dakota

Christmas came and went. It was now spring and time to plant again. Anna managed to get all the vegetables planted and was now having a little time to tend to her flower garden . Chuck was out in the fields every day.

Evening came. All the children were home from their various activities. June and Onna helped Mother with dinner while Chris and Clare helped Father with the outside chores. Sue, Jeff and Fredrick played at the end of the kitchen where Anna could keep an eye on them.

Chris, Clare, and Chuck stopped by the wash basin just inside the kitchen door. Chris pumped water for his father. Chuck finished and gave the wash basin to Clare. "Well Chris, pump me some water," Clare demanded.

"Pump your own," Chris shot back.

"Meat head," Clare sneered shoving him out of the way with her hip.

"Settle down," Chuck scolded. "Get the washing done and get to the table."

Chris grabbed the pan and held it under the pump with one hand as he pumped water for himself with the other hand. Setting it down, he splashed water over his face swiftly and dumped the water handing the pan to Clare to do whatever she wanted while he smoothly sat down at the table.

Everyone ignored the banging from Clare. They had learned to do that with their mean tempered sister. June and Onna set the food on the table before sitting down. Everyone folded their hands waiting for Father to say the dinner prayer.

Once dinner was finished, Onna called Jeff to help clean up while June put Sue and Fredrick to bed.

"Anyone want to join Father and me in a game of cards?" Anna asked.

Onna was already on her way up the stairs and June had never come down. Chris said he was going outside for awhile and Clare sat reading a book.

"Well, guess you and I will have a go at it by ourselves," Chuck said winking at Anna.

The house became quiet and peaceful. A few hours later all were in bed except Chuck and Anna and they were just finishing up their card games.

"Well, I beat you three out of seven. I guess that makes me winner for the night," Chuck teased.

"Oh well," said Anna. "It was a good evening all the same. Perhaps we can have a few more good evenings like this before the crops are ready to harvest this fall."

Jeff was now in school with the rest of the children leaving Sue and Fredrick at home with Anna. Chuck often took them out to work with him in the barn so that Anna could get the baking and washing done as well as the big chore of spinning. It was less expensive to make materials out of the threads she spun herself using the weaving rack. This material she used to make the work clothes and those the children wore at home to play and work. Some of the threads were a little coarser than that used for dress clothes.

*   *   *

Time passed. It was now time to take care of the vegetables she had so carefully planted in the spring. They would spend all day Saturday and perhaps Sunday as well canning peas and beans.

Saturday morning Anna already had her canning jars washed
ready to can. The peas and beans had been prepared the night
before. All the older children had been up late with Anna preparing the vegetables. The big boiler was on the stove and a good fire
had been built so it would hold as the jars sat in the water bath to
preserve. The jars were filled with blanched vegetables. A half teaspoon of salt was added to each jar and the lids secured. The jars
were placed on a wooden rack that covered the bottom of the boiler
so the jars would not touch the bottom and get overheated while
they processed.

While the girls had been in the house canning, Chuck and
Chris had dug up the carrots and taken them to the cellar putting
them in the huge box that had been designed to hold them. They
were then covered with river sand to keep them crisp all winter.

By midnight Anna was pleased to see twenty jars of peas,
twenty jars of beans and several jars of tomatoes ready to carry to
the cellar when they cooled.

Tomorrow they would dig up the turnips, parsnips, and ruta-
bagas which would be stored in the same manner as the carrots.
When this was finished they would harvest the onions, but they
would have to be put in a dry cool area so they would not sprout.
The field of potatoes would have to be dug up and put in the
cellar before frost as well as the pumpkins and squash. Anna decided to take the corn in to prepare it to dry so it would not be
necessary to can. Corn easily spoiled in canning jars so it was better to dry it. The corn had to be blanched in hot water to set the
milk in it. Then it was laid out in the sun on racks that had been
covered with cheese cloth or canvas. The corn was stirred often so
it would dry evenly. Apples were dried in the same manner. They
became delicious treats in the winter as they tended to sugar a bit.

*   *   *

One day when the children arrived home from school, they could tell
that Mother had a special project lined up. "Hurry and change your

clothes," Mother ordered pointing her wooden spoon toward the house. "Today we are going to make kraut." Sauerkraut making was a big project, especially if one were going to fill a twenty gallon crock.

When the children came back from the house dressed in the clothes made out of the material Anna had weaved from the threads she had spun, the orders began to fly. "Chris, you get the grater. June, you get the salt and tell Onna to start cooking dinner. Jeff, you are responsible for Sue and Fredrick. Clare, get washed up. You are going to start the process."

"Why do I have to be first!" Clare whined.

"Because, you are the most impatient, "Mother said as she pointed sternly toward the grater. "If your turn were later, you would be out riding your horse until it was all done."

"Ha!" Laughed Chris. "Isn't that the truth."

"Don't be so foxy, young man," said Mother." You're next. I don't plan on hunting you down out there on the river where you spend all your time either fishing or skating."

"Ah, Ma," he complained.

By this time June had several cabbages washed and peeled, she cut them in halve so it would be easier to run up and down the grater. Clare grated and June lightly sprinkled the salt and lowered the press—a block made out of wood and polished very heavy to be a weight. Once a third of the crock was full, it became Chris's turn. Chris worked a little faster than Clare had and with his powerful muscles finished his share in half the time that it had taken Clare. "Now it was June's turn to grate," Mother said taking over the salting and pressing job. When the kraut was finished, Chuck and Chris carried it down to the cellar just as Onna's shrill, high-pitched voice announced that dinner was ready. Chris wondered how anyone that tiny could have developed a voice that could carry long distances. She had hollered "Din nun err!" only once, but everyone had heard and were at the table by the time he had gotten back from the cellar. It must be the way she holds the last note he thought. She could be heard calling them to dinner even when they were in the fields a mile away.

After dinner June dressed the little ones and put them to bed while Clare and Onna cleaned up the kitchen. Chris had taken his skates to his room and Mother figured he was polishing the blades getting ready for the first deep freeze since it was snowing now and the river would soon be frozen solid. Mother sat with Chuck in the kitchen enjoying the quiet and thinking. It was late fall and most of the preparations for winter were done. Thanksgiving is just a few weeks away she thought as she congratulated herself for having raised turkeys this year. They would help make a good meal for Thanksgiving and Christmas. The snow had come exceptionally early. It was good that the harvesting and butchering were finished. She was proud of the children. They had been a big help. She thought of each of their children. They all had such interesting personalities. Even with their angry, uncompromising natures. Clare and Chris were willing, hard workers in the barn and fields, if not in the house. She wondered what she could have done differently that would soften their personalities. June and Onna were little mothers. Already able to run a household. They needed very little direction. Onna, her tiny frame, no less sturdy than June whose large-boned body resembled that of her mother.

Jeff was a loving helpful little boy. He enjoyed using the little wagon Father had built for him to fill the woodbox for Mother. Today Jeff had filled both wood boxes and gotten the kindling to pep up the morning fire in the kitchen stove. Anna smiled into her son's blue gray eyes which were looking up at her for approval. She realized that he was never going to get very tall. Anna pulled a cookie from the crock and poured him a glass of milk. "Thank you Jeff. You have been a big help today."

Sue was in the corner of the kitchen playing with Fredrick. Seeing Jeff with a cookie, she jumped up—her dark curls bobbing around her face. Her cute little cupid mouth smiling expectantly.

"Please Mama, can Fredrick and I have a cookie too?"

"Of course. You have done a good job taking care of Fredrick," she said, "and he has been a good boy so he has earned one too."

The next day Anna decided it would be good to get an early start on baking the holiday cookies. This being a weekend and Saturday, all the girls except Onna were asked to help with the baking. Onna volunteered to take care of the little ones. Father had plans for Chris for which Chris was silently grateful. Baking he thought, was for girls as he quickly escaped to the yard.

Night came and with it several crocks filled with cookies. The children were pleasantly tired. After dinner and chores were finished they all headed to bed early.

Chuck and Anna sat in their favorite chairs in the front room. Anna knitting a sweater while Chuck whittled away on the new whistle. As they worked they updated each other on the plans they had for the children's Christmas. After a long while Chuck stood and stretched. "Perhaps we had better go to bed, Mother. Morning comes early. Since we are having company through Thanksgiving, I need to get some work done in the shop before they arrive."

Anna woke earlier than usual. She slipped out of bed leaving Chuck to catch a little more sleep while she prepared breakfast. Chuck appeared in the kitchen soon after Anna finished. They both sat down to a fresh cup of coffee and Anna dished up thickly sliced crisply fried potatoes, country sausage, and fried soft yoked eggs. A tray of thick sliced bread was toasting in the oven. No toaster could keep up with her family now, thought Anna. When the family had been smaller they had used the toaster. Bread was placed between the double wire racks. The children had taken turns holding the long handle over the wood stove until the bread was toasted on one side, then they would turn the rack over to toast the other side.

"It appears to be very cold today," Anna said scratching the frost from the window pane. Turning from the window, Anna decided that a hot cup of chocolate would be good for the children. It was just what they needed to give their bodies fuel to keep them warm on their trip to school. She poured a gallon of fresh milk in the cast iron pot on the wood stove to heat while she grated 3 squares of chocolate. She added this to a half cup sugar mixing well. She made it into a liquid to stir into the hot milk adding a pinch of salt and a touch of vanilla and a little hot water out of the teakettle.

"Anna that looks real good," Chuck said holding his cup up. "Oh! you do make a good cup of chocolate, Anna." he exclaimed after taking a sip. Each of the children dipped a cup of chocolate before sitting down to their breakfast. Finally they filed out the door for school as Chuck headed for the barn.

Fredrick followed his father out to the barn to help with the few chores he had learned to do. Children learned to be quite helpful at a very young age and took pride in being able to do the big jobs. Usually by the time they were five years old they were assigned their first cow to milk.

18

Friends from Chicago

It was finally Thanksgiving week. Their friends from Chicago had arrived at the train depot and Chuck had gone to meet them. Anna was so excited. Sheila and Jim had lived on the farm next to theirs for five years right after Chuck and Anna were married. Anna and Sheila had spent many hours together before Anna's babies began to arrive and Sheila had moved with her husband to Chicago. Jim had gone to Chicago to be an apprentice in a rug laying shop. So far Sheila had not been able to have any children so she was looking forward to spending this holiday with a big family.

As the buggy pulled into the yard, Anna stepped out on the porch wiping her hands on her apron. Sheila got down as soon as the buggy rolled to a stop and the two friends met with a hug. "I have missed you so much!" exclaimed Anna looping her arm around her friend as they walked into the house. "I know Chicago is a good life for you, but I do so miss our exchange of recipes, gardening and afternoon tea. Here, sit down and have a cup of coffee," Anna said showing Sheila to the table and handing her a cup, walking back with the pot of coffee and talking nonstop "You will need to get some rest after your long journey because tonight there is a barn dance at the Koontz place. I know it will go on for most of the night." Anna went on breathlessly. "I have made a big basket with summer sausage, homemade beer, milk for the little ones, lots of bread and cookies so we will be well prepared no matter how late it lasts. Chuck is playing his violin tonight."

"It has always amazed me that Chuck can play so well with his hearing loss," Sheila exclaimed.

"I know," agreed Anna as she poured a cup of coffee." Now, you drink this then go upstairs and get some rest before those children of ours start making so much noise that you won't be able to sleep."

The door opened and the girls burst through running up to hug Sheila, "Oh, we have missed you so." cried June.

"Are you going to stay?" asked Onna.

"No," Sheila said sadly for the girls benefit. "We are only here to visit for the holiday." Then turning Sheila exclaimed, "Oh look!" picking up Fredrick. "What a big boy you have become. And Sue . . . my my such a pretty little girl you are becoming," stooping down and hugging her as she set Fredrick down. Where are the boys and Clare?" quizzed Sheila.

"They are probably out with Chuck," Anna answered. "That is unless Clare is riding her horse. Clare is such a moody child. I just can't seem to reach her no matter what I do so I leave her be and hope someday she will come around. Well, you go on up to your room at the head of the stairs and take your nap. The boys will bring your bags up when they come in," Anna coaxed.

*   *   *

Chuck and Jim had gone ahead to the dance so Chuck could get ready to play the violin. They had taken the buggy with one team of horses. Anna sent Chris out to hook up the other team to the sleigh which had already been loaded with the basket of food and blankets. The children piled in laughing and excited. It was going to be a glorious night, thought Anna as she and Sheila also climbed into the sleigh.

As they pulled up to the barn, one of the men unhitched the team and led the horses away to the corral. He put the harness with the sleigh so it would be easy to find if the need came to go home before the others. The children piled out and ran in the direction of the large group milling around. The music was already playing and a small group was dancing a waltz. Finding Sheila Jim took her in his arms and moved out to join the group of dancers. Looking down, he saw the joy shinning in her eyes. He knew she had missed her friend and all of the farm activity. He was glad he had been able to bring her home for a visit during this festive season.

When the little ones began to yawn and rub their eyes. Anna gave them cookies and milk. Then she put them down in their little feather beds where they were soon fast asleep.

Chuck seeing that Anna had the little ones asleep put down his violin. "I'm going to dance with my wife." Crossing the floor swiftly, he was there just as groups of four were gathering for a square dance. Taking Anna by the hand he led her out to the nearest group.

The old time caller picked up his megaphone and began to sing out, "Ladies and Gentlemen, choose your partners for the River Run square dance." As the music began the caller led the dancers.

As the music ended, Chuck led Anna back to where she had been sitting. "I will be back for you again when we get another chance," he said bending to kiss her on the cheek.

"It's alright," she said with a smile. "Don't fret about me. I enjoy just sitting here listening to you play too."

At one end of the barn, the women were directing the older boys to set up tables as they pulled out their picnic baskets. The music stopped and the dancers headed for the tables lined with all kinds of meats, preservatives, breads, pickles, and desserts. "Oh look at those delicious looking cinnamon rolls," exclaimed Sheila!

Mrs. Koontz observing the pickles said, "My pickles did not turn out as crisp and nice as these. What did you do to make them so crisp?"

"Well I don't know as I did anything special. I just soak the cucumbers in water, salt and alum."

"Well," said Chuck, "It seems to me we men had something to do with helping get that sausage done." Seeing the older children in the corner with their friends he called them to join them at the table.

Sheila helped Anna dish up food for the little ones who had waken from their naps, while the men followed their noses to the coffee which had been brewing in the big community pot.

The older children filled their plates and then went off to eat with their friends. Everyone milled around chatting and catching up on the news of their friends and neighbors.

After everyone had eaten, the ladies picked up the food putting it away for later while the men gathered in groups to discuss their crops and how each was doing on their respective farms. Chuck's group had been talking about how many acres they had managed to get planted. Then the subject changed to how many children each had. "How about you, Chuck?" asked one of the farmers

"Well," said Chuck, "I would have had a hundred if my seeder hadn't broke down." The men all began to slap him on the back as they roared with laughter.

Jim, enjoying Chuck's confusion, finally wiped away the tears of laughter as he explained why they were all laughing. Chuck joined in laughing at himself. He made a mental note that he would have to tell Anna about the good laugh everyone had at his expense.

The women had gathered in another corner of the room, their little children sleeping beside them. They were talking about the things they had canned that year. Each had a new recipe to exchange. Sheila had a few new recipes she had acquired from her new friends in Chicago. "Welsh Rarebit is a specialty if you can get the cheese," she said. "It is named this because the peasants were not allowed to hunt on the estates of the noblemen so they used cheese as a substitute for rabbit. If you have a piece of paper, I will write it down for you then each of you can copy it."

Welsh Rarebit

Melt over hot not boiling water 4 cups nippy cheese, about 1 pound. Be sure it does not boil. Gradually stir in 3/4 cup cream. 1/2 teaspoon dry mustard. Pinch salt. Dash pepper. Serve on crisp toast and if desired top with a piece of summer sausage.

All of a sudden they heard a commotion outside with the older children. Some got up quickly to see what was going on. It was apparent there was a snow ball fight the excited squealing from the girls and loud laughter from the boys as they teased the girls. Coming in they all gathered around the huge stove shaking the snow from their clothes as they snuggled up to the fire to get warm and dry. "Perhaps you children would like some hot chocolate," Mrs. Koontz suggested pointing to the big pot by the coffee. " Help yourselves."

"About the only creative gardening I get to do these days," shared Sheila as she turned back to the ladies conversation, "is in my herb garden. Herbs take up very little space when contained in pots. Some even produce beautiful blooms. They all produce a wonderful aroma not to mention the flavorful variety they add to foods. One of my favorite blends for oven roasted potatoes, lamb or pork contains three tablespoons dried leaf marjoram, three tablespoons leaf thyme, three tablespoons leaf summer sanary, and one tablespoon leaf basil."

"Wait, I want to write this down," interrupted Mrs. Koontz rummaging for a pencil and paper.

". . . one and one half teaspoons dried leaf rosemary," Sheila continued after the interruption produced paper and pencil. "One half teaspoon rubbed sage, one half teaspoon fennel seed and one fourth teaspoon lavender."

Once again the musicians returned to their instruments. When they began to play a fast two step, even the young ones were up on dance floor. This dance woke everyone up even though it was well past midnight. They followed this two step with a three step, then a few waltzes and then another square dance.

The last dance of the night was a slow cuddly waltz. Chuck laid down his violin so he could dance with Anna. Snuggling close, Chuck nuzzled Anna's ear. "Thank you for the wonderful night, Anna." he said as he pecked her on the cheek.

Chuck helped Anna situate the sleeping children in the sled. The older children helped Sheila gather the food baskets. Sheila climbed into the sled with Anna. Jim and Chuck trotted along behind the sled in the buggy. It was almost time to milk the cows by the time they arrived home. Chuck and Jim put the teams away, changed their clothes, and went out to do the milking. The older children helped get the sleepy little ones out of the sled and into the house. Mother sat the children down and dished up a bowl of oatmeal which she had prepared in a double boiler and placed on the back of the wood stove ready to eat when they got home.

"I'm going up to bed," Clare said not able to finish her cereal.

June and Onna asked if they were needed, and if not could they lay down for awhile?

"Ya, that is a good idea," Mother agreed. "That way you both will be ready to watch the little ones while we get a little rest after we finish the morning work."

Jeff, Sue and Fredrick were playing in the corner of the kitchen. Sheila enjoyed watching. Having no children of her own, this was a special time for her. Before the move to Chicago, Sheila had been close to Anna's children.

Anna could hear Jim and Chuck stomping the snow from their boots. They stopped just inside the kitchen door to clean up in the wash basin before sitting down to the table for breakfast. Sheila poured them each a cup of coffee as Anna handed them a towel, then dished up ham and egg's for each of them. Eggs were usually boiled because the family was so large. There wasn't time to please everyone. They just had to like what was put before them or not eat it at all.

The week sped by fast. They talked and played cards and did chores and enjoyed each other. Sheila could hardly believe that Thanksgiving was almost here. It had been a week filled with memories. "I hate to think about leaving the day after Thanksgiving. It's been so much fun being here with all of you."

The children were out skating on the river, except the three little ones who were taking a nap after having played so hard all morning. This gave Anna and Sheila some free time to gossip and get the pies baked for tomorrow.

Since there would be a big feast tomorrow they prepared a light dinner. When the children came in from skating, they fed them first so the adults would have a quiet evening together. June and Onna took the three younger children up to bed while Chris and Clare went out to clean the horse stalls. Once they were done, the older children went up to their rooms for the night leaving the adults alone.

Sheila helped clear the table and Anna got out the cards ready to play a few hands before going to bed.

"Shall we play partners," Chuck asked elbowing Jim.

"The women against the men?" Sheila challenged.

"Hey, that's alright with me," Jim countered winging his arms and strutting like a peacock. "Chuck, you deal," he said as he sat down and handed him the cards.

"You bet. We'll show these ladies who can count cards," Chuck agreed.

"Anybody for pie and coffee?" Anna asked after they had been playing for a couple of hours.

"Oh yeah," Jim and Chuck responded simultaneously.

While they ate their pie, the men chided the girls for beating them.

"Don't worry, guys, we'll give you a chance to beat us next time," Sheila gloated. "You know what they say, Pride goeth before a fall."

"Hey, is anyone beside me ready for some sleep?" Anna said yawning and getting up from the table.

"I sure am," Sheila said standing and stretching, "the morning comes awful soon around here."

"You're right. I think it's time for all of us to get some sleep," agreed Jim. "We aren't used to these early hours."

Thanksgiving day came with a heavy layer of snow. "This will keep the children inside all day," Anna reflected with a sad note.

"Oh Mother," the girls argued.

"No, Girls," Mother insisted. "The weather is just too bad today. You will just have to get out the games. Now stop your arguing. It won't do you any good," she sighed turning toward the kitchen.

The children spent much of the early afternoon upstairs playing games with occasional disagreement. The three little ones played on the floor at the edge of the kitchen. June and Onna took turns during the day either helping with the dinner or taking care of the little ones. Chris and Clare put on their warmest clothes and helped father and Jim in the barn.

The table had been extended across the front room to make enough space for all. Eleven places had been set with the high chair for Fredrick by Anna's place. The smell of roast turkey and fresh pumpkin pie filled the air. Once again Anna was glad that she had decided to raise turkeys.

Chuck blessed the food and thanked the Lord for the Jim and Sheila's company. The prayer said, dishes began to rattle and the voices around the table created a memory that Anna would hold in her heart for years to come.

Helping himself to the baked acorn squash, Chuck passed it to Jim on his right. In the meantime Jim had served himself mashed potatoes and poured a generous covering of giblet gravy, apple butter and home churned butter sat in the middle of the table waiting to compliment the homemade dinner rolls. As the dishes came her direction, June helped Sue to some apple walnut salad made with fresh whipped cream. "No cranberries," said Jeff as Onna began to dish some from the bowl coming her way.

"It's just amazing that you grew and preserved everything on the table," complimented Sheila sending the mashed potatoes to Anna.

"Yes," Jim remarked before taking a bit of turkey. "We city folks have forgotten how to live the simple life.

"It's not always so simple, " Chuck reflected looking down the table and remembering how Anna had looked that day after the death of Lill. Seeing her so content now, he was grateful for the visit of Sheila and Jim. They had helped bring some excitement back into their everyday lives.

Once the meal was finished the men went out to do the evening chores, Chris going with them. Clare and Onna helped clear the table while Anna and Sheila put away the food. June took the little ones upstairs, washed and dressed them, and put them to bed. June had already taken water up in the pitcher that was used in the upstairs dressing room. The stand that sat in the dressing room had a beautiful wash basin and a pitcher to match. It was always necessary to take the water up. Tonight, since there was company, June would make sure the pitcher was filled with hot water for the guests after she finished with the little ones.

Once the kitchen was cleaned and the chores done, Anna set the pies out with dishes and silverware so that everyone could help themselves.

Sheila breathed a sigh of relief when Chuck went upstairs to settle the children down. They had been making so much noise that she was deciding maybe having children wasn't so wonderful after all, at least not that many.

In the morning the sun was out and all was crisp and clear for Sheila and Jim's trip home. Chuck helped hitched the team to the sleigh. Sheila and Anna stood hugging and crying. Jim and Chuck shook hands and promised to stay in touch.

Chuck climbed up in the wagon waiting.

"Come Sheila. We'll miss the train," Jim shouted standing ready to help her into the buggy.

"Coming," Sheila called moving away from Anna and tying her scarf around her neck. As they drove off, Anna continued to wave good-bye until she could no longer see the sleigh. Wiping her eyes she went back into the house to begin another day's chores.

19

Another baby

December came with more snow. There was still much to be done before Christmas. For each child's first Christmas, Anna had knit a Christmas stocking with their name embedded in the cuff. The stockings had to be cleaned and ready for hanging on Christmas Eve. They would stuff the stockings with oranges, apples, candy, and a small toy as they had every year. Anna thought she must also finish knitting one for the baby that would most likely be here by Christmas.

With the Christmas plays, barn dances and skating parties along the river, time flew by quickly. Soon it was the week before Christmas. Anna was pleased that she had finished the baking for the holiday. She was rocking by the heater in the front room with Fredrick and Sue playing at her feet. She was thankful that the older children would be done with school for their Christmas vacation in a few days.

Onna and June were already home and had started fixing dinner. The door opened and Clare came in along with a big gust of wind. Using both hands she turned to push the door closed before taking off her heavy plaid jacket and hanging it behind the door with all the other coats. A puddle of water had formed on the floor below the boots. "Burr," she exclaimed holding her hands over the fire. "It certainly is cold out there."

June moved to wipe up the water just as Chris stuck his head in the door yelling, "Is dinner ready yet? I'm starved."

"No," June answered, "It will be another half hour. Why don't you go help Father finish in the barn?"

"Oh, alright," Chris said with a shrug of resignation taking off his skates and putting on his boots.

In the house, Mother still sat rocking in the front room.

June called the little ones and Jeff to the kitchen. After they washed up, she sat them down to a plate of food. "Jeff quit horsen' around and get to eating," June scolded a little less patient than usual.

"Sue stop putting your meat under the table for the cat," Onna nagged.

"Fredrick, you poor little guy. You're almost asleep in your plate," June said soothingly picking him up and dressing him for bed.

"Onna," called Mother, "please put a large kettle of water on to heat."

"Alright Mama," Onna called back. She bagan pumping the water into the big pan from the pump on the shelf at the edge of the kitchen and wondered why Mother needed it.

"June," Mother called a little more frantic this time. "Please get the children to bed as soon as possible."

"I already have Fredrick in bed," she said coming in to Mother's side so she wouldn't have to keep yelling. "I am getting Sue ready now. Is there anything I can get for you?"

"No. Not right now," Mother said wincing with the effort of talking.

"Come on Jeff. Get up to bed now." June demanded firmly.

Chris and Father came in from the barn, the chores finished for the night.

"Clare come on down to eat," yelled Onna. "Mother wants things finished early."

Chuck and the older children sat down at the table. Since Mother was not feeling very well, June dished a plate and took it in to her.

"Thank you," Mother said, "I will be fine in the morning. You go ahead and eat."

After dinner the girls cleaned up the kitchen while Chuck went to sit with Anna. "You feelin' poorly tonight." It was more a comment than a question.

"I think perhaps the baby will be here before the night is through," Anna informed him.

"Do you think I should stay up?" he asked wringing his hands. These births were such an emotional drain. With each child Anna grew weaker he thought.

"I don't think it will be many hours now. Perhaps by the time the girls finish and go upstairs. This one seems to be coming very fast," Anna whispered confidentially.

The house had grown quiet. Anna and Chuck sat talking. Every little while Anna got up to walk around the room panting heavily. Finally Anna turned to Chuck, "You had better bring the hot water to the bedroom." Chuck hurried to the kitchen to get the pan of hot water. When he entered the bedroom, he found Anna in agony pacing back and forth changing direction with each new pain. Chuck coaxed her to lie down on the bed.

A shrill cry from Anna caused Chuck to check. He found the head of the new baby visible. Another cry from Anna and he held the baby in his hands. "We have a new son Anna," exclaimed Chuck.

"Shall we name him Caleb?" suggested Chuck.

"That sounds fine," agreed Anna weakly.

After cleaning the baby and laying him in Anna's arms, Chuck cleaned Anna and then the area around the bed. He took it all out of the area so it would be clean when the children awoke.

Chuck went out to build up the fire and then put a big pot of oatmeal on ready for morning breakfast for the children as they woke.

It was now two in the morning. "I think I will try to catch a little sleep before the children wake up," Chuck said tucking the covers around Anna and rubbing the furry top of his new sons head.

"Ja, you lay down awhile. We will be fine," Anna replied weakly.

The house grew quiet. Chuck and Anna managed to get about four hours sleep before the baby began to cry to be nursed.

Chuck got up dressing quickly. He stocked up the fires and put on a pot of coffee. Coming back to Anna, "What can I get you before I go out to milk the cows?"

"I am fine for now. Thank you for all your help," Anna said reaching up to take his hand and kiss the palm.

As Clare and Chris came down the stairs, Chuck looked up and said, "Both of you put your coats on and start the milking. I will be out in awhile to help finish. Then you can eat and head on to school with Jeff."

"Oh Father, how come?" complained Clare.

"Don't argue," snapped Chuck.

Putting on her coat, Clare walked slowly to the barn head down kicking the snow as she went.

Chuck turned from watching Clare just as June and Onna came down the stairs. "Girls," he directed. "I'm going out to help with the milking. I need the two of you to stay home from school to day. Please get Fredrick and Sue dressed and fed. When you have finished, clean the kitchen and see that the children are occupied. Do not disturb your mother."

When Chuck came in from the chores, he went in to see Anna. "Do you feel like eating a little breakfast?" he asked as he bent over to kiss her forehead.

"I would love a cup of coffee and a cup of oatmeal," Anna smiled weakly.

June could stand the suspense no longer. "Father, what is wrong with Mother?" she asked as he returned to the kitchen.

"You have a new little brother," Father informed a concerned look overshadowing the twinkle in his eye. "His name is Caleb."

"Is Mother alright?" June asked.

"She will be fine as soon as she has a day of rest. She seems to be a little weaker this time. I want her to stay down and get her strength back."

"Can we go see her?" June asked.

"You may take her lunch when it is time and see her then. We will not tell the rest today. Keep them busy. She should not be disturbed until she is stronger," her father commanded.

"I could take the kids out sledding," suggested June. "That should tire them out and make them ready for a nap. Perhaps Onna would help me."

"That is a good idea. As soon as you have finished sledding bring Jeff to me. I have a job to keep him busy," her father said.

"I think I will take Mother a little something to eat before we put dinner on the table," June told Onna.

"Can't I go with you and see Mother and the baby," Onna begged.

"I don't see why not," June declared making a command decision.

June dipped some of the stew she had heating on the back of the stove ready for the evening meal. "Come on Onna," June whispered. "We have to hurry before the rest of the children get in here."

As they entered the room, Anna looked up and smiled.

"Can we hold the baby while you eat," Onna asked.

"That would be nice," Anna said handing little Caleb over to Onna's waiting arms. "It will give me time to wash up as well." Anna pushed herself up and took the dish of stew from June. June went to the kitchen and returned with warm water for the basin on the dresser.

Mother finished her dinner and washed up while June took the baby. Onna returned to the kitchen to begin setting dinner on the table. Finally Anna was took the baby. "Thank you for the nice dinner and keeping the house quiet today," she said.

"You're welcome, Mother," June said smiling softly as she headed back to the kitchen.

Everyone came in from the barn just as they finished getting dinner on the table.

As the washed up at the basin, Father said in a quiet voice so the little ones couldn't hear, "I want all of you to help get the tree set up tonight, so hurry and get done eating and clear up the kitchen."

"Oh boy," exclaimed Onna jumping up and down.

"Then I can depend on both of you to get the children to bed early?" Father asked.

"Yes Father, you can entertain Mother for awhile after dinner and we'll get everything ready," Onna said in her quietest voice that wasn't very quiet.

"Thank you," said Father. "I'll go see if she is hungry."

"Oh, we already took her something to eat," Onna chimed then put her hand over her mouth.

"That was good of you," Father said with a stern voice but a soft look from June to Onna.

Coming in to Anna, he bent down to kiss her on the cheek.

"How are you feeling, dear? Would you like a cup of coffee?"

"That would be nice," Anna said.

Chuck went to the kitchen and poured a cup of coffee then picking up a few cookies returned to Anna. "I have a project to do with the children tonight." Chuck said handing the cookies and coffee over. "Will you be all right for awhile?"

"Go ahead," Anna said waving her arm. "I think I will catch a little nap before baby calls again."

Chuck went out to find the children already eating dinner. It pleased him that his children could manage could take over when there was a crisis.

After dinner Chuck went out to the barn to get the tree ready while the children cleaned up the kitchen and got the little ones in bed.

"I have the decorations out," Onna said as Father came in with the tree.

They all worked steadily, putting each decoration in the place they had remembered seeing it in years past. Each one put something on the tree and soon it was beautiful. Special cut out snow flakes, popcorn ropes the girls had popped and strung, little rose petals that had been made into beads by rolling them on the kitchen stove.

"Chris," Father directed, "can you put the angel on the top for me?

They all stood back and looked at the tree.

"It is the best ever," Jeff declared clapping his hands together.

"It is getting late so you had all better get up to bed," Father ordered.

Chuck and Anna sat for a long time enjoying the quiet after the children had gone to bed. For a time even the baby was asleep and everything seemed so peaceful.

"Oh Anna, the baby is so cute. I do love all our children, but I am afraid this family is getting too big," Chuck said taking her hand and rubbing it to comfort her seeing the exhaustion in her face. "This is getting to be too much for you."

"Don't worry Chuck," she said. "I enjoy our family. Besides I think it will be lonely when they all grow up and go their own way. The girls are growing up so fast already. It won't be long before the young men start to notice Clare and Onna and even June is starting to round out in all the girl places. Clare already has her eye on the Hanson boy," Anna reflected.

"Well at least Caleb will still be in the buggy when the spring work begins," remarked Churck. "It will be easier to care for him if he is not able to get to mischief on his own."

Anna pondered what the next year would bring with Jeff in school now and Sue going next year. Fredrick would still be home to help with Caleb for another year thought Anna coming back to the present.

"Come Anna," Chuck invited patting the bed beside him. "You had better get some sleep. I already have the fires banked and the cereal is in the double boiler so everything is ready for the children. No need for you to get up and help tomorrow. I will do the milking and outside chores while the girls attend all the rest."

"It looks as though it is snowing," Anna commented looking out the window. "If it starts to blow and drift perhaps the children will stay home from school."

"I will make sure it is safe. You just rest," Chuck reassured.

Morning came brisk and clear the snow had stopped and the wind had died down.

Chuck put on his heavy coat and hurried out to do the morning chores as well as the milking. The cold brisk weather made the cows restless.

The milking done, Chuck took it to the house ready to be separated. Since the weather was clear, he thought perhaps he should take the cream in to the creamery if Anna was able to be left alone.

Reaching the house, he found all the children up and making

ready for school. June had Fredrick dressed and at the table eating his breakfast.

"Have you checked on mother?" Chuck asked June

"I took her a cup of coffee, oatmeal and toast. She seemed better today," June replied.

"Thank you. I'll take over here. You make sure Jeff gets to school alright," said Father sitting down to the breakfast June had set before him.

"I am leaving now," June hollored to Jeff as she put on her boots and grabbed her coat off the rack."

"I'm coming," Jeff called back, "are we skating to school?"

"Yes, hurry up and get your skates," June coaxed putting her skates over her shoulder.

"Come little one," Chuck cooed lifting Fredrick out of his chair. "You need to wash up if you're going to visit that new little brother of yours." Setting him on his feet he pointed him toward the wash basin that Fredrick was just barely tall enough to reach.

"Okay boy," Father said taking Fredrick's hand. "Let's go see Mother."

Fredrick peeked over the side of the cradle at the little face. "Oh," he said eyes wide and full of surprise.

"Well, what do you think?" asked Father.

"Puppy better," Fredrick said emphatically.

"Chuck and Anna," laughed and Anna invited Fredrick to come sit by her for a little while.

"Would you like a cup of coffee Anna?" Chuck asked still smiling at Fredrick.

"Thanks," Anna said, "but I think I will go to the kitchen and get some things done while the baby is sleeping and before the children come home."

"Do you need me to help with something?" Chuck quizzed lifting an eyebrow but not saying that he thought she should remain in bed for another day. He knew Anna and she would not be held down. In fact if he made an issue, she might just work harder to prove she was strong and healthy.

"Perhaps you could watch Fredrick awhile. I would like to get some things started for dinner as well as wash out a few diapers. If I hang them by the heater, they could be dry by the time the children get home."

He took Fredrick by the hand and walked with Anna to the kitchen. "Can I get you something from the cellar?" Chuck asked heading toward the cellar door.

"Yes please. You could bring up a jar of meat and some vegetables," Anna said moving slowly toward the stove.

"I will be right back up," Chuck said to Fredrick. Sit here on the chair and take care of Mother for me."

Anna dipped water from the big boiler that was kept at the end of the stove. She poured the water into the small wash tub, added the soiled baby clothes, some lye soap, and a bit of soda to sweeten. Then she made a pan of dish water to clean up the breakfast dishes.

Chuck came back up from the cellar with his arms full and opened the jar of meat for Anna to put it in a big pot at the back of the stove to simmer.

Anna had the diapers and baby clothes hanging on a rack by the heater and had the kitchen cleaned. She looked over at Fredrick and found he had fallen asleep on his arms at the table. At the same time she heard Caleb begin to cry.

"Chuck would you please lay Fredrick down while I tend to the baby."

Anna went to get the baby while Chuck picked up Fredrick and placed him down for a nap. Anna sat in the rocking chair nursing the baby and Chuck brought a cup of coffee and sat in a chair beside her.

"Have you talked to the children about their new brother?" Anna asked. "I have only seen June and Onna since the baby arrived. I have been wondering why they haven't come looking for me."

"I only told June and Onna. The rest just think you are sick," Chuck said. "I thought it best to give you and the baby time to yourselves before dealing with Clare and Chris. We'll tell them tonight."

"While the babies are asleep, I am going in the kitchen for awhile. I want to get some things done before the children get home from school.

"What are you planning to do?" questioned Chuck apprehensively.

"Well maybe they will all be a little happier if I they smell a nice hot meal when they get home. Maybe I'll fix a special apple kuchen for their treat," Anna said giving Chuck her best I-am-strong-and-healthy look.

"Do you have a little cream left over?" she asked.

"I will have it whipped by the time the kuchen is out of the oven," Chuck said as he moved to find the hand beater. "You know," he said with a twinkle, "I can't let the men see me doing this."

"Well, I won't be telling on you."

20

Lisa in Idaho

It was Christmas week. The town of Sandpoint was lit up with lights and colorful decoration. Since Father worked as night watchman at the Ponderay Mill, they did not often get to leave the farm. This was a special occasion. A band was to play Christmas music in the town square. Most people had very little money for entertainment so these events were special and well attended. Tonight Father had decided to take them into town in the Model T Ford. Lisa would ride on her mother's lap while her brothers and sister Mercy would sit in the back. The Ford would be a special treat as they usually used the horse and wagon to go into town. Lisa turned from side to side looking at all the lights. "Sit still little one," Mother scolded, "your little bones are poking me."

Arriving in town, they parked in the area where the concert was taking place.

"Oh Mama," Lisa yelled with excitement and running ahead to the decorated tree. Mercy caught up with her and quickly took hold of her hand. Lisa wiggled trying to break free eyes intent on the lights and colors. Mercy knew that it would have been difficult for her mother to catch up to Lisa. For one thing Lisa never stood still any where for very long. It was a trying job keeping up with her.

Gus, the stern faced brother who always acted like a miniature Grandpa, caught up to them and picking up Lisa swung her up on his shoulder.

"Thank you," Mother said as Gus took over relieving Mercy who was having trouble keeping Lisa in line.

Phil had run on ahead of them unmindful of anyone but himself. As Mother watched her children and thought how Lisa and Phil would always be the ones getting into trouble and Mercy and Gus would probably be trying to bail them out.

"Phil, come back here with the family," Father spoke sharply. Though a soft spoken man, he could still put authority in his voice when speaking to an errant son.

Reaching the bleachers that had been set up for the occasion, Father took Lisa from Gus's shoulder and held her in his lap. He wiggled his ears and teased her with his eyebrows making them go up and down entertaining her until the music began. Lisa liked to sit on Father's lap. He had a pretty watch bob that he allowed her to play with.

The music began and for a while the sights and sounds kept all the children quite awed. Lisa had finally worn down and had fallen asleep in her father's arms.

Phil asked to go to the outhouse at the edge of the park, and when he had not returned after some time Father turned to Rena and said, "I'll go find Phil. Gus can help you get the rest to the car."

Gus took Lisa from his father's arms and headed for the car. Mother took Mercy by the hand and paced her steps to Mercy's smaller ones.

"Mama, can we have some candy at the store?" Mercy quizzed.

"I think Santa will bring us some."

Mercy puckered her cute little cupid mouth and looked up at her mother pleadingly. Mercy rarely made a fuss but it was apparent she was upset.

Mother bent down and gave her a kiss. "It's alright honey. I think Grandma Anna has something special for you when we get home."

Mercy knuckled the tears from her eyes and smiled up at her mother.

Father had found Phil with a group of older boys. He stood for a while on the outskirts of the circle watching his son and another boy as they jabbed and punched and wrestled each other to the ground. "Phil," Father said with quiet authority. The circle parted and the boy fighting with Phil stood and ran off. The rest of group scattered as well. One sleeve of Phil's coat hung loose from the seam. The patches on his pants had new rips and Phil had blood dripping from a cut over his left eye.

"So, what is this all about?" John said in a quiet controlled voice as he approached Phil.

"George was teasing Gus at school and I came to settle it for him," Phil said with his fists clenched. He stood with his shoulders back, hips cocked forward, feet apart, anger still evident in his stance.

"Well, it's settled now," John declared smoothly. "You may head to the car now."

Phil took off for the car. He knew it wasn't settled as far as his father was concerned. His father would settle behind the barn tonight.

Arriving home father stopped in front of the house letting everyone out before parking the car in the shed.

Getting out of the car, Phil headed for the house quickly hoping his father had forgotten about the punishment.

Mother went over to the stove and built up the fire where she had things ready to heat for dinner. Anna and Amos had not gone to the park. Grandpa Amos found it difficult to walk around extensively with his crutches and Anna preferred to stay home and mend the stockings that had piled up.

Anna set the table while Grandpa Amos entertained Lisa and Mercy.

Mother put the heated stew on the table along with home-made bread and huckleberry jam.

"Wash up and come to dinner," Mother called.

Once dinner was finished, Grandma Anna helped clear the table. Then had Mercy help wash and dry the dishes. Once the dishes were done, Amos and Anna went up to bed.

Father sat in the rocking chair where he rocked Lisa for a while, once asleep he put her to bed. He came back to his rocking chair and lit his pipe ready to settle in to his own little world listening to the crystal set radio. These crystal set radios operated with a needle that sat on a crystal rock and only one person at a time could listen to it with a set of headphones.

Before putting the headphones on, he called Phil over to him. Phil came slowly wondering what was going to happen. Since Father was already sitting, Phil thought he had escaped a rendevue behind the barn with the strap.

"Phil," Father said. "What seems to be your problem?"

"I just wanted to protect Gus. Those boys are always teasing him."

"Well, fighting is not the way to solve a problem. Should you continue this behavior you will have a trip to the barn. Do you understand?" Father said in his quiet but dominant voice.

"Yes Father. May I go now?" Phil replied respectfully relieved to have escaped the strap.

"You may go up to bed right now, and don't let me hear any more from you tonight."

Phil quickly left and went upstairs with Gus following close behind.

"Mercy," Mother called pointing her finger toward the bedroom indicating that she was to go to bed. Mother didn't need words, thought Mercy. She just looked or pointed and the message was loud and clear.

Father finished listening to the news and took the headphones off and laying them carefully on the stand by the chair.

Mother seeing Father no longer was listening to the radio said, "I suppose now that you have rented that property up near the mountains you won't be able to get our Christmas tree there this year."

"They have only rented the building not the trees."

Before they were married, John had spent some time as a bachelor on this property up near the mountain just above Kootanai while she taught school in Latah.

"I will go up after church on Sunday,"

Sunday arrived and after church, John took the boys with him cut down a nice tree out of the top of one of his trees on his farm.

Bringing the tree down, he found Grandfather Amos had already built a stand to put it in. They set the tree up in the room reserved for Mother's organ and special occasions.

Gus was given the job of keeping Lisa busy in Mother's bedroom while the tree was being trimmed and the special jars of Christmas ribbon candy were set under the tree. Mother had prepared some men's stockings to put nuts and other small treats for the children.

Christmas was celebrated Christmas morning so Mother locked the door to the special front room and went out to set dinner on the table.

Amos and Anna sat at one end of the table. Father sat at the other end of the table. Mother, Gus and Phil sat on one side of the table. Lisa sat in a high chair and Mercy sat on the other side of the table and next to Father.

Amos sat quietly passing food and eating. Anna was full of complaints and was attempting to pick an argument with John. John, a quiet patient man, went about the business of tending to the girls and let what she was complaining about fall on deaf ears.

Amos grinned to himself but said nothing. He was enjoying the sight of Anna fuming because she had not been able to get John ruffled.

Amos had a habit of letting Grandma Anna scold and complain about something then when she finished, he would put his hand to his ear and say, "Eh—eh, what did you say Anna?" Anna would become so furious she would stomp off.

Amos enjoyed seeing this spicy lady get upset and stomp off so he often set her up just to see her show her spirit.

Gus was frowning at Phil who was punching at him but trying to hide it from his parents. Gus never made a fuss about anything, he would just frowned. Mother was usually aware of this. "Phil, take your chair and plate and go on the other side of the table and sit by Mercy," she said in her sharp teacher voice. "See if you can leave her alone so she can eat." Phil did not argue with her knowing things would not go well if Father saw a problem. He would like to avoid the barn and the strap that hung by the door.

Dinner finished Mercy helped Grandma clear the table while Mother washed the separator. Mother did not trust anyone to do the separator since it had to be put back together in the right order. She soaked it in scalding water then sterilized it before drying each piece carefully.

Gus left the table and went out to get the wood to fill the wood box.

Phil headed out of the door to the outhouse which was his way to dodge work. Coming back in, Phil noticed the wood box was full and breathed a sigh of relief. Then Father ordered, "Phil, dump the ashes out of the stove. You can spread it on the road to help keep the ice from forming."

Christmas morning arrived with heavy footsteps on the stairs leading down to the kitchen. Putting her robe on quickly, Mother knew the boys were on their way down. She hurried to meet them at the stairs. "Merry Christmas boys, I guess you got up early so you could get the milking done before we go in to share the tree," she said handing them each a coat and hat. "I will get the girls up while you are getting the chores done." Anna looked up to see her mother coming down the stairs with her father right behind. "Good morning and Merry Christmas," Rena snag with a lilt.

"Merry Christmas Rena," her parents chimed together.

The boys had just gone outside when John came into the kitchen putting on his coat and hat. "Good morning everyone. Merry Christmas. I am going out to see how the boys are doing. It shouldn't take us long. We should be back in by the time you have the girls up and the coffee brewing."

"We will be ready," Rena said pumping the water into the pot and adding the coffee grounds. Rena set out a plate of hot cross rolls which she had kept warming over night. Her mother set the table and added butter, jam and milk.

The warming oven was a helpful item for farm women who often had to keep dinner warm when their farmer husband had a problem with one of the machinery or a sick animal that detained them. The warming oven sat about two feet above the top flat surface of the stove.

John and the boys came in stomping the snow from their
boots and hanging their wet coats on the rack by the door. Gus
put the milk through the separator saving some for Mother to
put in shallow pans in the screened cupboard on the porch.
Later, when it cooled, she would be able to skim the thick
cream for use on the table.

Rena put the separator parts in cold water to keep the cream
from forming on all the separate discs. When she finished, she
went to help Mercy and Lisa finishing dressing. Finally, everyone
was seated at the table. She placed a hot cross roll on each of the
girl's plates then passed them to John. Mother Anna had poured
the milk and coffee and they were ready to say the blessing. "Thank
you Father for this thy bounty. Make us truly grateful," prayed
Grandfather Amos.

"Oh Mother," John said to Rena with a twinkle in his eye.
"Do you hear something in the room where you keep your organ?
I do believe someone is moving around in there?"

Lisa's eyes opened wide leaning her head forward she strained to
hear what Father was hearing. Everyone got really quiet. Grandfather
Amos scratched the underside of the table with his cane. "Hear that?"

"Oooooh," said Lisa pushing back in her chair and holding on
to the arms.

"Oh that's just . . ." Phil was interrupted from his revelation
with a jab to his ribs from Gus.

Father opened the door and Mercy peeked in to see the Christmas tree in the center of the room. "Look Lisa," called Mercy with
wonder in her voice.

Lisa slowly climbed down and peeked into the room from
behind Gus's pant legs. "Ooooooh," she said again, and then she
ran to the tree.

Mercy, with her fingers entwined tightly behind her back,
was looking at the big jars of ribbon candy. She was careful not to
touch the jars because Father must give his permission.

"Gus," Father said placing his hand on his oldest sons shoulder. "I think you may pass out the gifts this year."

A big grin spread over Gus's face. Gus picked up the doll that sat near the front of the tree and handed it to Lisa. "To Lisa from Santa," said Gus flair. Lisa jumped up and down with excited pleasure. Cradling her doll to her chest she sat next to Mercy and they began to look over the doll together. The doll had been made by Grandmother Anna from an old wool man's sock. Its head was out of a piece of shiny slip material. Two white buttons with smaller blue buttons sewn on top of the white buttons made up the eyes. The button eyes were sewn on with black thread to accentuate the black center of the eyes. A tan button made up the nose. The mouth was embroidered in red and the hair was made with brown yarn curled in wringlets.

While the girls were enjoying the doll, Gus took a present to Grandmother. Grandmother carefully took the wrappings off then looked up at the family in unmistakable joy. In her hand she held a beautifully built wood sewing kit with trays for spools of thread and a place for scissors, embroidery needles and thread. There were also several crochet hooks and a new thimble. It was evident this gift was put together by the whole family since grandfather had certainly been the one to make the wooden kit.

"Oh thanks be to the hands that brought this special gift," Anna with a sparkle of tears in her eyes acknowledging all.

In the meantime, Gus had given Grandfather Amos his gift. He ripped the wrapping quickly but took his time opening the box, waiting to catch Rena's eye so she could enjoy his surprise. He held up the plaid flannel pajama set. "My legs will be warm now," he said holding the plaid flannel pajama set up for all to see. "Thank you," he said with a broad smile.

Gus had given both Mother and Father their gifts. Father held up a new pipe along aith a can of prince Albert. "Looks like someone knew what I had need of," he said looking at Amos and thanking him with a nod.

Standing up and holding the dress in front of her to show how the blue color would bring out her extremely white complexion and enhance her jet black hair. "Thank you," she said looking at all of them but giving an extra smile to her mother. "This dress will be perfect for church.

Finally Gus reached under the tree and pulled out presents for Phil and himself.

Phil unwrapped his present first and held up a B B GUN. "Oh boy!" he yelped. "Thank you, Thank you, Thank you."

Father went over to Phil and showed him how to shoulder the gun. "You treat this as though it is a real gun. Do not ever point it at anything alive, that means animals or people," he quietly instructed.

In the meantime, Gus had unwrapped his gift and sat grinning. Finally he stood up. "It's an erector set," he said with obvious pleasure. Phil seeing this came over to have a closer look. When he reached out to take the box, Father said, "Let Gus look it over for now. You can help him later."

Mother looked over to see if Mercy had her present and was happy to see she had a little homemade doll buggy that Grandfather had made for her. The wheels had been whittled out of wood and the axles were made with long pieces of pipe threaded through the wheels with washers on the end to keep the wheel in place. Grandmother had made a hood like regular baby carriages and in the buggy was a special doll with a china head. Mercy sat quietly talking to her doll and placing it in the buggy. Finally she pushed the buggy over beside her mother. "Look Mommy. Isn't she pretty."

"Oh my yes!" her mother exclaimed as she leaned down to peek in the buggy. "You have a very pretty baby in there."

Mother stood up and said, "Would anyone like to sing while I play the organ?"

"Sing," the children yelled in unison. Mama sat down and began to play. She seldom had time to play these days so this was a special treat. The children all set down their toys and ran to the organ while Father, Grandfather and Grandmother sat listening and enjoying the young voices.

"A-way in a manger, No crib for a bed, The lit-tle Lord Jesus Laid down His sweet hea; The stars in the sky Looked down where

He lay,—The little Lord Jesus A-sleep on the hay." The children sang all three verses then asked for "Silent night, Jingle Bells, In the Garden, I Heard the Bells on Christmas Day, and Old Rugged Cross."

Phil had a clear voice that was beginning to change, but still he could hold a tune, Mother thought. It won't be long before it will float around on him. Having been a teacher she could tell that his voice was going to end up a tenor. Phil loved to sing to the cows as he milked so he kept in practice.

Gus's voice was changing but he could still lend a little base though it often peaked at the wrong moment. Today they even ignored the squeaks. Well maybe there was a few chuckles from the listening section.

Mercy's quiet little voice was swallowed up in Lisa's shouting melody.

Before the children could ask for another song, Grandfather Amos moved to his favorite chair in the kitchen. Anna poured him a cup of coffee then began putting breakfast on the table.

The meal finished father headed to his favorite chair near the crystal set radio. After lighting his pipe, he put on the ear phones and sat back listening to the news.

Grandfather took up his place near the kitchen stove. This was perhaps his favorite spot because it kept his legs warm. Lisa was sitting at Grandfather's feet looking at her image in the chrome piece that trimmed the stove. Lisa entertained herself with the strange images that became distorted because of the rounded pieces of chrome of the stove.

Grandfather seemed content to watch her play with her doll and talk to the images.

Gus took Mercy out to pull her on the sled. When Phil headed outdoors with his BB gun, Father again cautioned him to be careful and not to play with it near the other children or the animals.

John finished his pipe. Getting up he declared, "I am going up to the dairy and invite the Andersons to come down and spend tomorrow afternoon with us."

"That would be nice," Rena said her hands covered with flour as she rolled out the dough for the apple, pumpkin and mince-meat pies. "They have so little time away from the dairy."

Getting cold, the children returned to the house. Mercy sat down to play with Lisa while Gus invited Phil to play with the erector set with him. The erector set had been given to them by the local preacher whose boy had outgrown it. It was a very expensive set with a lot of small pieces and some small motors.

Gus put together a wind mill and Phil hooked up one of the motor to it. When they turned it on, the blades began to turn and Gus smiled with pleasure closing his hands and turning his thumbs up in triumph.

Hearing their excitement, Mother came over to see. "Why don't you put the windmill some place where your Father can see it when he gets back," she suggested letting her pride in them show in her tone.

Grandmother Anna was busy mixing pumpkin for the pie.

Lisa and Mercy were playing along side grandfather. Mercy was coming up with all the dialog. "Pretend you are my friend and have come to visit Lisa." Lisa put her doll in the buggy with Mercy's doll. She pushed the buggy back and forth. "Pretend you are my husband Grandfather," Mercy said. Grandfather chuckled enjoying being part of their make believe.

Mother was busy getting Christmas dinner ready. Today she would have baked winter squash, Lisa's favorite vegetable. She needed lots of mashed potatoes because both the boys would empty the bowl if she wasn't careful. Grandma Anna was good at making the with giblet gravy. They would have big homemade pan rolls and preserves. Roast chicken stuffed with dressing, and of course, her very special apple nut salad. This salad was made with washed and diced tart winesap apples mixed with shelled chopped walnuts and a generous amount of whipped cream flavored with almond extract. The pumpkin pie would be ready later in the evening.

John returned just as Rena was taking the chicken out of the oven. Her hair was covered in a floral dust cap to keep her long Jet black hair free of cooking residue. "John," she called, "we are ready to eat if you would call every one to the table."

Mother prayed, "Thank you Lord for all we have received through the year. Continue to keep us safe and well throughout the next year. Bless this food and use us to thy service. Amen."

The Andersons would indeed come calling tomorrow afternoon Father related as the dishes began to move around the table.

When dinner was finished Mother set the pies and whip cream out for everyone to help themself when they were ready.

Father went out to milk the cows leaving the boys to play with Gus's erector set. They were busy putting together a fence for imaginary animals. The girls were again playing with their dolls. Grandfather watching chuckled now and again at some of their silly conversation.

Mother and Anna sat at the table each with a cup of coffee. Grandma Anna was looking through the Ladies' Home Journal which was a fairly new magazine working for social causes. "Look here," Anna said pointing to a page, "Men are wearing raccoon coats and golf stockings. "Can you just see our men wearing these socks."

"Maybe the boys would find them stylish," Rena said looking up from her crossword puzzle. John saved the crossword puzzles out of the any newspaper that had been discarded. He knew how much Rena enjoyed challenging brain teasers.

A crossword puzzle is a word game which is made up of a diagram and a set of definitions or clues. The diagram has numbered empty squares and black squares. The defintions are numbered to match the empty squares. Every letter used appears in both across and down words so it is necessary for the words to be correct. The numbers start with 1. across and follow in order horizontally. One number appears in the first square of every series of empty squares, both across and down. The first crossword puzzle appeared in the *New York Sunday World* on December 21, 1913.

Father returned with the milk and Mother got up to put it through the separator setting her crossword puzzle in a safe place. She washed separator thoroughly as she did after every use. She knew how important it was to protect against germs.

It was dark and getting late. Everyone began coming in for the pie Grandmother was dishing. After every had eaten their favorite pie, Mother gathered the dishes and washed them as Father headed for his crystal set to hear the news and smoke his pipe.

Grandfather headed for the stairs to go to bed. It was a wonder how he managed to get up there with his crutches but he got up as well as down with no help from anyone.

Grandmother had Lisa in her night gown ready to crawl up into Father's lap for her nightly story. She never ever heard the end because she always fell asleep before he finished.

Mercy had listened to Father's story and was already in bed and asleep by the time Father carried Lisa in and put her beside Mercy.

Grandmother, having finished with the girls, was upstairs with Grandfather. Mother was washing her face as usual. She took great care for her delicate complexion. Rena never used any kind of lotion on her face. It was clear and smooth and very white. She used talc powder to take the shine off.

The next day Gus raced into the house with the announcement that the Anderson's wagon was coming up the drive.

Mother hurried to her bedroom to smooth her hair in place and checked to see if the girls dresses were soiled. Mercy was clean as usual, but Lisa's dress needed to be changed. What could she expected, she thought, that rambunctious child was always into something.

After dinner the two Andeson children joined Phil, Gus, and Mercy out in the field throwing snow balls and taking turns on the sled. Lisa, her snappy blue eyes drooping, had worn herself out earlier and was ready for a nap. She struggled against taking a nap and missing the fun but was fast asleep in minutes.

Rena set out the left over pie and rolls and poured everyone a cup of coffee while Grandmother went to get the Ouige board. This board was a great conversation piece. For those who believed, its mystery held great promise. To the rest it was a chuckle inside themselves. No no one would ever let anyone else know how their believeswere. The board had various symbols which inclued the letters of the alphabet, numbers from 0—9, and the words yes and no on it. A smaller three-legged table serves as a pointer. This table had felt pads to make it easy to move when two people placed their fingers on their side of the little board. One of the people with fingers on the little table would ask a question. The little table had a pin in the end that pointed to the letters and it would move around and spell out answers to questions. According to people who believed in the Ouija board, spirits guided the pointer. Others thought the fingers of the questioner influenced the pointer. It was always a mystery how it worked. Grandfather said perhaps magnetism from the people's hands caused the movement. The board was invented around 1890 by William Fuld of Baltimore.

They took turns changing partners for the greater part of the afternoon. When they grew tired of that game, someone suggested another spirit conjuring game called "Up Table". This was played where all the occupants around the table placed their hands on the table and chanted Up table Up. Lisa woke from her nap and crawled under the table to see what was making the table tip. Sometimes, one of the boys tipped the table with their knee. Other times Lisa couldn't see anyone tipping the table and she decided she didn't like that game.

Late in the afternoon, the Andersons said their goodbyes and headed home to do the chores. It was an interesting afternoon, but something left a bad feel. Rena gathered the children and they all said evening prayers together before going to bed that night. "I don't think I will get out that Ouija Board again," said Rena to John as she climbed into bed.

21

North Dakota 1925

Christmas eve would be tomorrow and Anna knew this would be one of the first times for a long time that she would not be able to go to the church for Christmas eve service. Little Caleb was only a few days old and it would be too cold to take him out. The coldness of the weather reminded her again of Lill who had been lost to the flu when she was almost a year old. She had not been able to deal with the harsh winter weather.

Chuck came in from doing chores and she poured him a cup of coffee. "Where are the children?" she asked.

"They are all on the river skating. I told them to come in soon by noon because you would need some help," Chuck replied sitting down to the coffee she had poured and taking a *Springale* from the dish on the table.

"That is fine," Anna responded, "I wanted to talk to you about tomorrow night anyway. I have decided it would be best for me to keep Fredrick and Caleb home for Christmas Eve. I can read my Bible and sing a Christmas lullaby to the babies. Caleb is so little and I worry about the cold. Would that be all right with you?"

"Of course it is. You do what you think is best. I would not want to risk the babies getting sick either and I want you to feel at ease, Anna," Chuck reached over and put his arms around her shoulders giving her a squeeze.

"We can put the presents under the tree after you return and the children are in bed," Mother suggested.

"That will be fine. Perhaps you will make us some hot chocolate for when we get back," he said looking at Anna with a pleading almost boyish grin.

"Of course," Anna said, "There will be enough for all and a snack too.

Returning home Chuck found Anna had the promised snack and Chocolate ready. They all sat down and out did each other telling Mother about the evening's events.

Finally, the house grew quiet. Chuck and Anna began putting the things under the tree. The nuts had been placed as usual with a few spread out on the floor, the stockings with the oranges, apples and a small toy hung by the fire place but not close enough to be in danger of getting burned, the presents were placed carefully under the tree.

Chuck and Anna stood back and looked at the tree. "Another Christmas, Anna. It seems we just did this a very short time ago,"

"Yes and it will be a very short time before children are down here wanting to get at this Christmas," Anna reminded him going to the kitchen to bank the fire while Chuck busied himself with the fire in the living room.

The sky had barely become light when Anna heard the children. The morning sky held a promise of a good day for the children to enjoy skating and other outside pleasures.

"Mama Mama," Fredrick shrieked as he ran into his mother's room pulling at her. "Santa. Santa," he squealed with eyes round and hands windmilling forward.

"Alright, I'm coming. Don't wake Baby Brother," Mother shooshed in a whisper holding a finger to her lips.

Chuck dressed quickly. Picking up Fredrick, he put him on his shoulders for a ride out to the tree.

Mother dressed and went to the stove and fireplace to feed them wood. She wanted to get the house heated quickly. She intended there be no chance where the children could catch a cold from a drafty floor.

Fredrick found a teddy bear under the tree and began to hug it. Sue found a real china headed doll. Chris spotted a store bought sled that had his name on it, and there was a bow and arrow with Jeff's name on it. Clare got a new pair of riding boots and Onna unwrapped a store bought sewing box with thread, needles and thimbles in it. June went through the beautiful jewelry box which held some jewelry she knew had once been her mother's and was very special. The children each found a wrapped pacage that held a new outfit made with Mother's sewing machine.

Finally, the children got their stockings from the fireplace and wandered into the kitchen one by one to open them at the breakfast table.

"What baby get?" Fredrick chanted.

"Look here Fredrick. Baby has this rattle. Let's see what he does when I shake it." Mother said drawing the baby cradle closer and shaking the rattle.

Fredrick let out a little chuckle and wrinkled his face in a smile of approval.

The holiday was uneventful. The skating, dances, neighborhood parties, and baking parties went on around them, but they spent most of their Christmas and New Year celebrating at home because of the new baby.

22

Spring in North Dakota

Anna pulled the little wagon holding Caleb up along side the tilled piece of ground that had been made ready for her garden. The area was fenced with white pickets lashed together with wire so the wild animals would not eat the young plants as they came up. In the wagon, Caleb lay cosily wrapped in blanket, coat and hat. Fredrick also was bundled in a hat and warm coat. He followed Mother with the bucket of seeds and the tools that he dragged behind him.

"Mommy, can I put the seeds in the row?" Fredrick begged.

"Yes Fredrick. You can put the carrot seeds in the row I have just made. Be sure you put only a few at a time. And make sure the seeds are evenly spaced or you will have to pick them all up and do it over again," Mother cautioned in a loving but firm voice.

Fredrick spread the seeds evenly being careful to cover all the area. Every once in a while he would stoop and pick up seeds that were too bunched and spread them out more evenly. Mother, hoe in hand, gently put the dirt over the seeds and stamped the dirt lightly to be sure the birds would not eat them.

Fredrick and Mother planted carrots, peas, beans, and corn. It was getting late and time to go in and wash up. The children would soon be home from school and she needed to get dinner started.

Brusing the dirt from her dress, Anna went over to the wagon and found baby had fallen asleep curled up in the folds of his blanket. "Fredrick, take the tools and seed bucket to the shed before you come into the house," she directed as she began to pull little Caleb back to the house.

Without a word, Fredrick began to gather the tools. Anna stood and watched him for a bit. He is such a big help to me and such a perfectionist she thought. I can trust him to do what I ask.

"When you are finished, I'll have a cup of chocolate ready for you," Mother called to him. "Then I would like you to play with Caleb while I get dinner ready."

Chris came in from school banging the door behind him. He ran upstairs and was back in a short time wearing play clothes and carrying his BB gun. Clare was right behind him. She had changed her clothes and come down to the kitchen dressed for riding.

"Don't even think you are going anywhere until your chores are done," Mother said pointing her stirring spoon in the direction of the barn.

June, Onna, and Sue all had changed out of their school clothes and were asking Mother what she needed them to do.

"Onna please get the basket of darning and see how many stockings you can darn before dinner," Mother pleaded.

"Sue please take over playing with Caleb so Fredrick can have some peace. He has been helping all day."

"June you can start peeling the potatoes."

Jeff was in his play clothes and heading out to the wood pile with his wagon to fill the wood boxes.

When he had finished, Mother thanked him and asked if he would like a cookie.

"No thank you," Jeff replied, "but I would like to go, fly my kite before the wind dies down."

"Go on then but be back in by the time the milking is done. That's when dinner should be ready." said Mother gently.

Chris was back in from helping Father with the milking. Jeff had returned and was sitting by the heater doing school work.

The family was just sitting down to dinner when Clare appeared at the door. As Clare made a place for herself at the table, Father began in a stern thunderous voice, "I guess since you have had your time free riding your horse while the rest were doing their chores, you will be doing the dishes and cleaning up the kitchen by yourself." When Clare did not answer he continue, "Is that clear, young lady?"

"Yes Father," Clare answered not looking up.

After dinner Anna and Chuck went into the sitting room with a cup of coffee. Chuck sat next to Anna who sat in the rocking chair nursing the baby.

Fredrick and Jeff sat building an imaginary structure with the blocks their father had cut out for them. Sue was reading *Burce* by Albert Payson Terhune, a book she had borrowed from her teacher. It was a story about a collie who had turned from an ugly duckling into the pride of his owners. The dog was a devoted friend who saved lives. Sue had already read *Lad: A Dog* by the same author and could hardly wait until another book came out. June and Onna sat at the corner table playing Dominoes.

Chris was working on a map he was drawing for his school project. He kept asking Father about different things related to the German area of the map.

Everyone ignored the banging and clattering from the kitchen. Father knew Clare avoided helping Anna. Long ago Anna had quit trying to get Clare's acceptance, but Father knew she didn't push her to help either. It was Father who watched and when he saw she was not doing her share stepped in to see to it that she helped.

Finally, one by one the children finished their separate projects and went off to bed and taking Fredrick with them. Anna had Caleb asleep and in his own bed. "Would you like to play a little Gin Rummy before going to bed, Chuck?" Anna asked holding the deck of cards in her hand.

"Sure, I could use a little change of pace," he said, "and you have put in a hard day as well. I see you have a lot of the garden in."

"Yes," Anna said cutting the deck and dealing ten cards to each of them. "I had a lot of help from Fredrick," she continued talking as she layed a card face up in the center of the table beside the deck. "He is getting to be a real help. I will hate to see him go of to school next year."

Chuck took a card from the deck and layed one from his hand down on the discard pile face up.

The game continued while Anna described the things she needed to do to get the hens ready to set. "I will need to get things ready for the turkeys as well."

"I can do that," Chuck said melding his entire hand with a big grin. "You have enough to do with the garden and the babies."

"You think your are so smart," she said with a chuckle. "Deal those cards."

After playing for the better part of two hours, Anna rose from her chair and heading to the stoves to bank the fires for the night asking if Chuck would like a little snack?

"That sounds good," Chuck said getting up to help, "Perhaps a bit of hot chocolate and some cookies."

*   *   *

It is the fourth of July and the neighbors are all gathering in the grove of trees by the river to celebrate. The day is beautiful and warm. The children hear noise and run out of the door to see the great procession of buggies coming up the lane. In the grove, saw horses have been set up with four by eight sheets of board on top to make tables. These tables are covered with sheets as tablecloths and food is beginning to be lined up. Anna has large pans of home-made rolls, jars of pickles, and huge pans of fried chicken. Chuck unloaded a wash tub full of ice taken from the icehouse. In the ice he placed a five gallon cream can filled with the ice cream mix that Anna had made that morning.

The men and older boys took turns turning the cream can in the ice to make ice cream while other men challenged each other in a wrestling match. The young children gathered around to pick up the loose change that fell out of the pockets of the wrestlers. Fredrick and Jeff had dreams of what they would spend their money

on when Father took the cream to town and they went along. The
girls were down wading in the river until they were called in by
the women to help feed the young children. Everyone gathered to watch the boys play softball. When the game was over,
the ball players went to the river to wash up and cool down
before loading up their plates with food. Opening the cream
can and swinging a long spoon in the air, Chuck announced,
"Ice cream is ready." Every one filled their bowl and sat down
to relax and visit. Nearing chore time every one filled their
plates once more, then the women packed up the food not
eaten and loaded it in their buggies.

The children yelled their goodbyes to friends and the women
hugged each other knowing this would be the last get together
until harvest was over.

Anna, Chuck and the children stayed behind to clean up the
grounds and put their things in the wagon to haul back to the
house.

Once home everyone lent a hand to get the cows milked, the
wood in, and the other chores done before calling it a day.

23

Clare falls in love

The night was warm. Anna had brushed her hair back in a soft pomp framing her soft, loving features. She was just finishing the final touches on the last of the baskets for the basket social at tonight's barn dance.

"Is every one ready to get in the wagon?" Chuck asked as he came in from having finished the last of the chores. "We need to head now so I will have time to set up the music before all the rest arrived."

"Girl's get your coats on. It will be cool coming home," Mother directed. "June, if you could please get Fredrick ready, I tend to Caleb".

Coming in from outside Clare said, "Mother' can I have a basket for some one to bid on instead of the children's basket we share?"

"Yes dear. I have made one for you and Onna as well. You are both old enough," Mother answered handing them the baskets to carry out to the wagon.

Mother carried the baby's feather bed and one for Fredrick out to the wagon and directed June to watch over them until they left.

Sue, in a pink flower print dress, ran quickly to the wagon. Her black hair was cut short framed her round face. The sparkle in her eyes revealed a glint of mischief as she climbed into the wagon holding her special rag doll. Jeff, his blonde unruly hair falling over his eyes, carried a wooden horse and buggy his father had carved out for him; the wheels were made from empty spools attached with rubber bands. He raced to get in to wagon before Sue but then stood waiting for her.

Arriving at the dance everyone took a basket with them and placed it on the auctioneer's table near the music stand. Mother noticed Clare had drifted off into the corner where a group of young people were milling around. Young Olaf Swenson stood near where Clare had stopped to talk to a girl with whom she went to school.

The music started and June came over to her mother. "I'll sit with Caleb and Fredrick until they went to sleep. You go, visit with your friends."

"They need to eat something," Mother said, "they will not sleep if they are hungry."

"I fed them some soup before we left home Mother."

"Thank you," Mother said with a smile, "then I think I will just go over there and visit with the ladies setting up their tables."

Watching her go, June sat down on one of the hay bales that lined the room.

After the music had been playing a few hours, the women noticed the old farm hands were beginning to droop from hunger, having put in a full day in the field. One of the ladies whispered something to the auctioneer.

The auctioneer in his bid overalls and plaid shirt took his place at the table with the baskets and waved his hand for the music to stop.

"I believe we have a bunch of hungry men here so we better get them fed," he said with flouish and winked at the women who had whispered to him. "The bidding will start in five minutes. Remember the rules: you bid on a basket. You win the basket and the lady who brought the basket will be your meal partner."

Chris was standing by his mother when Chuck joined them. "Son, here is five dollars. That should get you a big basket. Now bid carefully," his father chuckled as he handed him the money.

Clare and Onna came over to stand by Chris while June sat at the family table with Sue and Jeff.

Clare's thoughts were deep but she kept them to herself. She did so hope Olaf would bid on her basket.

Arin Swenson, a young man from school, came over to where June was sitting. "Which basket is yours?" he asked sitting down beside her.

"I don't have a basket this year. Mother said I am not old enough. So I will be eating at the family table."

"Oh!" the young man sighed in disappointment.

"That big yellow basket is my sister Onna's," June pointed to a huge basket with the yellow ribbon Onna had tied to the top. "It has lots of good food in it."

"Thanks," Arin said as he walked closer to the auctioneer.

The biding was halfway through and the auctioneer was just picking up the big yellow basket. "Do I have one dollar?" started the auctioneer.

"One dollar," yelled a big fellow with red hair and a beard.

"Four dollars," squesked Arin with a tremble.

"Four dollars. Who will make it five," said the auctioneer. "Four once. Four twice. Sold to the Lad with the red hair."

With that Arin ran up and grabbed his basket, then coming over to where Onna bashfully stood, he took her arm and led her off to the other end of the long set of tables. "Your sister said this was your basket. I am glad I was able to get it," Arin said smiling timidly up at Onna. Arin had enjoyed the basket of food and found that he could talk easily to Onna. "When we have finished eating perhaps you will dance with me?"

"That would be nice," Onna said in a soft bashful voice.

"How come June doesn't have a basket. I thought she was older than you ?" Arin brought up. "My brother Jacob wanted to eat with her."

"Well," said Onna waving her hand toward the family table. "There certainly is enough in the family basket for him to join her. With all those kids, Mother always packs a lot of food. Mother also packed a basket for Father to buy so they could eat by themself. Don't you think it is so cute?"

"If he comes this way we will tell him," he said losing interest in his brother's concern for the moment while he furthered his own concern. "I have seen you at school and wanted to talk to you, but you always have so many people around you."

"Oh! They are probably just my brothers and sisters."

Arin's brother, Jacob, came by the table just then, and Arin called him over, "Heh! If you want to eat with June," Onna said, "just go over to where she is watching her brother and sisters."

"I'll set it up," Onna said standing and getting ready to go talk to June.

"Thanks, I would like that," Jacob said following Onna to where her sister was sitting and then passing her.

"Hi," Jacob greeted as he reached the table.

Seeing Jacob could take care of himself, Onna returned to Arin and her own basket of food.

"Your sister said you might have a lot of good food here. Since you didn't have a basket for me to bid on, Onna thought you wouldn't mind sharing your family basket with me. Is she right?"

"Sure come join us," invited June. "Mother and Father have their own basket and Mother always packs enough for a harvest crew. I guess she is afraid her family will starve."

June had been scanning the hall for Olaf. She saw Clare still standing in the corner where several of her friends had gathered to chat. June could not see Olaf anywhere she hoped he had not left the basket social. June knew that Clare was interested in Olaf. She had worn the yellow dress that went so well with her blond hair. She had spent a good part of the day curling her hair with the flax seed they had boiled. It made a nice jel that held the curls firm and hold in place. "She looks beautiful tonight don't you think," said June thinking out loud.

"Who?" asked Jacob looking around.

"Clare, my sister," she said pointing over to where Clare was standing. "Olaf should be smitten with her."

Looking in the direction June was pointing, Jacob saw that Clare was watching the auctioneer.

Three baskets remained on the table. "We have three baskets left," called the auctioneer as he held up the basket belonging to Mary Erickson. "Who will open the bid?"

Coming in the door, Olaf held up his hand and offered a dollar.

"Who will make it two?" called the auctioneer.

"Two," Olaf and the crowded laughed.

"You're bidding against yourself," said a big fellow from the back of the loft as he said, "Three."

"The bid is three." yelled the auctioneer. "Who wants to make it four. After a pause he said, "Three once. Three twice. Sold to the fellow in the back. Come get your basket Mary young fellow and have a nice evening."

"Okay," the auctioneer said picking up another basket. "I have another fine basket. Who will open the bid?"

"One dollar," Olaf yelled once again.

Then a fellow in the far back yelled, "Two."

"Five," yelled a young man just coming in the door.

A pause and then the auctioneer hollered, "Going once. Going twice. Gone for five to the young man by the door."

Clare was in deep despair. Olaf had not out bid any of the rest so she decided she was probably going to be stuck eating with one of the area farm hands.

The auctioneer held up Clare's huge basket. Anna had done a nice job making it appealing in size and color. "Who will start this bid at two dollars," he said, "remember the money helps to keep this place repaired."

Olaf held up his hand and said two. Clare's heart pounded hoping no one else would bid for on it. Clare had seen how far he had gone before and she felt he would not go further.

Her heart began a fast beat as she heard a fellow up on the music area yell three.

Then without her notice, Olaf came up to the auctioneer table and said, "Six."

A pause held as the auctioneer waited to see if anyone else would bid.

Clare let out a sigh of resignation when she heard the auctioneer say gone to the highest bidder. She looked around for the last bidder but couldn't tell who it was.

When Olaf went up to claim her basket, she caught her breath.

"I thought your basket was already gone," he said when he came over to take her by the arm and lead her to a seat where there were no others sitting. "I was outside when the auction began. Then when I came in every one in your family seemed to already be eating."

"That was the younger ones," Clare said sitting down beside Olaf.

"Well I am glad I got here in time to get your basket," he said looking into Clare's eyes to reassure her.

As they sat eating and talking about the school and farming and who was going calling on whom, Olaf all of a sudden said, "Could I come calling on you Sunday afternoon?"

Clare flushed pink with embarrassment. This was her dream come true she thought. "I would love to have you call on me." Clare said smiling up at Olaf her eyes shinning like a maid in love.

"Well then, I will be there after church Sunday."

"Why don't you ride over on your horse. Then we can go riding together?"

"That is a good idea," Olaf agreed.

"I will seeask Mother if she will let me take a picnic lunch. Perhaps can eat by the river. We can spend the afternoon away from the rest of the family and the babies."

"Great," Olaf said standing and brushing the crumbs from his pants. "Thanks for the dinner," he as he waved goodnight and headed for the door.

Clare packed up the remaining food, cleaned up the area, and took the basket to Anna.

"Can I make a picnic lunch and go riding with Olaf on Sunday?" Racing ahead before her parents could answer, "He asked if he could come over on Sunday. I suggested a picnic lunch by the river." she pleaded looking first at Father and then to Anna for approval.

"Will you be picnicking with him alone?" Father questioned.

"Well yes," she said looking down at her feet then up at Father for approval ignoring Anna. "We thought we would ride awhile and then have lunch by the river."

"That will be fine," Father said, "but you can expect that I will be riding down that way just to make sure your young fellow minds his manners."

"Oh Father, do you have to? He is a fine boy. Just ask June. He goes to school with all of us," Clare whined.

"Well Clare, I guess you will have to accept it on just those conditions. You know I really I didn't have to tell you what I was going to do. If fact I could have demanded that you take Chris or June with you. Besides it is open area," he said with a private chuckle and a nudge to Anna, "I might just tell each of the children to ride on by and check on you."

"Oh Father, can't you please tell all of them they can't come near there?" Clare complained knowing her plea was a waste of time.

"Don't you fret," Father continued, "you'll be taken care of just fine and your young man won't even know anyone is around."

Sunday afternoon arrived bright and clear. Clare stood in the window watching for Olaf to arrive. Anna had helped her pack a nice picnic basket. Soon she saw his horse sauntering up the draw along side the bank of old trees that bordered the river . Olaf jumped down, tied his horse to the hitching rail, and then made his way to the house. Olaf smoothed his hair back with the palm of his hand and knocked gently on the door. Anna opened the door.

"I have come to call on Clare Mame," Olaf said bowing to Anna in respect his hat in his hand.

"Come in," Anna said calling to Clare and showing Olaf into the sitting room.

Clare greeted Olaf as he came into the sitting room. She knew he was at the door, but she thought it was not lady like to meet him at the door so she pretended to be surprised that he was already there.

Grabbing up the picnic basket and handing it to Olaf, she invited him to follow her to the barn where her horse was already saddled. Olaf assisted her as she climbed up. Then hanging the basket on her saddle horn, he walked to where his horse was tied while she trotted along side. Once he had mounted, they rode off together.

They rode in a comfortable silence for some time. Sparse conversation helped them get better acquainted. They found they had common interests.

Having been riding in the hot sun for about an hour, they dismounted and tied their horses to the tree alongside the river where there was a nice flat grassy area. Clare brought out the jar of lemonade she had made. She spread the blanket that had hung in a roll on the back of the saddle.

Clare pushed her straw hat back on her head and wiped the sweat from her brow where it had beaded under the hat band. She busied herself laying out the lunch while Olaf stretched out on the blanket looking up at the sky, his straw hat over his forehead with just enough room to peak out under the brim.

The afternoon floated by. They had been in deep conversation when out of the corner of her eye, she saw her father riding just at the edge of the hill above them. She knew Olaf had not seen him and was pleased that Father had not stopped.

It was beginning to get hazy and Clare decided it was best to head back to the house. She didn't want the day spoiled by a storm.

When they arrived back home, Olaf got down and helped Clare unsaddle her horse. "I would like to call again," he said taking her hand in both of his.

Clare looked up at him. Her eyes sparkled with the love she had for him. "Yes. I would like that. Perhaps next weekend."

Clare watched Olaf ride down the lane and out of sight. She walked slowly back to the house. Coming into the kitchen, she saw all of the children standing at the window. They were all snickering but she didn't care. "He wants to see me again," she told Anna. "I told him next weekend."

"Have you spoken to your father about it?" Anna inquired softly.

"No," Clare said with defiance. "I already told him he could come."

Anna bit her lip. This statement seemed a little disrespectful, but Anna let it be, knowing Chuck would handle it his way.

Chris came in teasing Clare and trying to make her believe he had been spying on her.

"Shut up Chris. You don't know anything."

"Saw you kissing," declared Chris.

"Well, you must have been spying on someone else," Clare retorted, "since we did not kiss."

"Bet you did," Chris shot back stretching his eyes, cocking his head to the side, and smirking.

Chuck came in with the milk ready to separate. Hearing the yelling back and forth, he called Chris to come get the separating done. "Stop tormenting your sister," he reprimanded in a low tone. Father knew where he had been all afternoon and it wasn't near the picnicking area.

24

A Wedding in 1927

It is early spring and Clare and Olaf have been keeping company steadily, church, barn dances, and Sunday horseback rides with culminating picnics.

This Sunday as they sat on the blanket with the picnic basket open between them, Olaf suddenly turned and took Clare's hand. Looking into her eyes he said, "Clare, we enjoy each other's company, wouldn't you say? You like to ride horseback as do I. You seem content to watch while I fish. We have a lot of things in common."

"What are you trying to say, Olaf?" Clare questioned confused by his conversation.

"I . . . I. . . . Well I am trying to ask you to be my wife," he stammered. I am now full time at the Chevrolet garage. You would not have to be a farmer's wife. I know you do not much like the work on the farm."

"I think you will have to ask my father for my hand," Clare said with a soft smile. "If he will agree then I accept."

Clare reached the barn and prepared to unsaddle her horse. Olaf tied his horse to the hitching post by the barn and headed for the house, turning long enough to call over his shoulder, "I am going to find your father, Clare."

Arriving at the porch door, he gently knocked and then walked into the house and found his way to the kitchen where Anna busied herself getting dinner.

"Would you like to join us for supper, Olaf? We have it almost ready."

"I would be pleased to have supper with you. Besides I have something to discuss with Chuck when he has finished his chores and has a little time, perhaps after dinner."

Dinner finished Onna and June cleared the table as Sue took Fredrick in the sitting room to play. Jeff headed out the door but turned to tell his mother he was going to get the wood in for the night. Chris headed upstairs to his room with a book in hand. As Chris climbed the stairs his thoughts were on what Olaf could possibly want with father. Perhaps he had seen him kill some of the birds with his sling shot. He knew this was something that was strictly forbidden. Arriving at the top of the stairs, he looked out of the window that was at the end of the hall into the yard below. He saw Olaf and his father deep in discussion. Olaf waving his arm the direction of the upstairs window where he stood.

Chris was the furtherest thing from Olaf and Father's thoughts at this moment but Chris was consumed with guilt. He had used his sling shot on several birds that afternoon but he didn't think anyone was near enough to see. "I have a time job at the garage in town sir. I am sure it will take care of rent and food."

Chuck, looking the boy straight in the eye said, "There is more to marriage than money, boy." Putting his hand on Olaf's shoulder he said, "I don't think you understand what you are getting into. Clare is a very determined young women. When she wants something she usually goes after it. Are you sure you can handle this?"

"Yes sir," Olaf said lifting his head to look Chuck in the eye. His feet set apart and his shoulders back. His head came a little higher in a very determined stance. "I have been keeping company with her a long while now. I believe we will be a good match."

"Well, then you have my blessing. When had you figured this wedding should take place?" Chuck said with a twinkle of amusement at the boys assertiveness.

"I would like it to be the first part of May."

"Well that only gives the ladies a few months to get ready boy."

"I know but sir I . . ."

"It's okay," Chuck interrupted not wanting to frustrate the boy any longer. "I will tell Anna your intention. If Clare has agreed and Anna thinks they can get the wedding plans done then I don't see a problem." Chuck shook his hand before Olaf climbed into his saddle and headed down the path toward home.

Chris lay on top of the covers of his bed hoping Father would not come up to scold him. Laying very still, he waited for the footsteps on the stairs.

Chuck came into the kitchen and poured himself a cup of coffee. "Anna," he said sitting down, "come sit with me for a minute. I need to talk with you.

Anna cocked her head sideways to look at Chuck then she poured herself a cup of coffee and brought a plate of cookies. "What is troubling you?" she asked hearing the seriousness in his voice.

"Olaf has asked for Clare's hand in marriage and I have given him my blessing. Olaf wants the wedding to be in May and I know that doesn't give you much time to put a wedding together." Chuck looked at Anna searching her face for signs of frustration and stress. "I know this is the wrong time of year for adding to your work load but I need to ask if you will do what is needed to prepare for Clare's wedding?"

"Oh Chuck, I love our daughter. I know she hasn't accepted me, but that hasn't stopped me from taking her on as my daughter. She is not any more difficult than Chris other than she cannot seem to let go of her own mother's memory to accept me. I will be happy to make her dress and prepare what is needed for the wedding and the get together after the wedding. We will get the girls to help and some of the ladies of the church."

"Do you need to go to Bismark to get what you need?" Chuck said finishing the last bite of his cookie and taking a sip of coffee.

"Oh yes. Please take me to Bismark. They will have much better material there" Anna exclaimed taking on an excited flush.

"Okay then. Be ready in the morning. As soon as I have finished the chores we will go to Bismark. The girls can take care of things here."

Chris waited and waited and soon everything in the house was quiet. Perhaps his father had decided to let it ride until later. Chris took off his clothes and climbed under the covers perhaps his father would forget all about it he thought as he rolled over and went to sleep.

Chuck got up early. He finished the chores and then went out to start the old Maxwell touring car and let it warm up for the trip to Bismark.

Anna came out carrying a bag she had made to carry purchases. It had an elaborate embroidered flower on its face. Anna stepped up and into the car, her weight made the car list to one side until Chuck got in and help level it out some. The kids watching noticed the car still leaned a bit more to Mother's side but it did not hinder the movement. Anna was a beautiful woman with a pleasant disposition and, in spite of her great weight, her children as well as her husband adored her. With all those babies so close together it was especially hard to keep weight down. The sausages they made were a big part of their food source. Since there was no way to keep foods cold, meats needed to be cured, smoked or canned with plenty of salt.

As they pulled into Bismark, Anna's thoughts began to consider the type of dress that would make this skinny young woman a beautiful bride and please her future husband and father.

Chuck parked the car along side the busy mercantile and Anna hurried inside anxious to begin her shopping. "I will meet you back here. Just take your time. I have plenty to keep me busy," Chuck hollored with a chuckle as she disappeared into the store. Is she excited, Chuck thought to himself. There is nothing like a family event to bring new energy to that girl.

After searching several sections, Anna finally found a piece of white satin that she liked. Calling to the clerk she ordered her to cut enough material to make a bridle gown that would be long and sleek and enhance Clare's slim figure. "Do you have fine lace for trim," Anna asked?

"Oh yes, Ma'am. We have the finest lace just in from New

York. How much would you like?"

"I believe it will take ten yards." Anna replied her pointing under her chin eyesthoughtfully looking up calculating measurement.

"I will need some buttons to make the opening in the back and the sleeves pretty," Anna said looking around.

"We have these beautiful cut glass buttons," the clerk said moving to the button section and picking up the buttons. "See how the lights makes them sparkle."

"Thank you. Those will be perfect," she said choosing twenty-five for the back and eight more for each sleeve. "I also need some thread," she said but her eye was on the small white garland of flowers and bead handing on a rack.

"This garland will look lovely on the bridal veil," the clerk coaxed taking it down and handing it to Anna. "You think about it while I get the thread."

As the clerk finished wrapping the material in a package she said, "I would love to see this dress when it is finished. Your daughter is going to be beautiful with that garland accenting her hair."

"Oh, I hope so," Anna sighed wistfully.

With her purchases tucked under her arm, Anna stepped outside the door wondering how long it take her to find Chuck. He stood from where he had been sitting on the bench just outside the merchantile. "I bought some special treats for the children," he said. Anna liked the way Chuck always made sure that all the children were noticed especially when one was getting special attention.

Now in the car heading home, Anna began to reminisce. It has been a good life she thought. Oh there had been the bad times, but Chuck had loved her and been a loving father. Anna's mind wandered to Clare all the times she had tried to make friends with Clare. She had not been successful in all these years. She didn't know if there was anything else she could have done. Perhaps she had been too patient. Oh well, she shrugged perhaps after she is married or maybe after she has babies of her own she will want to become friends.

As they pulled into the yard, the children all came running knowing they would get a special treat. "Whoa stand back," Chuck yelled as he slowly guided the car into the shed and put a cover over it. Getting out of the car, Chuck reach over and squeezed Fredrick's shoulder before picking Caleb up and putting him on his shoulder. "How have my boys been today?" he teased giving Caleb a bumpy ride to the house.

Chuck reached in his pocket and brought out the special ribbon candy they all liked so much.

Chris and Jeff came up and stood in line along with the little ones. Chuck grinning handed them new sling shot he had in his oversized pocket along with some of the ribbon candy.

Anna went into the house anxious to show Clare the material she had bought for her wedding dress. She hoped she would be pleased.

She called Clare over to her as she lay the package on the table and began to unwrap it. Clare gave it a quick glance and said, "It is nice." then waving her hand and smiling with her mouth but not her eyes she headed for the door dressed to go riding.

"How will I ever get the measurements to sew this dress Anna," thought to herself. Anna wondered if Clare really wanted to marry Olaf or just wanted to rid herself of the family. Well she began to tell herself as she rewrapped the material and took in into her bedroom. I will just have to catch her when her father is around. Clare does not refuse a request from her father.

Dinner was over and the kitchen cleaned up for morning. The chores were done and Chuck sat reading a book in his favorite chair. Anna opened the package she had rewrapped and spread it out on her work table. She took out the pattern pieces she had made for Clare's other dresses. She would use it to create a new pattern for the wedding dress. "Come here, Clare," Anna pleaded, "let me get your measurements so I can start your dress."

"I am reading," Clare shot back without moving.

"Well young lady," Father scolded in a stern voice. "Perhaps I should ride into town and tell Olaf you have changed your mind and will not marry him after all since you will have no dress."

"Oh alright!" Clare begrudged slamming her book down and coming over to Anna.

Anna brought out her tape measure and swiftly jotted down the measurements. She had begun to lose the excitement of creating the dress since Clare was showing so little interest. She laid the material and pattern aside to work on later. Maybe tomorrow I'll work on it tomorrow when the children are at school and Caleb is napping.

In bed that night, Chuck stroked Anna's hair. "I know she is difficult. I don't know what makes her so mean spirited. She is deliberately unappreciative of the things you do for her. I have talked with her about it and she promises to be better, but she never is. I wish I could make it better for you."

"Thank you Chuck," Anna said feeling revived by Chuck's understanding.

Anna hummed as she pressed the seams of the dress. She was careful to press the back opening flat so the buttonholes would not hide the glass buttons. Anna drew a straight line with a chalk marker so each button hole would be even. She did the same in the area where the buttons would be placed. Next she made a mark where each button would sit to match the button hole. She worked with pleasure throughout the day.

Finally she hung the dress up for inspection. Anna was pleased with it so far. The seams were all sewn by her new Singer sewing machine. But now the lace, buttons, buttonholes and hem would all be done by hand. This would take several evenings after the children were in bed. Anna looked at the sleeves. They were almost like the ones she had made on her wedding dress so many years ago. They puffed out from the shoulder down to the elbow and then fitted from there to the wrist. Anna began to plan just how much she would need to leave the sleeve open from the wrist up to make it easier to get into. She decided with Clare's skinny arm it would only be necessary to make six buttons up from the wrist. She wished she could try the dress on Clare. It would make her feel more comfortable about the fit.

Having marked and cut all the buttonholes, she hung the dress in her bedroom until tonight. She could hear Caleb waking from his nap and Fredrick was asking for a snack. The rest of the children would be home from school soon. She didn't want the dress out for Clare to see until it was finished she would probably want changes that were impossible to make. She had decided that Clare would just have to accept what she got since she was not making it easy.

*   *   *

May was almost here. The wedding was planned for as soon after graduation as possible. Anna had worked diligently every evening and finally finished all the button holes in the sleeves and down the back. In all there were thirty-two button holes. She would put the extra buttons away for something special. Tonight she planned to sew the fine lace in rows on the bodice to flatter her small bustline.

The wedding was set for May nineteenth, she calculated how much she needed to do each night to be ready. Once the lace was on she would need to hem the dress and then make a nice slip and veil. She thought she should be able to have it ready for Clare to try on by the seventeenth. Anna hoped Clare would be willing. She had not asked about the dress nor involved herself in the wedding plans.

On the evening of the seventeenth, as the family sat at the dinner table, Anna looked at Clare and then at Chuck, "I think tonight would be a nice time for Clare to show you how she looks in her wedding dress. Besides the wedding is only two days away; I will need time if anything needs to be changed.

"Ya, Clare," Chuck said sipping his coffee then setting it down slowly. He knew Anna needed his support right now. "Anna has worked many days on your dress. Tonight I will see it on you, ya!"

"Alright Father," Clare said looking at Father and avoiding looking at Anna. She resented her having gone to Father to get her to do what she wanted. She didn't know why she was always angry at her.

"Good," Father said and sat back in his chair wiping his mouth with the coarse napkin Anna had spent hours making for her large family. He looked at the napkin, always clean and ready for the next meal, and thought how Anna did so many things for their family.

Finally the family gathered in the sitting room, all except Jeff who darted out the back door to get the wood and Chris just to get away.

Clare came out of her parent's bedroom with the dress on all buttoned with June's help. Her skinny body flattered by the clever bodice Anna had created of fine lace.

Chuck beamed with pride at his oldest daughter, "Anna," he exclaimed. "you have made her into a young women with that dress. She is no longer the Tom Boy we all know."

"She already is a young women," Anna said looking at Clare with love and pleasure at the job she had done. "It is not the dress that makes a women."

Anna followed Clare back into the bedroom to help her out of the dress. Her thoughts drifted again to her own wedding day. She had been so much in love with Chuck. That love has only grown with his nurturing. "I pray you and Olaf will be as happy as your father and I are, Clare," Anna said taking a chance that Clare would not reject her attention.

"Thank you, Anna," Clare said as the dress came over the top of her head.

It was a simple acknowledgement but one Anna would hold on to for the rest of her life.

*   *   *

All were assembled at the church. Clare was in her dress and wait-ing with Father in the church office waiting for the music to an-nounce walk down the isle. Many other guest had already been seated. Anna had been ushered to the seat researved for Mother of the bride. Olaf stood with the pastor and the best man in the front of the church.

Chris and Jeff had joined some of the other boys to tie cans on Olaf's wagon. As they headed into the church to take their seat with the family, one of the boys hollored his reminder to meet back there late that night.

The music changed and Anna looked back to watch as Chuck brought his daughter down the isle. Tears formed in her eyes and one escaped rolling down her cheek at the sight of her handsome man. For a moment in Anna's mind the years had all gone away and it was them standing together before the tall preacher, except she thought coming back to reality this preacher was not tall and thin, in fact he was short and plump.

The wedding vows had been said and the ministers blessing given. The wedding was over all too soon. The guest rose and followed the bride and groom down the aisle and into the Sunday school room for cake and punch. As they entered the room they shook the new couple's hand wishing them well. For the first time ever Anna saw a smile on Clare's face that reached her eyes. She seemed to shine with a special glow that had never been a part of her character before. "I do hope she will be as happy as we have been," Anna sobbed looking at Chuck through her tears feeling as though she were Clare's real mother and losing her first daughter.

The couple left the church through the side door . Olaf had a small house in town that was left to him. That is where they would be living.

The guests began to leave and the ladies who were in charge of church socials began cleaning up. "Go home," They commanded sending Chuck and Anna on there way.

Arriving home, Chuck took Anna in his arms and thanked her for all she had done for his daughter.

"Too bad their house is so small. Their friends won't be able to give them the three day chavari we had," Chuck commented with a twinkle in his eye as he gave Anna a squeeze.

Chris had come in just before the comment and said, "Well father the boys up town and I are going to take care of that tonight after dusk if it's all right with you. I was going to saddle up and ride into town along with the rest of the boys.

"They have no room in the house," Chuck admonished, "so don't you guys all go piling in."

"No, we won't," he assured. "We are going to go with the noise makers and keep them up awhile. It will be fun and I'm sure Clare will be fit to be tied."

"You don't be causing trouble in town. No guns. Just pans for noise makers okay?" Chuck demanded firmly.

"Don't worry, Father. We are not going to get drunk or get out of hand. We just want to frustrate Olaf a little."

Anna looked at Jeff who appeared to be getting ready to go. "And where do you think you are going, young man?"

"It's okay Mom," Chris said. "Let him go. He is old enough and I will watch out for him. Besides, his friends will be there too."

The house was quite, but Anna had not been able to go to sleep. Her boys were still out. She was not used to them being out so late on their own. "They were all growing up so fast and she didn't like the way it felt.

"Don't be troubled Anna," Chuck comforted taking her hand. They are grown and will soon be going out to find work for themselves."

"Oh Chuck, Chris is only thirteen," she sniffed. "And Jeff is only ten. They are still boys."

"Ya Mama, to you, but they must learn to be self sufficient. No one can hold their hands if another war should come along. They must learn to take care of themselves. It will be fine," he soothed. "They are many together," Chuck said giving her a little peck on the cheek before falling asleep.

Soon she heard the foot steps of the boys trying to tiptoe up the stairs without their shoes. Anna, satisfied all were home, turned over and went to sleep.

25

Clare and Olaf come for Christmas

Summer was coming to an end and though Anna had taken the buggy to visit Clare in town several times, it didn't seem Clare was interested in her visits. As Anna drove back to the farm, she thought about what she could do to get closer to Clare. Perhaps when the harvest was done, Anna thought, she might take them some vegetables and canned meats. Being a garage worker did not give them much money and living in town did not allow them a place to raise a garden or raise meat. Anna noticed that Clare was in the family way. She knew it was important for Clare to eat better, especially since she was such a scrawny little thing. How could she be giving the baby what it needed she thought.

*   *   *

It was nearing November. The crops had been harvested. Anna had canned and dried extra things from the garden in hopes Clare would accept some. They would need them for the harsh winter ahead. Next week they would make the sausages and can some of the beef and chickens.

As they sat down to dinner Anna looking at Chuck, "Will you be going into New Salem any time soon," she inquired with concern in her eyes.

"Ya, why do you ask?"

"I would like you to take some sausages, and canned vegetables to Clare. I don't think they have enough stored away for winter and it looks as though she is in the family way."

"The family way huh! Well, I'll be," smiled Chuck inwardly trying out the name Opa. "Ya, I can take it in with me when I go this week. But Anna, why do you not take it to her yourself."

"I am not sure but what she would be offended. She has such a hard time accepting things from me," Anna returned. "Anna you are so kind."

"Stumm Frau!" exclaimed Chuck as he rose from his chair and poured them each another cup of coffee.

"She is not a dumb womon Chuck," Anna defended. "Just a very hurt one. She has never wanted to betray her mama's memory by excepting me, that's all."

Chuck returned from New Salem with lots of news from town. He put the Old Maxwell in the shed, covered it, and hurried into the house anxious to tell Anna.

Caleb had just awakened from his nap, and Anna was putting him in the high chair with milk and cookies when Chuck raced into the house.

"Whoa, what are you all excited about?" she asked pouring some coffee and getting a plate of cookies for them as Chuck sat down and took off his hat.

Chuck tipped his chair back as he began to describe what he had seen in town.

"The kids were telling me about a new motion picture called *The Jazz Singer*. In it the actor, Al Jolson, actually talks Anna." These new motion pictures are called Talkies. Clare said they try to go once a week if they can save up a nickle.

"By the way, Clare was happy to get all the nice things you sent. I made sure she knew it was what you had fixed for her and Olaf. She said thanks."

"I am happy that she found it something she could use."

"Well she had better be happy."

Anna rose and started the evening meal. "Chuck," she said turning to meet his eyes. "Do you think we could go see one of those talkies some time?"

"I was hoping you would want to do that Anna," Chuck said putting on his hat and returning to the barn to complete the evening chores.

After dinner Anna sat in her rocking chair finishing a piece of embroidery she would give Clare and Olaf for Christmas. It was the last of a set of pillow cases. They would be added to the tea towels she had already finished and wrapped. She was pleased with herself. She had managed to finish all of the children's new clothes and had them wrapped so they would not find them before Christmas. Chuck had made Caleb a set of train cars. Fredrick would have his ice skates. Anna had been able to get them when she had been in town last. With most of the Christmas gifts done she could now concentrate on Thanksgiving preparations.

Anna put aside her work and heading for the bedroom. Calling back to Chuck, she said, "Please fix the fires tonight. I am so tired. I just need to lie down and sleep."

Anna undressed. Before lying down she found some extra pillows. She was having difficulty catching her breath and she hoped that raising her head would help her to breath better through the night.

Chuck finished fixing the fires. His thoughts on the many times lately that he had seen Anna slip away to rest. He knew she must be feeling poorly. It was not like her to sit unless she was busy with her hands sewing or fixing things for canning. Chuck had found Anna in her rocking chair quite a bit of late with her eyes closed but not really asleep. Going in to the bedroom, he reached over to pat her hand, "You feeling badly tonight Anna?"

"Just a bit tired. I will be better in the morning."

Anna returned Chuck's pat, "Goodnight Chuck. Sleep well."

Chuck found it hard to fall asleep listening to Anna's heavy breathing. *Please God, help Anna to breath better*, he prayed before turning over.

Anna rose early. She had breakfast on the table before Chuck was in from the milking and the children came down dressed for school. Little Caleb sat pounding the tray of his high chair trying to get attention from any one in ear shot.

"Ya, here is your porridge little one. Eat it all." Anna patted the little fellow on the head as she handed him his dish.

Caleb picked up his spoon. It was made just for baby hands with a loop at the end for baby his thumb and finger. He began to eat as though he had missed a few meals. That was not possible with Anna for a mother.

The family all finally made it to the table, a prayer was said, and then they all began to dish up, arms reaching across the table, plates of sausaged, eggs, fried potatoes and toast going this way and that. The chatter of the morning, clatter of dishes, and baby noises comforted Anna.

"How come you fixed us such a big breakfast this morning," Chris questioned taking a bite and looking over his fork at his mother.

"Oh, I just thought it would be nice to see all of you together this morning. We need to plan our thanksgiving. Since all of you are older and may have plans of your own, I thought we should find out each one's plans. Thanksgiving is only a week away."

"I'll be here," June said quickly. "Me too," piped Sue and Onna at the same time. "I'll be here," Jeff said hesitantly looking at Chris for confirmation. He and Chris planned to go visit some neighbor friends, but he didn't think Chris meant to get together before dinner.

"Well that is fine," Mother said and turning to Chuck, "You can see if Clare and Olaf want to come out to dinner. I don't imagine Clare feels much like getting a big dinner ready."

"Ya, I will stop by the garage and tell Olaf when I am in New Salem," Chuck said knowing he was putting Olaf in the spot of convincing Clare to come to dinner. Olaf always enjoyed Anna's cooking. If anyone could talk Clare into coming it was Olaf.

Thanksgiving arrived. Olaf and Chuck were in deep conversation in the sitting. Clare had dressed for riding her horse and was out getting him ready with Chris, Fredrick, and Jeff's help. She missed more than anything the chance to ride her horse every day. Funny how Chris was being so helpful with this sister he had fought so constantly with when she was home, thought Anna looking out of the window. Jeff, of course, was always a loving brother to all his siblings. June and Onna were helping Mother with dinner. Sue was entertaining Caleb.

Finally dinner was ready, "Come to the table," Mother called.

As everyone took their place at the table, Anna's heart filled with pride. She bowed her head and thanked God silently as Chuck said the blessing.

"I would like to thank you all for making me feel so much a part of this family," Olaf reflected. "Mama, you are a good cook."

As Olaf and Clare put on their wraps to leave, Anna looked at Olaf. "Would you like to bring Clare and join us for Christmas morning since your little one is not here yet?"

"Oh you bet we'll be here," Olaf said rubbing his tummy. "I can't wait to have another one of your cinnamon rolls."

"The children will probably all be up early so come early. "Or better yet, you may come after Christmas eve service and stay the night," she said.

"That would be so much better. What do you say?" Olaf pleaded looking at Clare.

"We will come after the Church service if you like," Clare responded knowing it was what her husband wished. A man's stomach dictates many decisions she thought, and I am a long way from being the cook Anna is.

*   *   *

With Thanksgiving over, the neighbors had decided to herald in the Christmas season with a barn dance this Saturday.

Anna brought the children in the wagon with the food basket packed for the lunch break that would be halfway through the dance. The bed roll were laid with the rest where all the young children could be put down to sleep as they became tired. The ladies or one of the older girls took turns watching the group of sleeping children. Chuck ridden ahead on his saddle horse and was already tuning up his violin ready for the first dance to start.

Everyone came in full of excitement and began singing along with the song Chuck and the rest of the band members were playing. "Jingle bells Jingle bells Jingle. . . . ," they sang as the children joined hands and began to dance around the floor.

The music stopped and the children found their way to their mothers who had dipped up a cup of hot chocolate to warm them after the ride from their farms. A cold wind was blowing. The hot chocolate and a cookie usually settled their little ones right down and before long they were fast asleep.

Sue and Onna were the first to offer to watch them. Onna had brought a set of cards. Using one of the bales of hay as a table to play, she shuffled the cards and dealt out the hand.

It was past midnight when the lunch was spread out for everyone. The food was all shared as one big meal by all the neighbors. Coffee and hot chocolate had been made by those in charge of tonight's dance. Onna and Sue had long ago been replaced by other child tenders and they sat at the lunch table. Arin Swenson came by with his plate of food and asked to sit with Onna. "Oh yes," she said moving over and making room. She liked this handsome young man.

Sue seeing Arin's brother, Jacob, coming their way got up from sitting next to June to make room.

"May I sit with you, June," he inquired?

"Yes," June said inviting him to sit as she slid over on the bench to give him room. As the young people began to talk about what they were planning to do while school was out, Jacob suggested they all get together and go ice skating on the river by June and Onna's place.

It was agreed by all at the table that Saturday before Christmas would be a good day. The brothers suggested that they should all bring along their sisters and brothers. Onna agreed to make the hot chocolate to warm them up afterward.

"I know Mother will insist on fixing lunch so come early. We don't want it to get dark before we have time to skate," June added.

Saturday came and all the children were dropped off by their parents for the skating party. True to June's statement, Mother had lunch waiting. She had made a giant pot of soup thick with vegetables and thickened for body to fortify the skaters.

The children skated most of the afternoon. Finally they began to grow cold and hungry for the fresh cinnamon rolls and the hot chocolate warming on the back of the stove. As the young people put away the last the cinnamon rolls the first of the parents were heard coming up the lane.

Anna laid the evening meal out on the table as Chuck came in from finishing the chores. Sitting down with a cup of coffee in his hands, "looks like you fed half the valley's kids," he said stretching his toward all the dirty dishes. "They must have had a good time , ya."

June answered before her mother had a chance. "Oh Father you should have heard them talking about Mother's cooking."

"Well I think you had better not repeat that or their mothers might not want to feed them anymore," Chuck said with a laugh.

*   *   *

It was Christmas eve. Arriving at the church the family met up with Clare and Olaf. They went in together, Clare and Olaf sitting next to Father. Fredrick sitting next to Mother with Caleb on her lab. The rest found their place at the back of the church.

Anna sat mesmerized by the beautiful portrayal of Christ's birth. The manger scene, the shepherds, the star, Joseph and Mary, the baby Jesus played by a real baby. The songs were especially sweet this year. What was it that was making her so mellow she wondered. She supposed it was that her family was growing up and leaving home. Fredrick too sat quietly spellbound. His mother had told him about the time when he had been the baby in the manger. He watched to see if the baby cried.

When the program was over the preacher invited the children up front to receive their treat. Fredrick ran up to receive his treat, then waited with his left hand extended. "This one is for baby Caleb," he said shaking the treat in his right hand. The preacher smiled and handed Fredrick another sack for his baby brother. Running back to his seat, Fredrick handing Mother Caleb's treat.

"Thank you," Mother said reaching down to hug him. "You are a loving brother." While the treats were being handed out to all the children, the congregation began greeting their neighbors and the visitors who had come to stay with relatives for the holiday. All were in high spirits as they found their way to the door leading their children beside. They shook hands with the preacher and wished everyone a Merry Christmas. "Are you coming straight out to the farm," Father inquired of Olaf.

"Ya," Olaf said taking Clare's hand. "We are ready. It will be a jolly time. Clare is impatient to go horse back riding though I have thought it not good."

"It will be alright," Anna said, "For years it has been the only means of getting around. All the farm women have ridden out of necessity not just for fun."

Arriving home, Anna quickly fed the fire in the kitchen stove and put on a pot of soup and made some sandwiches. She could hear the happy chatter of the children and their excitement about tomorrow. Anna was happy to have Clare home for the holiday and hoped she could get closer to her while she was here.

After dinner Chuck and Olaf went out to finish the evening chores while the girls did the dishes and cleaned up the kitchen. Anna sat in her rocker slowly rocking with her eyes closed as she often did lately. Sue helped get baby Caleb ready for bed at the same time coaxing Fredrick to make it a night reminding him Santa couldn't come until all in the house were fast asleep. The girls having finished up in the kitchen headed up to bed, Chris and Jeff had already gone up. Clare climbed the stairs to go to the spare room that she and Olaf would be in tonight. Lighting the lamp by the bed and having dressed in her warm flannel gown, she took out a book and propped up on pillows to read while she waited for Olaf.

Chuck and Olaf sat down with a cup of coffee and a piece of pumpkin pie. Having finished their snack, Olaf bid him goodnight and headed up the stairs. Chuck going in to the sitting room found Anna in her rocker with her eyes closed. This was not at all like Anna on Christmas eve. She was usually busy putting things out under the tree.

Chuck put his hand on her shoulder. "You seem very tired tonight. Shall I find the gifts and put them out for you," he asked with concern in his voice.

"Oh no!" Anna said slowly pushing herself up from the chair. "You bring the toys from the shed, and I will get the things from our closet. I have had them wrapped and ready before thanksgiving."

"Don't exhaust yourself. I will get the things from the closet, and you can put them under the tree while I get the toy. You have done enough for today. Save your strength for tomorrow. It is going to be a big day," Chuck cautioned. He went to the closet and pulled down a big box from the top shelf. Anna had carefully wrapped all of the gifts after she had made them. He put the box by the tree and went out to get the toys that had been hid in the machine shed. After helping Anna arrange the gifts under the tree, he took her by the arm and led her to their room. He helped her get into bed seeing she was unusually exhausted. Then he went back out to bank the fires.

Chuck lay awake for a long while listening to Anna's heavy breathing hoping that it would be better by morning.

Anna woke to the excited sounds from Fredrick. "Mama come see what Santa brought me. It's a sled with a box on top. I can give Caleb a ride in it. Come see," Fredrick pulled on Anna.

"I'll be right in there, Fredrick. You go help June get baby

Caleb." Anna dressed as quickly as she could having to stop a little to catch her breath. Chuck had already dressed and gone out to greet the children. Fredrick already had Caleb in the box but since it was a sled he couldn't pull it anywhere.

Chris, Jeff, and the girls came down dressed for the morning. Clare followed Olaf who was singing "Merry Christmas to you, Merry Christmas to you," to the tune of Happy Birthday as he came down the stairs.

All in unison called back, MERRRRRY CHRISTMAS Olaf.

Anna pulled a chair up near the tree and sat down heavily. June looked at her questioningly. She determined that she would breakfast and encourage her mother to sit and rock Caleb.

Chris and Jeff had taken charge of distributing the presents. One of which was passed to Clare.

"Oh!" Clare exclaimed as she opened it and found the embroidered pillow cases Anna had made for her. Clare, in all the years she had been with them, had never showed such excitement or pleasure over anything.

Anna's heart leaped with joy to see this from Clare knowing that at last she had been able to please the girl.

June, Onna and Sue all were excitedly opening the special clothes Anna had made each of them.

Chris and Jeff had taken their gifts outside with permission from their father. Fredrick asked Father if he could take the sled outside and put Caleb in it for a ride.

Onna offered to go with him so Mother agreed. "It will be good for Caleb to have a little fresh air," she decided.

June had already slipped into the kitchen and was preparing breakfast and Sue had the table set.

Clare and Olaf sat keeping their mother company in the sitting room. Everyone had noticed Mother was exhausted or sick and were trying to prevent her from doing any work. Mother had tried a couple of times to get up, but Olaf started another story about the talkies which kept her interested and sitting.

When breakfast was done, Father called the children in from

outside. June finally called everyone to the table. Mother's relief and pleasure was evident on her tired face, "What a wonderful Christmas this is. Thank you for the rest. You children are quite sneaky," she wheezed.

Breakfast over, Olaf rubbed his tummy showing how much he enjoyed the meal. "If I keep coming out here, I'll look like the one carrying our baby," he said laughing.

Olaf and Chuck joined Chris and Jeff in the barn to finish the chores. After the kitchen was clean, the girls took their new clothes up stairs to try on.

Onna brought Caleb in when he started getting sleepy. She washed and changed him and laid him down in his crib for a nap.

Anna remained in her rocker and Clare sat on the couch. "Thank you Anna," Clare said looking at Anna with full appreciation in her eyes. "The pillow cases are very pretty. The doilies will really dress up that old house."

Tears pricked Anna's eyes. "You are very welcome dear. I enjoyed every minute of the work."

Chuck and Olaf came in from the barn. Chuck had picked up two beers and handed one to Olaf. The two men sat down with Anna and Clare drinking their beer.

"Where are the children?" Anna asked. When Chuck assured her that they were all busy doing and taken care of, she said, "I think I will lay down for awhile before I start puttingChristmas dinner on the table. I put the turkey in last night and it won't be ready for another hour or so."

"That is good Mother. Olaf and I will play cards. How about you Clare, do you want to join us?"

"No, I think I would like to go riding if you think it will be alright."

"Clare, I know you have been wanting to go riding. If you are feeling up to it, I don't see what it would hurt," Mother put in.

When June, Onna, and Sue came downstairs and saw Mother lying down, they went into the kitchen and began getting things ready for the Christmas dinner. June peeled a large pot of potatoes. Onna went to the cellar and brought up the pickles, vegetables and sausage. Sue set the table and gathered all the chairs to around the table. She would have to wait for the two Chuck and Olaf were using. Onna helped Sue get the butter and pickles in a dish and set them in the middle of the table. June cut the bread and put it in a napkin basket.

"Onna," June inquired. "Do you suppose we can get enough broth out of the turkey pan and make the gravy."

"Well, the turkey should to be done. Mother put it in after church last night. Help me clear a place on top of the stove."

June cleared a place on the far end of the cook stove where it would be just warm not hot. Between the two of them they took the big pan of turkey from the oven and sat it on the stove. June ladled out enough broth to make gravy.

Onna called to Sue, "Do you have the beet pickles as well as the dill. You know Mother alwasy likes to have them for Christmas."

"Yes," she said coming into the kitchen. "I have everything on the table. I am just getting ready to pour the milk."

Clare had returned and helped the girls finish the carving of the turkey.

June went in to tell Father they had everything ready for dinner.

"Father smiled up at her and patted her hand. "Ya that is good. Mother is feeling poorly. She will be surprised and pleased I think."

Caleb woke up from his nap and began to cry. As Chuck went in to wake Anna, he found her startled awake with the babies cry.

Onna had gathered everyone and had them sitting around the table when Chuck brought Anna and the baby into the dinning room.

"Oh!" Anna exclaimed when she saw dinner already on the table. She was speechless. The girls could see the appreciation in her eyes.

"Merry Christmas Mother," the girls choired.

"I guess we are old enough to do things to help you," June added. "Look already Clare is married. It will be our turn before

long," she said pointing to Onna and including herself. "It is time
we learn to do more on or own without being told."

Anna and Chuck sat down. Chuck said the blessing before the
dishes began to move around the table with noise chatter and
clanking of silverware.

Onna took charge of helping Caleb with his food leaving
Mother to enjoy her dinner.

Dinner finished, the girls encouraged Mother to go in the
sitting room and visit with Clare while they cleaned up in the
kitchen.

Clare sat on the couch. Before Mother sat down, she went to
her closet and took out the baby things she had finished. She
wanted Clare to have them now so she would know if she needed
to add anything more before the baby came. She handed the bundle
to Clare and then sat down in her rocking chair. Little Caleb came
in and started to crawl up in her lap, but Sue followed behind him
and took him with her upstairs to play.

Clare opened the bundle and let out a cry of joy. She looked
at Anna. Always at a loss for words where Anna was concerned
she just smiled and then began to take things out one at a
time. There was a whole layette of beautifully embroidered
baby clothes and blankets some with crochet lace. "Thank you,
Anna," she finally said looking up and revealing a stain of tears
on her cheek.

Mother too had tears of joy. This was the best Christmas present
of all. All these years she had waited for just such a response from
Clare. She tucked this peace of joy deep inside herself.

Onna had brought the mince pie in from the ice cooler where
it had been kept since Mother baked it . She placed it in the oven
to warm. Mother always said it was necessry to keep mince pie
cold since it was made with portions of meat as well as apple and
raisins. June had cut the pumpkin pie and laid out dishes as well
as whip the rich cream. When the men came in from finishing the
chores, June invited them to sit and have pie and coffee.

"Well that sounds good," Olaf said not waiting for Chuck. Clare came into the room and pulling a chair out sat beside him dipping a fork into his pie. "Hey, get your own pie," he teased.

"Anna has made a beautiful layette for the baby, Olaf," Clare said softly. "I want you to come see it."

Poor Anna thought Chuck. She has wanted Clare to call her Mother all these years. Still she calls her Anna.

Anna came and looking at each girl with loving care including Clare she said, "I have had some very special gifts today girls. Thank you very much. It has been a most blessed day."

Having finished the pie, Olaf got up and beckoned to Clare, "We must go home before it gets dark. Thank you very much for everything," he said giving Anna a hug.

"Come any time. Anna gets lonesome. She could use some company when the children are in school and maybe Clare would like to learn how to make the cinnamon rolls.

"That would be nice. What do you say Clare," Olaf teased moving her toward the door. Clare didn't answer.

26

Mother is ill

Fredrick went in to Mother as she once again sat in her rocking chair. He sat at her feet looking up at her. Taking her shoes off, Fredrick began rubbing her feet. Sue had brought baby Caleb downstairs and was in the kitchen having her piece of pie. The baby crawled into the sitting room. Fredrick picked him up and they both sat at Mother's feet. Mother reached down and picked up Caleb, putting him on her lap she began to rock and hum. Finally Fredrick went in search of Father who picked him up and held him as he had his last cup of coffee. The girls banked both fires for the night and then asked Father if there was anything else he needed done before they went upstairs.

"Perhaps one of you could get the baby to bed and one could get this young man to bed he needs to get up and help me milk the cows early in the morning."

Fredrick jumping off his fathers lap, "Really, I am going to milk the cows?"

"Yes Fredrick, you are a big boy now. When the milking is done, you can learn how to take the cows out of the stations. This summer you will take them to pasture."

"Oh boy," yelled Fredrick as he headed upstairs with June and Onna.

Sue went in to get the baby and found Mother had rocked him to sleep. She picked him up gently. She cleaned and changed him, careful not to wake him fully, then she put him to bed.

Sue came back and bent to kiss her mother good night, "Merry Christmas Mother," She said once more.

"Thank you for all the help Sue," Mother said hugging. "It has been a good day, don't you think?"

"Yes, Mother it has been." Sue went upstairs and as she reached the top of the stairs, she met June and Onna coming down on their way to tell Mother goodnight. They reached the bottom of the stairs just as Anna was coming in to the kitchen. Together both said, "Merry Christmas Mother," each giving her a big hug and a kiss.

"Thank you for the wonderful day," Mother said to both hugging them. "You have been so very helpful today." She headed for her room as the girls headed out the back door to the outhouse then stopped when she saw Chris and Jeff at stair landing. "Good night Mother," they both chimed.

Mother patted their hand and said, "Merry Christmas boys." The boys flew up the stairs and Anna went to dress for bed. Anna was propped up on two pillows when Chuck came in to get ready for bed. "You feeling any better," he asked, "or should I call the doctor. I know you have to feel quite bad to sleep through the girls in the kitchen."

"No, I need no doctor. I think I was just tired. I don't sleep well because I am not able to breath well. The girls have been so helpful today. I have rested all day. Tomorrow should be better."

Chuck blew out the lamp and lay down beside her. He took hold of her hand as though she were going to slip away. He fell asleep holding her hand.

Anna lay awake a long while. Finally she moved his hand to his chest so it would not get a cramp. After a long struggle she was able to breath easier and fell asleep.

June and Onna rose early, going down to get breakfast for father and the boys while Sue woke Chris and Jeff to go help father. Next she helped Fredrick dress before taking him down stairs to be with June. She picked Caleb up out of his crib, bathed and dressed him. This done she put him in the high chair next to Fredrick.

Chuck and the boys came in just as the girls were putting breakfast on the table. Jeff and Chris took the milk in to separate while Chuck went in to Anna. "Hi there he greeted. The girls have breakfast ready, Anna. How about coming in and having some?"

"Oh Chuck, how could I have slept through everything. I'll be right there. Just let me get dressed." Anna got to her feet and began to dress as Chuck went in to the table. Anna came in to the kitchen slowly, and Jeff had a chair pulled out for her seeing she was in difficulty.

Fredrick jumped down from his chair and ran to his mother hugging her leg since he couldn't reach up any higher. Caleb began to fuss wanting his mother, but Father patted his head and he calmed down. All the children seemed to sense that their mother was not feeling well.

The girls took over the cooking and cleaning during the Christmas holiday, but now it was almost at an end. This last week they decided to catch up the washing so Mother wouldn't have to do it after they went back to school. Jeff and Chris were being unusually helpful. They brought the water for the wash and dumped it into the wash tub. Onna got out the scrub board while June gather up the lye soap and bluing. As Onna scrubbed, June rinsed and rung them out. Sue, Jeff and Chris helped get the clothes on the line. Father had a troubled look but said nothing to the children. He thanked them all for taking over Mother's work to let her rest. He checked on Mother frequently and took Fredrick with him to do the chores.

It was New year eve and Chuck had already promised to play at the barn dance held to celebrate the New Year. He went in to where Anna sat in her rocker, "Would you like to go along, Anna. I can help you get into the sled," he said putting his hand on her shoulder and kissing her cheek.

"No, I think I will be better here. You go along. Every one is expecting you," Anna said reaching up and touching the hand he had placed on her shoulder.

"I will stay if you need me," Chuck responded looking anxiously and uncertain.

"No. The girls are here, and Jeff and Chris can help if I need anything," Anna replied.

The children finished cleaning the kitchen. After making sure Caleb and Fredrick were down for the night, they checked on their mother kissing her goodnight before going off to bed.

Anna laid her head back in the rocker. Closing her eyes, she managed to fall asleep, something she had had difficulty doing these past few weeks.

The dance over Chuck didn't waste any time greeting people. He got his violin and made a hasty retreat to get on his saddle horse and hurry home to Anna. Coming in the house, he found Anna asleep in her rocker. He went to bank the fires, but one of the children had already done a good job of that. Coming over to Anna, he put his hand on her shoulder. "Anna," he called, "Why are you here in the chair? It can't be that comfortable?"

Anna woke startled but saw Chuck and smiled, "You here already?"

"Yes Leipshin. Come I will help you to bed. Taking her hand, he helped her up out of the chair. Then putting his arm around her shoulder led her into the bedroom.

New Year's morning came, and the house was a bustle getting things ready for the big New Year's Dinner. Breakfast was finished. Chris helped Father with the chores while Jeff took Fredrick out to play in the snow. Sue charge of Caleb while June and Onna worked on the dinner.

Chuck had brought breakfast to Anna in bed. Sitting next to her he felt her head. It was clammy and though it was a cold day it seemed she was heavily perspiring. Going outside, he found Chris. "Get the horse saddled up. I want you to ride into town and get the doctor. Tell him to hurry. Your mother is quite ill."

Chris rode swiftly. His thought sifted through all the things that could be wrong with Mother. He didn't want her to have another baby but babies she survived. He didn't want her to have the flu that had taken Little Lill. Washing these thoughts from his mind, he focused on getting to the doctor. He reined up by the doctor's house and ran to the door pounding soundly to be sure he was heard.

The old doctor came to the door. His wife right behind him. "My father sent me to fetch you," Chris said out of breath more from fear than running.

The old doctor knew it was serious. Anna never complained and if she was agreeing to see a doctor it was bad.

"You ride on back and tell your dad that we will be on our way. I will bring my wife along to help."

Chris raced back. Running in the house he reported to his dad that the doctor was on his way.

In the meantime, June had gathered all the children around the table to feed them before the doctor arrived. While she was feeding the children, Chuck came in and dished up two plates of food and asked Onna to make a cup of tea for her mother. Chuck handed a plate of food to Anna then sat down beside her to eat.

Anna picked at the food until Onna came in with the tea. She handed her the plate of food and took the tea. "Thank you for the tea. I don't think I can eat the food."

After dinner the June and Onna swiftly cleaned up the kitchen while Sue took Fredrick and Caleb out in the sled. Chris and Jeff went out to the barn. they were worried and they didn't want to hear that something awful was wrong with Mother.

June went in to see if she could do anything for Mother. "Everything will be fine," said Father in an unusually strained voice. "Just go upstairs with Onna. I will call you if you are needed."

June and Onna went upstairs just as they heard the doctor's sled speeding down the lane. They watched out the upstairs window and saw the doctor and his wife hurrying toward the house faster than they had ever seen old doctor move.

Chuck went to the door before the doctor could knock and ushered him in to where Anna sat in her rocking chair, the sweat pouring off her forehead.

He took her temperature but knew when he did it that it was not going to be high, if anything it would be subnormal. Looking at Chuck he asked, "how long has she been this way?"

"Anna has been tired the entire Christmas holidays. She is not her usual self. When I wanted to call for you, she said no that she was just tired."

The old doc got up from where he had been feeling Anna's pulse. "How about giving me a cup of coffee, Chuck," he called devising a way to get Chuck to follow him into the kitchen leaving his wife to sit by Anna .

"Chuck," the old doctor said, "Anna is pregnant again. Her heart is not handling the extra load. It is not beating right. I think tomorrow you had better take her to Bismark and see if the doctor over there wants to put her in the hospital. I will give her something for now which should help, but she has let this go too long. She has too much strain on her heart." Taking some medicine from his bag and handing it to Chuck he said, "Give her this tonight. It should allow her to breath better and get some rest, Tomorrow morning without fail get her in to Bismark."

Before they left, Chuck offered them a cup of coffee and dinner.

"No, we need to get back. Holidays are bad," said Mary, the doctor's wife. "That seems to be when people get sick or hurt. We need to be available."

"I understand," Chuck said feeling the need to get back to Anna anyway.

"I hope she will find comfort tonight. I won't lie to you Chuck, she is in serious condition. Get her in to Bismark early," the doctored encouraged. "If you need help out here, I will send some one out."

"No, that won't be necessary. The children have taken over and done all the work seeing Mother has not been feeling well. They even made Christmas and New Year's dinners," Chuck told the doctor proudly. "Thank you so much for coming this far on New year's." Chuck stood in the doorway as he watched them get into their sled, then he shut the door and sat down to the table. *Please Lord help my Anna*, he prayed silently, head buried in his hands.

It was evening. The children had all come in and begun to prepare for bed. Sue washed Caleb and changed him into his night clothes. When he finished his snack, he toddled in to see Mother. Mother reached down and tried to pick him up, but Sue realized she was struggling and lifted him into her arms. Anna held Caleb close to her and rocked him to sleep. Sue helped Fredrick get ready for bed then while she took Caleb into his crib, Fredrick crawled up in his mother's lap and gave her a big hug and kiss.

"Goodnight Mama," he said. Anna patted his head and kissed him on the cheek. Fredrick lay his chubby hand along side his mother's cheek. "Don't be sick Mama," he said before climbing down and going to bed.

Anna lay her head back against the rocking chair content. Having kissed her babies goodnight, she closed her eyes and fell asleep.

The girls came in to tell their mother goodnight but found her asleep so they didn't disturb her. Chris and Jeff came in with Chuck. They all went in to see Anna just as the girls were leaving. The girls lay a finger to their mouth and tiptoed out of the room. The boys bid their father goodnight and went upstairs. Chuck banked the fires for the night. Then taking a cup of coffee, he sat down beside her. She seemed to be resting better than she had for days even though she was in the rocking chair. He guessed the medicine old doctor gave her must have helped.

Chuck fell asleep sitting in the chair beside Anna. He woke when she began to stir. Chuck reached over taking her hand so when she awoke she would not fall.

Anna sat up and seemed to fight for her breath.

Chuck stood and putting his arm on her shoulder, "I think it is time I get you in bed."

Anna responded to his touch and let him help her from the chair and to their room. Laying down, she didn't have the energy to undress so Chuck spread a blanket over her and put extra pillows under her head. It seemed to help.

Morning came and Chris and Jeff were out doing the milking while the girls got breakfast. Sue attended Caleb and Fredrick. Fredrick finished his breakfast and ran to find Mother. Finding her still in bed, he crawled up beside her.

Onna helped the children get ready for school. It is good I am no longer in school she thought. I will be able to help with Caleb. Onna went to find Fredrick and get him ready for school. When she found him snuggled up beside mother she decided that he could miss school today. It would be better for mother to have Fredrick there to comfort her.

The rest had gone off to school. Caleb was getting restless in the high chair so Onna lifted him down. He too ran in to find Mother. Onna lifted Caleb up, "Lie still or you may not be with Mother," she cautioned. She sat beside the bed making sure the boys were a comfort and not a hindrance.

After the chores, Chuck came in. Sending Onna with the boys, he sat down beside her. "I have the car ready to take you to Bismark," he said taking her hand. "We need to see the doctor over there."

Chuck put his hand on her forehead and found it wet with cold perspiring. Getting a washcloth and towel, he sponged her forehead and face and then wiped it dry. "How about a cup of tea before we go?" he offered.

Anna let out a sigh and said, "No, not now." Taking his hand she attempted to rise from the bed. When she reached the edge of the bed, she fell foreward into his arms. When Chuck looked down at her, he saw her looking up at him with a radiantly peaceful smile on her face. He knew at that moment she had left him. "No! No!" he cried softly. "Anna, you cannot leave me."

He lay her back on the bed. Sitting beside her for a long while, his mind went back to when he had first seen her and fell in love. He thought of all the wonderful years, the sad years at the loss of their little boy and girl, the fun years with their big family, and the loving mother she had been for his two daughters. He wished Clare had given her the one thing she had wanted, to be accepted as Mother to her. His mind raced ahead. How would he tell the children their mother was gone, especially Fredrick who was so attached to his mother.

Onna came and knocked on the door. "Do you need me to dress Mother?" she called. Coming in the room, she found her father in deep sorrow. Looking over at the bed, she let out a sharp cry, "Mother! Oh Mother!" But she knew her mother was gone. She would never again be able to hug her or talk to her.

Chuck rose from the side of the bed, "Please keep the children occupied while I drive into town. I will need to make arrangements for the funeral." He moved to the kitchen still talking. Onna following still in shock. "Leave it to me to tell the other children. I will have to tell Fredrick and Caleb a little differently," he went on as he took his hat down from the rack in the kitchen and opened the door.

"While I am in town, I will stop and let Clare know. I will have to stop at the preachers too. When the girls come home, have them get dinner and feed every one. The boys are to get the milking and chores done. I will be back as soon as possible, but don't wait dinner for me," he instructed as he went outside.

Every one moved through their chores automatically for the next few days. The children stayed home from school. The neighbors coming and going bringing meals, helping with the chores, and giving comfort and encouragement. Some helped tend to the little ones trying to keep them entertained so they would not start to look for their mother. The funeral was held quickly with all of their friends in attendance. Anna and the unborn baby were buried together in the cemetery behind the church alongside the baby boy and baby Lill.

27

Life with out Mother

Onna had taken on the responsibility of homemaker, tending to the young ones, cooking the meals, cleaning the house cleaning. June and Sue pitched in to do the gardening, harvesting and canning. Onna often thought it was good Mother had taught them how to do these things. Chris and Jeff helped their father with the farming the first year their mother was gone. Onna, being good with the needle, did most of the mending. Fredrick wandered around the house looking for Mother even though his father had explained that she had gone to be with little Lill, his sister in heaven.

It was the early part of February. Fredrick skated ahead of the rest. Something he had been told not to do. He felt particularly uncooperative today. He missed his mother and sometimes he just didn't feel like obeying. The girls had not wanted to be too tough on him so often they looked the other way when he was disobedient. They thought he seemed to miss Mother more than all the rest. Today though it turned out that perhaps they should have been more firm with him for his own protection.

Fredrick, skating well for his age, was taunting the girls by skating ahead of them. All of a sudden he hit a soft spot and went down through the ice. June and Sue skated swiftly to the spot, hearts racing. Careful to stay away from the soft spot, they stretch out to rescue him, but at that distance they couldn't reach him under the ice.

"Move back," Chris ordered as he and Jeff skated over. "We will have to break out more ice to reach him." Moving back June and Sue watched as Chris and Jeff broke out a bigger chunk of ice. Jeff, who was smaller than the rest, moved out onto the soft ice and looked into the hole seeing the top of his head he grabbed him by the hair and guided him to the edge of the hole while Chris held onto his feet. Jeff reached in and grabbed Fredrick by the hair and began pulling him out. Everyone could hear the ice cracking. They all remained quiet holding their breath. Finally, they had Fredrick out of the ice. Chris took off his coat and wrapped him inside. Dragging him by the coat collar, Chris skated swiftly toward the bank where he threw off his skates, picked up Fredrick and headed for home as fast as he could run, Fredrick becoming a block of ice.

Chris made it home in less time than the rest. He carried Fredrick into the kitchen. "Onna," he yelling relaying urgency in the sound of his voice. Seeing the blueness of Fredrick, Onna quickly set down the wash tub. She order Chris to pour water into the washtub from the boiler on the stove as she began stripping Fredrick of all his clothes. Fredrick was too cold to move, even his teeth had stopped chattering.

Onna checked the water temperature to make sure it would not thaw him too fast. Chris helped Onna get Fredrick into the water. While Chris worked at getting all the ice off Fredrick, Onna made a wash basin of kerosene to thaw his feet so they would not be damaged.

Chuck came in to see what all the commotion was. He went into action. Grabbing a wool blanket he wrapped it around Frederick's shoulders where he sat with his feet in the kerosene. Then he fixed him a hot drink with a small amount of brandy to warm his body from the inside, hoping and praying that he would not catch a chill or get pneumonia.

Sue and June had come in and Father turned on them, "How could you be so careless as not to keep him by you," he barked thinking he just couldn't bare to lose another member of his family.

June listened patiently knowing he was right.

"He has been hard to handle lately," Sue interceded for June. "He misses Mother so much."

Father sat down beside Fredrick. Looking him in the eye, "Do you think Mother would like it when you don't follow orders?" he questioned his eyes softening with understanding.

Fredrick knuckled his eyes with his little fists as the welled up tears began to over flow. Chokingly he whimpered, "Noooo," and then the dam broke and Fredrick cried like he had never cried before. His body wracked with sobs as his father held and comforted him.

When his sobs had died down, Father asked, "Can we depend on you to be more obedient from now on Fredrick?"

"I will try to do as they tell me," hiccupped Fredrick.

*   *   *

That year Chris and Jeff finished school. After they helped with summer harvest, they bought an old Ford and headed out west.

The 1929 Stock Market crash had made grain prices fall sharply. The dry season had not yielded a good crop so they had bought an old Ford, and with their father's blessing headed out west. He had hoped they would be able to get a job and send a little money home. With the boys gone and Clare married, there were still five children left at home. How would he ever get them raised without their loving mother he thought. Chuck sat at the table drinking coffee. He found himself wishing often that Anna could be there to help him. She had always been the one to get them through the bad times. Anna always seemed to make things easier. Through the loss of their babies, through sicknesses, through bad financial times it was always Anna who could see the good in every situation. Chuck felt his loss of Anna deeply. The nights were even more difficult. He lay awake in his bed long into the night. Sometimes he could feel her eyes on him and he would look at her picture and be comforted.

*   *   *

It was spring. June and Sue did their best to take the place of the boys helping Father bring in the crops. Fredrick was assigned to herd the cows. Onna kept Caleb and did the baking and meal preparation. June and Sue helped in the fields and in the barn.

It was a bright summer night and the neighbor kids came over after their chores to play kick the can. It was Saturday and Chuck had saddled up his horse and gone to play at the barn dance leaving the children to care for Caleb and Fredrick. Onna kept Caleb in the house, but Fredrick wanted to play kick the can all the kids.

One of the boys got the bright idea that if they filled the cans with gas and lit them, when they kicked them toward the river they would light up and be a fun sight. Everything was going along fine, and the river definitely had a stream of light flowing when a yell from Fredrick pierced the night.

June saw the fire on his pants and ran to catch him rolling him in the dirt. Apparently some of the gas and fire had spilled on him as he had attempted to kick the can away from him. After the fire was out, June ran with him into the house to get Onna. Together they stripped off his pants and put him in a tub of cold water to cleanse the wound and the heat out to stop it from burning any deeper.

Sue and the rest of the kids got rid of the evidence and the neighbors went home not wanting Chuck to catch them in their misdeed. Sue went into the house and was troubled to see how badly Fredrick was burned. "What will we tell Father?" she asked.

June reached up in the cupboard and found the medicine Mother had used when anyone got burned with grease. She put it over all the burned area and wrapped his legs in a clean white sheet. June and Sue carried him upstairs and laid him in June's bed so that she could care for him throughout the night. "I will bring you your favorite pudding if you keep quite," she bribed. "We can't let Father know or he might make you go stay somewhere else."

"I don't want to leave you," Fredrick whimpered more from the fear of being sent away than from the pain although it hurt awfully bad.

"Well you stay quiet up here and I won't tell Father.," she coaxed. "We will bring your food up until you get well." Going back downstairs June told Sue, "We will have to take turns being with him and try to keep it from Father."

"How are you going to do that?" Onna inquired uncertain about leaving their father out of the picture. "You know Father will be looking for him."

"If we tell him that Fredrick has a cold and we are taking care of him, Father may not want to see him. You know he is still grieving for Mother and sometimes he gets so busy that he goes days without talking to the little ones." June answered.

The girls hurriedly cleaned the kitchen and went up to bed taking Caleb with them. All was quiet when Chuck got home so he went to bed without looking for anyone.

The next morning Onna rose early to be sure Father had his breakfast and would head for the fields to work without waiting for the rest to come down. "Father," Onna said, "June and I will do the milk so you can get an early start."

"That will be good," Father agreed. "If I get an early start, I might be able to finish the South field today."

The girls kept this up for several days knowing he would come in tired eat his dinner and go straight to bed. June made sure Frederick's burns were kept dressed and the sheets washed and sun dried to make them purified for wrapping his legs.

Two weeks passed like this, and finally June stood Fredrick up to see how well he could walk and if there was any evidence of the problem. Fredrick was a little weak since he had been down so long but in all he had been a good boy not fussing and the girls had taken turns entertaining him. It took two more days to get him to walk again without falling. Soon his natural rambunctious nature won over and they could not keep him hidden any longer.

The girls took him into the yard while Father was in the field and let him pull Caleb around in the wagon. Caleb was laughing as Father came back from the fields for lunch.

"Well, Hello there little fellows," he said grabbing Caleb and putting him on his shoulder. "It is a good thing I came home for lunch today. You two never seem to get up before I go out into the fields." He took Frederick's hand and they went into the house. Onna breathed easier. Father hadn't seemed to notice anything and appeared happy to see the boys.

28

Disobedience

It was a cold spring day. The snow was deep but getting soft and hard to walk in.

Lisa's family had moved closer to Sandpoint. Their new place was along side a river that flowed through rich bottom ground. John knew this ground would grow a quick vegetable crop to feed his family.

Lisa and Mercy were both now in school. This day Mercy walked with Lisa from their old school which was three miles from their new home. She was upset with Lisa who insisted on making snow fairies in the snow by throwing herself in the soft snow and waving her arms to make it look like angle wings. By the time they reached home Lisa was soaked to her skin though she had been bundled up for the wind.

Mother met them at the door and began to scold them for being such a mess. "Get the wash tub from its nail at the back door and bring it to the kitchen Mercy," she directed. Mother began to undress Lisa while she put the hot water in the tub. "Lisa, get yourself in that tub right now. You are going to catch your death of cold," Mother scolded as she began rubbing her down with a cloth and soap. She leaned her back and washed her long brown hair. Then leaving Lisa with soap-filled hair hanging over her eyes, she went to the stove where the water was heating in a resevoir. She dipped out a bucket of warm water to rinse Lisa's hair. Lisa began to cry theatrically as Mother poured the water. "Oh Lisa, hush up. You have been through this a hundred times," said Mother showing no compassion.

As Mother was toweling Lisa off, she directed Mercy to get undressed and into the tub. Mercy got the same scrub and drowning with the rinse bucket but she knew not to complain. Mother was no nonsense when it came to bathing, washing hair and combing.

The boys came bounding into the house just as Mother finished putting the rag curls in Lisa's hair. These curls were special since Lisa had two rows of curls with the top row going one direction and the bottom row going the opposite. The rags were torn strips of worn out clothing. The hair was wrapped around the strip of rag then the strip was rolled over and over until it reached the scalp and was tied at the top of the curl. When finished there were four curls on top and five at the bottom making nine curls all together.

Lisa was not happy with the curls in school because the teacher's son sat behind her and delighted in dipping her curls in the ink well making a mess on her clothes and face when she moved. Mother had to put her clothes in buttermilk to take out the ink.

While Mother worked on Mercy's hair, Gus took Lisa to play with the blocks Grandfather Amos had made for them while he still lived with them. Lisa missed Grandpa Amos. He and Grandma had gone to live with Uncle Clarence in Spokane, Washington.

Phil had made a butter and onion sandwich for himself and was heading for the door. "Where do you think you're going young man?" Mother questioned sharply with her no-nonsense teacher voice.

Jerking to a stop, Phil turned his shoulders and head but his feet stayed pointing toward the door. Over his shoulder he said, "Out to the barn to play catch with Old Pal. He's lonesome."

"Not before you take this tub out and dump it and put it away," Mother commanded pointing to the tub and then to the door.

"Why can't Gus do it," he whined?

"Well perhaps if you would like to change places with him and keep your little sister out of mischief while I get dinner, he would be more than happy to dump the water."

Phil laid down his sandwich and picked up the tub as he had no desire to watch Lisa in the house. She would probably want to play dolls or some dumb girl thing. It was okay to play with her when they were outside. She sometimes got into more trouble then he did. No way was he going to be cooped up in the house all night.

As Phil came back in to retrieve his sandwich Mother called to the boys, "From now on I want you boys to walk home with the girls. Mercy, I don't want you and Lisa to leave school until the boys are out, do you understand?"

"Yes Mother," Mercy replied looking up at her mother with a look of resignation.

29

A double Wedding 1932

Three years have passed since Chuck lost his Anna, two years since Chris and Jeff had gone out west to settle in Spokane, Washington. The boys had sent word that they were working in the Sacret Heart Hospital. Chris was a cook and Jeff was an orderly. Boy that was a laugh. Chris had spent no time cooking. They had both sent their father money to help out with the children's clothes. They had to be bought now that Mother was gone.

"Father," Onna pleaded one night. "Could we please go to the next dance with you. "What will you do with Fredrick and Caleb?" Chuck quizzed.

"We will do what everyone else does," June called out from the sitting room. "We will take their blankets and put them to sleep with all the other children."

"Well perhaps you would like to come to the basket social next Saturday," Father conceded. "Can you can fix pretty baskets filled with delicious food that any one would want to bid on," he teased.

"I can fix the food to put in the baskets," Onna came back spark in her voice almost as though she had been told she didn't cook well.

"I will get the basket ready for the family unless you want me to make a basket separate for you?" June inquired of her father.

"Well, it is supposed to be a way to raise money for hall up keep," Father said thoughtfully. "Why don't you make all of us our own basket. You could make a smaller one with snacks in it for the boys since they will eat early and go to sleep."

The Saturday of the box social came and the baskets were finished. June and Onna were proud of their work. They dressed carefully and tied their hair back in ribbons to match their dresses. Sue dressed in the skirt and blouse Mother had made for her last. It made her feel close to her.

They all climbed in the wagon with Chuck. He had to be there early to set up with the rest of the musicians, but that was okay with the girls. It gave Onna and June time to feed Fredrick and Caleb and Sue made several trips from the wagon to the autioneers table setting each basket down carefully.

As June and Onna settled the boys in their bedroll, a neighbor came over to greet them and commented on how well they were handling things with Mother gone. The girls thanked her but found it hard to keep the tears from welling up in their eyes.

The music started and Onna saw Arin Hanson moving across the floor in her direction. Right behind him was his brother Jacob, heading straight to June. They each claimed their partner and moved out onto the dance floor. They danced smoothly. They knew the music so well. It was music they had heard from the time they were very small. Father had played it whenever people came to their house. They remembered how happy Mother was to watch the dancers in her kitchen. They remembered her smile as she sat listening to him play his violin.

"Which basket is yours," Arin was asking Onna?

"The one with the yellow ribbon," Onna replied feeling special and singled out.

"And which basket is June's. Perhaps the one with the red ribbon. Ya?" Arin continued.

"Yes, but why do you want to know?" Onna said the special feeling deflating with his question.

"So I can tell Jacob silly," he said with a wink. "I told him I would find."

Onna smiled up at him in relief.

The auction began and the Hanson boys managed to outbid every one else for the baskets of Onna and June.

Chuck bid on the basket of his brother Fritz's wife outbidding his brother. "Come along Fritz," he said. "I know that wife of yours has packed enough for both of us and her too." With a chuckle he took the basket to the table where Sue had sat down with her basket.

"The boys asleep Sue?," Chuck questioned.

"Yes Father."

"Then you can go ahead and dance if you like Sue. I can see the boys from the band stand if they stir," he said putting his arm around his youngest daughter forced to take on so much responsibility with her mother gone.

The night came to an end and Chuck saw Sue move over to ready the boys for their ride home. Soon Onna and June were by her side helping. The Hanson boys seemed to be hovering over them and soon he saw each of the Hanson boys pick one of the little boys and follow the girls to the wagon. Chuck picked up his violin and quickly joined them not wanting the young boys to wake up. Several of the regulars stayed to help put things back in order and make sure the fire was out. No one expected Chuck to help. They knew he had more than enough to tend to with his big family and no Mother.

After getting the boys settled in bed, June and Onna discussed what the Hanson boys had said to each of them. It seems the boys had both indicated they would stop by after church Sunday to visit them. Perhaps we should ask father before Sunday comes and tell him we would like to get a special dinner to entertain the company.

"Company," laughed Onna. "They are coming courting, at least Arin is."

"I'm not sure about Jacob," June retorted he didn't say.

Sunday came and the girls had a special dinner prepared when the boys arrived. When the meal was finished, Sue took the boys outside to play while June and Onna cleared the table but left the dishes to do later. The two Hanson boys went into the sitting room with Chuck.

Arin was fidgeting. Finally he got up enough nerve and said, "Chuck, I would like to ask you for Onna's hand in marriage. I know it would be hard for you to part with Onna since she has taken on much of the responsibility of her Mother, but if you would agree we would gladly take the boys to live with us." He suddenly ran out of words and the silence was uncomfortable.

Chuck looked at him thoughtfully. "Have you asked Onna yet, Arin?" Chuck said finally breaking the silence. "It would be her decision you know. Parents do not arrange marriages now days."

"Yes, I asked her last night and Onna agreed to marry me if you gave your blessing." Arin was a tall strikingly handsome young man with a gentle spirit.

Chuck could not imagine anyone more suited to Onna's personality. "Ya, you have my blessing, but it will have to be a simple wedding in the church. There is no Mother to help with a big celebration." Chuck closed his eyes for a moment as he remembered the last wedding Anna had put together so well. *Clare* , he thought, the one who could not accept Anna as Mother. Onna truly deserved to have Anna prepare her wedding. It is strange how things turn out. He returned his thoughts to the present and reached up unashamed to wipe the tears from his eyes.

"I too would like your blessing to marry June," Jacob put in hastily and looked bashfully at Chuck. "I haven't talked to June yet, but if she says yes, will you give your blessing?"

"Well, Well," said Chuck with amusement. "A double wedding."

The girls having finished clearing the table joined the men in the sitting room. Father looked up and said, "The boys have asked for your hands in marriage. What do you say to that?"

June smiled at Jacob, her eyes dancing.

Seeing June's reaction, Father went on. "I have given the boys my blessing if that is what each of you wish. I have already told them there will not be a big wedding since Anna is not here to make it happen. It will have to be a simple ceremony at the church."

Onna seeing the tears in her father's eyes, put her arm around his shoulder and said, "We don't need a big celebration, Father. June and I can have a double wedding. The pastor can marry both of us at the same time. We will invite our family and close neighbors for a potluck picnic."

"That will be fine. You make the decision and tell pastor what day it will be," Chuck agreed getting up to go out to his chores. As he walked to the barn he thought *Oh Anna, what do I do?* There would only be Sue left at the house if Arin and Onna took the boys to live with them. *What do I know about taking care of young girls, Anna?*

Monday morning Chuck rose early. After finishing chores, he went in to tell the girls he was going to Bismark and would be back before dark.

Arriving at the house of a long time acquaintance, "How are you they said," answering the door. "Come in Chuck. Come in. How are you doing with that big family of yours out there on the farm?"

Chuck started to talk, then went silent.

"Sit down," said Otto as Martha poured them some coffee.

Chuck began again telling of Anna's death and how Chris and Jeff had gone off to Spokane to get work. They send a bit from their pay back home. "Since the crash things are tight as you know. That is why I have come," Chuck went on. "to ask if you would like to earn a bit to board Sue while she finishes school. June and Onna are getting married. Onna is going to take the two smaller boys, but I think Sue needs a woman around.

"We would be happy to care for Sue," Martha said with delight. "Anna raised lovely hardworking responsible girls. Sue will be a joy to have."

They said their goodbyes after finalizing the arrangements.

Chuck came home just before milking time, "Where is Sue?" he asked of June who was hanging the wash. Her hair flying loose from the pins.

"She is out here somewhere with the boys. I think she is pulling them in the wagon." June mumbled blowing the hair from her eyes as she hung another sheet on the line.

"Have you and Onna set the date to marry the Hanson boys?" Chuck asked enjoying watching her fumble with the big sheets. "I have made arrangements to have Sue stay with the Schlenkers in Bismark while she finishes school. Sue needs to be with a womon."

"That will be good for Sue," June agreed feeling happy for Sue but sad to see the family breaking apart. "We will be getting married on Sunday, the week after next . Pastor said it would be the best time for him to perform the marriages," June said turning to look at her father.

"That soon? I had not expected . . ." and then he could not finish. "I would like to tell Sue right away," he said thinking if he did not do it right away he would not be able to. "When you see her, send her to me and keep the boys with you."

June set down her wash and went to find Sue. She knew this was hard on her father.

Going into the house Sue hollored to her father, "June said you wanted to talk to me."

"Come in here Sue," he called.

Following his voice, she found him sitting in her mother's favorite rocker. Sit awhile," Father invited. "I need to tell you what I have found for you." Father looked thoughtfully at Sue hoping she would agree and be happy with what he was about to tell her. "I went to Bismark yesterday to see the Martha and Otto Schlenker. Do you remember them?"

"Oh yes, Father. They used to live on the farm near here. I have known them since I was a baby."

"Well I have been thinking that with Onna and June getting married and the little ones going to live with Onna that you would be lonely out here all by yourself." They have agreed to have you stay with them in Bismark and go to school. Would that be alright with you?"

"Oh yes Father," Sue said with obvious relief. "Being in town, perhaps I could get a job and help pay for my clothes since things are so tight here on the farm."

"Put your things together. I will take you in to town after the girls go to their new homes. The Hanson boys are joining farms. They both have small houses, but it is good enough to start out, and they will be near enough to help each other with the care of the boys."

"But you will be here all alone," Sue said feeling a pang of guilt. "Who will help you with the fields?"

"Ya, I will be right back to where I was seventeen years when I met your mother. I was alone then too." Chuck reminisced aloud, "but I will be busy, and I can get some of the young fellows around here to help me. My memories of your mother will keep me from being lonely."

*   *   *

It is a bright hot day the end of July Sunday afternoon Clare and Olaf decorated the church with simple flowers from the gardens of friends. Many close neighbors milled around outside the church waiting for the time to start the weddings, all took turns coming up to Chuck greeting him warmly.

The hour has come the designated ushers have begun to take the family in to be seated. Chuck was nervous how is he going to take two girls down the isle at the same time. He went into the hall where he was to meet his daughters giving them a hug then each took one of his arms ready to be propelled down the isle. Chuck was relieved the girls settled the problem. The music started the congregation rose and stood at attention turned to see the two brides being propelled down the isle by their father. The pastor came from behind the pulpit and standing before the two ladies with respective young men standing at their sides he asked who gives these two young ladies in marriage.

Chuck looked up at the preacher his thoughts going back to his wedding to Anna , Oh! how lovely she was how he missed her being here now to give away their daughters. I do, Chuck responded and turned sitting down by his eldest daughter Clare and her husband Olaf. Chuck went into a total trance his mind back all those years ago standing before Anna pledging to be with her until death do them part. Oh why did it have to come so quick. Chuck came out of his trance just as the pastor was finishing the last with June and Jacob. The music started again the congregation stood and the two couples arm in arm left the front and walked acknowledging the guests as they passed down the isle. Outside the church the young women stood waiting for the bouquet to be tossed their direction. Today they were lucky two ladies would be able to catch one. The men had a bowl of rice ready to pelt the couples as they left the church. Onna and Arin got in their buggy to head for their new home as did June and Jacob the young men decided to gather in the evening and make a call at each of the new couple's places with their noise makers .

The church ladies had brought things to serve the guests and though the couples had slipped away they served a delightful lunch with delicious desserts. The ladies had a great time along with Clare celebrating while the men gathered around Chuck patting him on the back and telling him how lucky he was to have the sons-in-laws he had, and inquiring after the well being of his two sons out west.

Caleb ran to jump up in his fathers arms while Fredrick looked on. Sue came to takeover and get them ready to go home. Sue knew Fredrick did not want to see Onna go he had become very attached to her since Mother's death. Well he would not be without her long shehad planned to get the boys the next week and Sue was to be sent to town then.

30

Lisa's illness

Lisa's father and mother were finishing the move from their old place. A month had passed since Lisa had come home wet from making fairies in the soft spring snow. The snow was gone but the wind was cold and brisk as things began to dry out.

Lisa woke up early in the morning calling for Mother, "I can't make my feet work."

"What seems to be your problem?" Mother, asked as she came to where Lisa lay in the bed she shared with Mercy.

"I tried to get up, but I can't find my feet." Lisa whinned. "They went away."

"Well I would say you laid on them, and they went to sleep. You probably shut off the circulation. Well no matter," Mother said with a shrug of her shoulders not feeling much concern. "I'll get Gus to carry you downstairs and we can wake them up."

"Gus!" Mother called cupping her hands over her mouth and yelling down the stairs. "Come up here and carry Babe downstairs." Following him down the stairs she directed him to put Lisa on the cot by the heater in the sitting room.

Mother went to the kitchen to get the rest of the children ready for school. "I am going to keep Mercy home with Lisa today," she said to the boys. "I need her to watch Lisa while we finish moving the last load of things from the old place."

Mercy tried to get Lisa up but all Lisa wanted to do was sleep. Finally she gave up and sat down beside her to read a book but found that Lisa was not hearing a word because she was deep asleep.

Mother came in and while father unloaded the things from the wagon she checked on Lisa.

"She has been asleep all day," Mercy stated with an anxious tone. "I read her a story but she slept clear through it."

Father coming in to see how Lisa was. When he found that she was still sleeping and had been all day, he became worried. "Tomorrow we will take her to the doctor. It doesn't seem normal for her to be sleeping that much. It is too late tonight and it is too cold to take her out this late."

Morning came and Lisa was still unable to move her body. Mother fixed breakfast and got the children ready for their long walk to school.

Gus came over to where Lisa lay. He sat beside her and tried to wake her. When he couldn't he left with a frown wrinkling his brow. Mother came in and seeing his distress said, "Don't worry Gus. She'll be fine in a few days."

The doctor got out a hammer with a rubber head on it and gave Lisa a sound tap on the soft part of each of her knees to see how they responded. One knee responded so well it came up automatically and kicked the doctor in the stomach. Mother was about to scold her when the doctor interceded and said, "She had no control of her leg. I hit her reflexes. Polio is going around so I was checking to see if she might have caught it. You are in luck. That is not what is her trouble. Her reflexes are too good especially in her left leg. However, the other leg moves slowly so something is wrong."

"What do you think the problem is?" Mother inquired.

"Well, your father has crippling arthritis, or I should say inflammatory rheumatism. I am afraid that Lisa may have inherited it. Remember when we took her tonsils out. They fell apart letting all the infection from them go through her body," the doctor informed looking at her chart and then back at Rena. "Also it has been a damp cold spring so that has not helped." Writing down a prescription for a tonic, the doctor explained this would help give her strength to fight the infection. "Be sure she has some oranges and lemons; they will help clear her blood. Be sure you wash them well. They could have polio germs since there are so many in the area. When the weather gets sunny and clear,' he continued with his instructions, "see that she is out in the sun with her legs uncovered. She will not be able to move herself for a while, but with care we can only hope that the paralysis is not permanent."

"Oh Doctor," Rena begged don't tell me my baby daughter is crippled. She is too young."

"We can only hope she is strong willed enough to fight this," The old doctor said patting Lisa on the leg tenderly as he looked up at her mother. "Some times a positive mental attitude can do more than medicine. That is often why children recover more easily than adults," reassured the doctor patting Lisa's mother on the shoulder. Dr. Montford pulled a piece of candy from his white smock jacket and handed it to Lisa. His eyes sparkling with love for this rambuncious child he had so often cared for.

Taking Lisa home, they put her to bed on the cot along side the heater. Mother rubbed her down with the wintergreen liniment. It had a penetrating warmth to it. She had rubbed this same liniment on her father's legs she thought, but his legs had never regained use. Shrugging off the thought she continued to rub. He was much older and had lived a good life before his legs stiffened up. Rena let her head drop back onto her shoulders and stretched the knots in her neck. Poor Lisa is just a little girl. She breathed deeply and let her eyes focus on the ceiling before closing them in prayer. *God*, she prayed silently, *Please heal my little girl.*

Lisa slept many hours a day only waking to eat a little chicken broth Mother kept cooking at the back of the stove. Mother had borrowed a heat lamp and spent many hours putting heat on Lisa. She continued to rub the wintergreen liniment into her leg muscles and once in awhile she thought she saw Lisa's toes work a little.

Several weeks passed. Lisa was not sleeping as much. She had even begun to move her legs, but as yet had not regained the ability to get up and walk. Mother continued to rub her down and use the heat lamp. Mother had begun to put her in a hot tub of Epson salt water each day to soak.

It was turning green outside and Lisa began to beg her mother to let her get up and go out side to play on the nice green grass.

Mother, of course, being a teacher and used to giving positive responses said, "Why yes Lisa. Be sure to dress warm before you go outside to play. Maybe your friend Maude will want to play outside with you when she comes today." Mother knew Lisa was unable to get up. She also believed that she must help her try or she would never get up again. Only her own strong will would be able to help her get up.

Lisa lay all day trying desperately to move her legs over the edge of the bed, but try as she would she could not budge.

Mother continued her regime of filling the tub with warm water and Epson salt, soaking Lisa in the tub until the water became cool, then rubbing her dry before putting the wintergreen liniment on her legs. Mother would give Lisa chicken broth to eat while she empied the tub and by the time she returned Lisa would be sound asleep from the exhasting routine. Every day for the next two months it was the exactly the same thing routine.

It was almost summer. Lisa had finally started getting stronger. She could almost stand on her own. Each day Lisa spent much her day trying to get up. Finally one day, her legs move. "Mother," she cried out in excitement.

"I'm commmmming!" her mother yelled in panic as she came running thinking perhaps Lisa had fallen out of bed.

"What is wrong?" she inquired as she reached Lisa's cot out of breath. Mother had been out tending the garden she had planted earlier in the spring.

"Look Mama! I can make my legs move out side the bed. See!" Lisa swung her legs over the edge and tried to put her feet on the floor.

Mother came close. Her hands went to the side of her face as she saw the wonderful sight. "Come Lisa. Walk to Mama," she encouraged holding out her hands for her daughter to feel safe. She felt like she did when Lisa had learned to walk the first time.

"Oh Mama do you think I can?" Lisa's eyes shone with excitement as she looked up at her mother .

"I will take your arms and hold you steady. You do all that you can by yourself. If you start to fall, I'll be here to catch you so don't be afraid."

Lisa swung her legs over the edge of the bed but having been down so long she did not have the strength to lift herself up from the cot. Mother lifted her to an upright position but her legs were like rubber and they buckled beneath her. Lisa sat down on the bed with tears in her eyes.

"It's okay Lisa. Keep working." Mother covered her and said, "you did very well. You will be walking again in no time I just know it. So don't you give up. You just have to build up some strength."

"Oh Mother, are you sure. I want so much to go outside and swing and play with old Pal."

"You just keep trying like you have been Honey. If you believe you can then you can," Mother promised with the strength of conviction in her voice.

                        *   *   *

Near the end of summer Grandfather Amos passed away at his son Clarence's place in Spokane. That meant Mother would have to leave for a few days. Lisa would be left with Father and the rest of the children. Lisa had gained her strength in the month since she had first tried to stand and was now able to stand on her own. As yet she had not learned how to walk again.

This morning Lisa dressed with the help of Mercy before she and the brothers left for the school. When Father came in, Lisa sat rocking back and forth in her favorite chair, "I am taking the car into town. If you can stand up and take a few steps to me, I will take you with me. If you can't, I will have to put you in bed and leave you here."

Lisa had a great fear of being left alone. When she had been six, she had a bad time going to her own classroom at Sunday School. Now she was eight but her fear of being alone was no less than it was then. Father was aware of her fear. He was using this psychology while mother was away to see if he could get Lisa to do what he knew she could do. He believed fear of falling was keeping her from trying. Mother was a little fearful too even though she had been a positive influence to get her this far.

Lisa stood up from the chair and though she wobbled a little, she was able to stand on her legs. "Keep your eyes on me Lisa," her father said standing only two feet in front with his arms out-stretched. "Now move your right foot towards me and the left foot will follow."

Lisa strained and soon her right foot moved forward. Just as her father had said, the other foot followed.

"Good," said Father smoothly trying to keep calm so Lisa would stay calm. "Now take another step. Good . . . Good . . . Good . . . There. See you could do it, couldn't you," he praised holding her in his arms and stroking her long curls. "Now we can go to town," he said moving two paces back and encouraging her to come to him again. Lisa followed shakily but father caught her and lifted her tenderly to the chair.

"See," Father said, "If you keep it up, you might be outside playing before Mother gets home. That will be a wonderful surprise for her, don't you think?"

Father put Lisa's coat on and carried her to the car.

Father and Lisa practiced walking often over the next two days. Finally Father took her out to her favorite swing and she spent half an hour swinging. Father thought this a good exercise for her legs since she had to use them to make the swing go high.

"You need to try and get down by yourself," Father said when she had finished swinging. "I have a stick here that you can use to balance yourself. I want you to see if you can walk back into the house by yourself. If you can, you will be able to come out any time you want and swing."

Lisa got out of the swing and Father handed her the stick.
Lisa started the long walk toward the house. First she moved
her right foot and set it down, then she moved the stick and
wabbled before setting it down. Next she moved her left foot.
She kept repeating this process all the while her father walked
right behind her. Reaching the house, Father opened the door
and Lisa went in by herself. Father gave her a big hug. "Wow.
You should be so proud of yourself Lisa. Mother will be home
Saturday so you will have to see how much you can do by
yourself so you can surprise Mother."

Lisa had been getting up each day the rest of the week and
dressing without Mercy's help . She took the stick Father had made
for her and went out to swing.

Lisa got to go with Father to pick up Mother at the train
depot. When Mother came down the walkway, Lisa walked to
her mother using the stick for balance. Mother saw her and
came running, tears streaming down her cheeks at seeing her
baby walking again.

"Oh Babe," she cried. "You are walking! How did she manage
that while I was gone?" Mother inquired of John who stood with a
sassy grin on his face.

31

Lisa and her family move to Spokane area

Lisa's uncle, her father's brother has come to visit. He is a heavyset fellow. Though he is several years younger than Lisa's father, his hair is balding.

Lisa could hear them talking in the kitchen. "John, I have bought Father's place at the edge of Spokane. It doesn't have much ground but there is an adequate house. You probably could farm some of the other farms around since most who live in the area work in town. You can live there rent free if you just care for the place. I felt the folks needed to move to town and be shed of all the work even though it is only fifteen acres."

"This comes at a good time for us Fred. The doctor has just told us we must move Lisa from this damp cold area or she will again become paralyzed. I believe Rena will agree to it since Spokane area is much warmer than it is here.

"Hello Rena," Fred called when she came in from the garden. "I just gave John a proposition that you should hear about it. I will need your decision right away."

"What is up, Fred?" Rena questioned. "You always have something going."

"I just bought Father's place at Keasling," he repeated for Rena. John tells me the doctor wants you to move Lisa to a warmer place."

Fred's arrogant ways had always irritated Rena. Fred was in the armed service and acted like he was above the rest of the family with his steady income. The rest of his brothers scraped to make a living since the stock market crash.

"I am offering Dad's old place rent free just for taking care of it for me," Fred said looking at Rena, amused at her opinion of him. Rena was a well-educated women. She had been a teacher before she married John. He knew she was capable of earning a good income if she would go back to teaching, but she was a good mother and stayed home to care for the children.

"If John thinks he can find a way to earn a living there, I have no objections," Rena said waving her arms around the room in which they were sitting. "But we will have to try and cancel the purchase of this place on which we have just put a deposit."

John and Fred left in Fred's new Ford car shortly after and drove over to talk to the man who owned the house they had planned to purchase.

They returned to the house in deep conversation.

Suddenly John saw Rena watching them from the stairs. "He gave me all the money back and wished us well when he heard about Lisa's problem," he called up to her.

"That was very nice of him," Rena replied, "he could have kept the down payment."

"Does that mean we have an agreement," Fred inquired looking at the two of them.

"Yes," said John. "We can have everything here taken care and be able to be there by the end of the month."

"The key will be at the folks home in town." Fred said gathering his things and preparing to leave. "I will be back on the base since my leave will be up next week." Fred said his goodbyes to John, Rena and the children and got in his Ford.

Fred had been injured in the war. He a metal plate put in his head where he had lost a part of his skull on the battle field. Having recovered from the surgery, he was now back to active duty. Though the war had ended he chose to remain in the service.

The end of the month was here and they were all packed and ready to go. Father had already made several trips to Spokane with the wagon taking the farm machines and the animals.

It was now time to take the family in the Model T Ford. The cat the girls had nursed in the barn loft was their treasure and they were determined the cat would go with them.

"How are we going to get that wild thing to stay still in the car," Mother scolded the girls who stood their ground refusing to go unless the cat could go.

John looked at the troubled girls and said, "If you are willing to give up your doll trunk, I will cut air holes in it and the cat can ride on the running board in the doll trunk."

"Yes, Yes, Yes," the girls said jumping up and down with joy at the prospect of having their cat.

"Girls," Father admonished, "it is up to you to catch the cat. You know he will only come to either of you. Make sure you have him here and ready to go by tonight."

This cat was special with its multi-colored coat and short tail. Some said it was a bob cat mix. The cat was big and heavy and John liked the way he kept the fields clear of gofers, moles and mice.

They were up at the break of dawn. The was cat in the little trunk and tied to the running board. The children piled in the car. The Phil and Mercy in the back. Father and Mother in the front with Lisa sitting on Mother's lap. The trip would be long and trying.

Gus was not with them. He had already left home to join the new project the government had provided for young boys. They trained them and gave them enough work to send a little money home. This helped keep families from starving. Since the 1929 stock market crash many had lost their jobs. There was very little money for food or medical. The local doctor in Idaho had helped Gus join. This money had helped provide care for Lisa while she was paralyzed.

Father grumbled when Mother picked a nice grassy spot along side the road for them to stop and eat. Mother had packed a huge lunch because she was a frugal person. Father wanted to stop in a cafe for hot food.

Arriving late in the evening, the children piled out of the car needing to stretch their legs. Lisa and Phil took off on a dead run up the hill facing the back of the house. The house set down a ravine with lots of trees surrounding it. The barn and corrals sat up against the bank. The alfalfa fields flowed to the side of the house, and in the front a great green grassy area invited them to play. The huge two-story house was one Lisa had always loved to visit when Grandma and Grandpa lived there. The house had many windows and the French doors had little square windows. With the help of the boys, Father set up Mother's kitchen stove which he had brought in the load just before bringing them.

Mother got a good fire going and started dinner cooking, while the boys helped Father move more heavy furniture. This would be their first hot meal since the night before last. Mercy was directed to find plates, cups, and silverware in one of the boxes that sat on the floor. Phil was sent to get some buckets of water for cooking and drinking. These had to be carried from the little spring at the end of the road. It was good water and provided for both them and their neighbors. The well on the property was apparently adequate for the animals, washing and cleaning but not for people ingesting.

Father had already put up the swing. It was something he always did whenever they moved. Lisa needed motion. She had always been an active child. That is why her paralysis was so difficult.

32

Fredrick and Father

Onna and Arin kept Fredrick for five years. When he was fifteen, he returned to the farm to help his father. He had grown into a strong young man. He had Anna's soft loving nature but resembled Paul, Anna's brother. Where Anna had dark hair, her brother was blonde and when Chuck looked at him he was reminded of that first night when he saw Anna and her brother.

It was a dark rainy night. The wind howled and the house felt drafty. As Fredrick fell asleep upstairs with a sliver of the moon peaking in his window, he once again saw the vision of his mother standing at the foot of his bed. Fredrick tried to talk to her just as he had when she first left him. Back then he had seen her every night at the foot of his bed until he went to stay with sister Onna. Now after all these years, he saw her again. There she was raising her hand to quiet him as she had done so often before she left. Waking in a sweat he tried to revisualize her but the vision had all evaporated. He lay for a long time trying to go back to sleep. In the early hours of the morning sleep finally came.

Fredrick was good with his hands. One day he saw a magazine with a heading *Make Your Own Electricity*. The article showed how to convert a Model T Ford generator into a slow speed wind charger which could be used to change batteries to use for electric light. He sent a dollar and fifteen cents for a kit which contained wire to rewind the armature, a small can of shellac to seal it, and a book of directions.

Finally the parts came and Fredrick worked on his generator in his spare time. He managed to get the armature rewound and

coated with shellac according to the directions. Then he built a
fire in the kitchen range to 200 degrees so the oven would not be
too hot. The directions said to keep the heat at an even slow temperature. Finally he put the armature into the oven to bake for six
hours. When the amatured was finished baking and cooled , he
reassembled the generator.

After the generator was reassembled, he climbed to the top of
the barn and attached a ten foot long 6x6 timber to the side of the
barn and braced it to make it strong. Next, he attached a twelve
inch long pipe an inch and half in diameter to the 6x6 timber. He
then took a six foot 2x6 and cut a twelve inch piece from it. After
this he attached a heavy barn hinge to the 12 inch piece and attached the other end of the hinge to the other part of the 2x6.
Then Fredrick fastened a one and quarter inch pipe to the 2x6 just
below the center of the hinge.

Frederick's father could see that his son had figured out something more than the directions had said to do with the generator
so he helped him make a propeller to attach to the generator.
Fredrick then attached the generator with the propeller already in
place to the twelve inch piece of 2x6 that was on the barn. The
inch and quarter pipe was put into the inch and half pipe to allow
it to swivel. A piece of plywood was nailed on the end of the 2x6.
This allowed the generator to face the wind at all times. Fredrick
put an eye hook on the top of the generator threading a cable
through the hook and down through the pipe to the bottom of
the building so it could be shut down if the wind became too
strong. A spring was connected to the bottom of the generator so
that when the wind blew on the propeller face it would not tip the
generator too far. The spring acted as a control when the wind
blew on its face. Now that the generator was in place and ready to
produce electricity, he had to run two more wires from the generator to the battery, one negative and one positive. He then had to
run two wires to the house the same as he had run to the battery.
Once this was done, he needed a receptacle and a bulb so they
could have light.

Chuck was proud of his son's accomplishment, so he drove into town to pick of the materials his son needed. That night they had lights in the house just like the people in town. There was always enough wind blowing from the north west to keep the battery charged.

Fredrick and his father kept busy. Along with the regular chores, they began to figure out how they could make their fields produce better crops. North Dakota was going through a period of extremely dry times. The crops lacked the moisture to produce.

"Why don't we plug every other hole on the seeder," Chuck suggested to Fredrick one day. "It will take half as much grain and the low amount of moisture that is there will last longer."

When it came time to harvest, they got thirty bushels to the acre while all the local farmers either had no crop at all or got half as much and used twice the seed.

1929 stock market crash had left the country in terrible condition. People who had been wealthy found they were unable to pay for the grains and goods from the farmers. Since the farmers could not sell their goods for enough to make a profit, some lost their farms. Whole families were suffering. In North Dakota and surrounding areas, they had yet another plague. The lack of enough rain or snow had caused the fields to dry up and the top soil began to blow away. Crops failed.

The government set up CCC Camp which was a plan to take young men into a work camp to train them as well as give them money to send home to keep their families from starving. When a boy was seventeen years old he could join.

Fredrick got permission from his father to join and when the harvesting was done that fall he went to sign up. Though he was only fifteen and a half, he was a big boy for his age and had a strong build so when he told them he was seventeen, they believed him . Fredrick soon earned respect for his ability to learn quickly and his willingness to work hard. Building a high rock fence to border the grounds was the first project he worked on. Fredrick seemed to naturally know how to use a proper plumb line to keep the wall straight. The foreman in charge taught him how to select the rocks and put the mortar around it. He learned what to do so quickly that the leader put him in charge of directing the other boys.

Fredrick and his crew finished their project in record time. Because the men in charge saw that Fredrick was knowledgeable about engines, they put him on the sand blasting equipment . It was used to take the burned charcoal out of signs they were making. They had cut down trees sliced them and burned the letters into the flat part that came from slicing the tree. It was dead of winter and the signs were put into a big building for them to work on. Fredrick understood how to operate the engines having helped his father on the farm from the time he was very little. But the projects at home had been done in the open in the spring or fall not in a building in the winter.

Fredrick had been left alone to do this project since the foreman saw he was very adept. A period of time elapsed and Fredrick began to feel ill, his head hurt and he felt he needed to throw up so he went to the big doors and opened them. When the air hit him full force he collapsed. Several hours later after a long struggle in the infirmary he regained conscience. Fredrick woke his head was fuzzy and he began to call out asking where he was. A nurse came to his side and griped his hand . The nurse was an older lady. A first in his fuzzy mind, he thought it was his mother. Then just as quickly he realized that was impossible.

"Hi there Sonny. You finally back with us," the nurse chirpped taking his hand and smiling down at him. "You had a close call. Why in the world did you run that engine in a closed building, you were overcome by exhaust fumes?"

"We never worked on machines at home during the winter. We always did our work outside," Fredrick returned with an embarrassed laugh. "I guess I thought the building was big enough. Once again it seemed Frederick's charmed life had saved him.

33

Lisa in school

Going to this new school was a real scary thing thought Lisa as she walked away from the bus. The school was in a field away from everything. There were no stores or houses around. Lisa walked slowly with her head down kicking at the clumps of dirt. She missed her two brothers and her sister. They had always been with her and now she had to go to this small little grade school that only held the lower grades.

The school where she had gone before always had houses and stores around so she never felt alone or afraid. There were always people she knew close by.

Getting on the bus with Mercy and her brother Phil was fine she thought. At least until the boy sitting on the seat next to her decided to get pushy and pushed her on the floor as they went around a curve. Pretending it was the fault of the bus swaying, Mike grinned at Lisa. Lisa knew he had shoved her, but she didn't want to get in trouble the first day by clobbering him like she would have in her old school. That time she had to stay in recesses for a whole week just for defending herself against David, her teacher's son. Lisa thought life wasn't fair.

Oh but David had deserved it Lisa remembered as she moved toward school. She had invited him out behind the wood pile and then beat him until his eyes were black and his nose bled. He had cried non-stop, but Lisa kept beating him while Mercy and her friend egged her on. Lisa had stayed in at recess for a whole week for that little incident but she felt good about it. She had paid him back for everything he had done to her and gotten by with it because his mother was the teacher.

No Lisa decided, she had better not start that here. It was a long way home if she were made to walk, as she had been back in Idaho. Besides, Lisa realized, she did not have to fight this battle alone. Mike was older, and he went to school with Mercy and Phil. All she would have to do is tell Phil which she would do tonight. That settled, Lisa entered the new school.

The next day, Phil managed to innocently smash a ball into the side of Mike's head while supposedly playing. Mercy had come home that night and told Lisa about it. Lisa felt defended especially since it was Phil who had come through for her. She and Phil had always been pals in mischief.

Lisa had always been able to defend herself before, but the fear of being punished or kicked off the bus in this strange new environment kept her meek and quiet for awhile. Finally though she ran into a boy bigger than anyone else in this small school. The word was that he had failed a grade or two. He had a habit of coming behind girls and hitting them on the back, the smaller ones fell on their face. Lisa had about all she was going to take watching this when he made the bad mistake of choosing her as his next challenge. Lisa saw him out of the corner of her eye. Just as he reached her, she swung her tin dinner pail around her head, and because she was tall for her age, the pail was just the right height to connect with his head. The sharp corners of the lunch box laid a gash in his head about three inches long and quite deep. A teacher seeing the problem hustled him into the school to bandage his head. This incident highlighted the problem of retaining a child in a grade for more than one year. The principal decided to move this bigger boy to the intermediate school due to his size and age.

The months past quickly and Lisa had been in this small school for two years. In that time span, Lisa had dealt with many such problems deciding to take the consequences of the punishment rather than endure the tormentor. One such problem was twin boys whose job it was to chop the wood for the heater that kept the room warm in the cold weather. The weather being cold and damp and Lisa having suffered with paralyzed legs chose to go to the basement near the furnace for her play time. One day when the twins were there chopping wood, they chased her around telling her they were going to chop her feet off. The next time Lisa went to play in the basement, she took a baseball bat to defend herself. It is a good thing she never had occasion to use it since she had developed a heavy swing with the guidance from her brother. God often protects us even when we don't deserve it.

34

Fredrick on his own

Fredrick arrived in New Salem and instead of going back to his fathers, made his way to June and Jacob's.

Onna had cared for him for a long time but as he grew older, it was difficult for Fredrick to deal with her husband Arin. He had some strange ways and the intelligent boy he was, he found it difficult to be with Arin who treated him as a little boy. Through Arin was a kind man, he did not trust Fredrick to be left on his own to work.

Fredrick had missed June. She had been the one to watch over him when he was very little, and she had always made him responsible to do whatever he was able on his own.

Fredrick arrived at sunset, just as the last of the chores were done. June opened the door just as he reached it having seen him walking up the lane. Wrapping her arms around him, she gave him a hearty squeeze revealing how much she had missed him and how pleased she was that he had came to her.

June had missed her little brother. She had felt the loss of his constant presence when he went to stay with Onna. Oh, she had him right next door, but it wasn't the same. and though she missed him, she knew baby Caleb needed him more.

Fredrick was her treasure. June had loved him from the day he was born. He needed her to keep him from hurting himself. He was active and always into one adventure after another. His mind always seemed to be experimenting to see how things worked but so often found himself in life threatening situations. She needed him too, he brought excitement into her life.

Hearing the commotion, Jacob came in to the kitchen greeting him with a healthy hand shake and then a hug and good natured pounding on the back.

"Well," Jacob said, "I see you have grown into a strong man. You look like you can handle a man's job. The farmer next to us on the opposite side from Onna and Arin is looking for a strong young worker to help them this summer. It pays thirty dollars a month and a place to sleep, and meals if you like. I will go tell him you are here and put in a good word for you."

Fredrick was honored that his brother-in-law would speak well of him to the neighbor. He also was pleased to find Jacob treating him as a grown man. "I would like to take that job if he offers it, Jacob," Fredrick agreed looking up at him with admiration and appreciation.

"Well, then come along and I'll introduce you right now. He should be in from the fields at this hour. Let's go before he gets someone else. Jobs are hard to come by these days." Fredrick and Jacob saddled horses and set out across the fields to see the neighbor.

"Hello," greeted Jacob seeing his neighbor coming out of his barn. They dismounted. "Harold, this is my brother-in-law, Fredrick," Jacob introduced. He has just returned from the CCC training camp. I believe this is the fellow you have been looking for to help you on your farm. As you can see he is strong and healthy. I can attest to his strong work ethic," Jacob recommended.

"Great, great," Harold said firmly shaking Frederick's hand. "I sure could use you tomorrow. I have a great deal of work that piled up."

Another man who treats me with respect thought Fredrick returning Harold's firm handshake and smiling warmly. "I'll make you glad you hired me, Sir," thanked Fredrick tipping his hat back a bit in a nervous gesture.

"I'll be here at sun up if you like," Fredrick said looking Harold in the eye. Fredrick was a quiet young man, not especially shy but gentle in manner. He had a way of carrying himself that showed his confidentce in himself. He was not afraid to try new things and his mind was quick and eager. He was not arrogant, but appreciated being respected for his abilities.

"Bring along your things. You will be here until Saturday after chores. Saturday evening and Sunday until evening milking is your time," Harold directed.

Fredrick spent a wonderful evening with June and her husband playing cards after dinner. Just before retiring for the night, June dished them up some Aufa Kucken topped with rich whipped cream. He finished the delightful desert with a loud smack and several scrappings of his spoon against the empty dish hinting for more.

With a twinkle in her eye, June said, "I see you haven't lost your appetite for Mother's good desserts." After his second helping, Fredrick wished every one goodnight and went up to enjoy his first night back home.

Fredrick worked through the season finishing in the fall. The work was heavy and tiring, but he enjoyed the way Harold respected his work making him want to please him and work all the harder.

Fredrick spent much of his off time with June and her family, but some times he rode a horse over to visit with Onna. One day while he was there, Onna talked about Chris and Jeff in Spokane and that gave Fredrick an idea. "What do you think about me going to Spokane Onna? Do you think I could find work with them?"

"Well you better ask Jacob," Onna said. "He could better advise you about that."

The next morning while he and Jacob worked together, Fredrick brought up his idea about Spokane. Jacob's reply was slow in coming. But he was like that. He was one to think things through, before speaking aloud. Fredrick waited patiently.

"Well Harold tells me you are a good dependable worker. Spokane might be your best bet. There is very little work around here until summer."

They talked about him going to Spokane for a few more days looking at it from every angle. Finally, they talked it over with June and though she clearly did not want to lose him, she agreed that it was a good idea.

"Have you thought about how you will get there?" she questioned.

"I have heard that some people are jumping freight trains," Jacob suggested. "It's a dangerous business though."

June didn't like that idea but once the seed was planted, Fredrick couldn't let it go. It sounded like an adventure worth the risk.

Finally Fredrick was ready to go.

"I'll take you over to Glen Ullen to catch the train in the morning," agreed Jacob. "I have taken others and that is the best place.

Morning came and Fredrick bid June and her family goodbye. He had already ridden over to tell Onna and her family goodbye the night before.

With four dollars in his pocket and the clothes on his back, he rode with Jacob over to Glen Ullen where he jumped the freight heading west.

Scrambling into the dark box car, he crawled over to a far corner so the railroad bulls could not detect him.

After several jostling hours, the train came to a stop at a water up and service station. Fredrick was hungry and in sore need of excercise. Seeing a store near the tracks, he jumped off and ran quicly to the store buying a bottle of milk, a loaf of bread, and three cans of sardines. The clerk was a lady dressed in slacks, something he had only begun to see since the stock market crash. Not only were ladies beginning to work more out of the home but they were beginning to dress like men he thought shaking his head and racing back to the train.

He got back to the train just as it was moving out of the station. Looking to the right and to the left to make sure no one was watching, he raced for the train scrambling on just as it was picking up speed. Once back in he scampered to the darkest corner of boxcar and waited until the train was at full speed. Finally he breathed easier feeling the bulls would not be bothering to check further. Fredrick sat back pushing his hat to the back of his head, he counted his remaining money before putting it in his money belt . Then he opened the loaf of bread. He heard rustling in the opposite corner and stopped in mid movement listening. Hearing nothing he opened a can of sardines. As he was putting it on the bread he heard the noise again. Stopping he listened and peered in the corner, but it was too dark to see anything. Finally he put another slice of bread on top of the sardines.

Just as he took a bite, a large dark figure loomed up out of the back corner of the car and started moving directly toward him. He stopped chewing and sat their immobile, cold chill traveled up his spine and into his scalp making the hair on his arm and the back of his neck stand out.

"Could ya'll spare a slice of bread," said the voice in the dark moving slowly toward him. "I hav' not eat'n all day." Gradually the dark figure came in to view. He could make out the shape of a tall black man.

Fredrick had been raised in an area of settlers who had come from Germany, Sweden, and Russia. He had not been acquainted with black people.

Trembling, Fredrick held out two slices of bread and a can of sardine.

"No. No, ya'll keep your sardines," the man said gently, "just the bread. "You'll need it before ya git to wh're you're goin'.

The man invited himself to sit beside Fredrick and eat. "Where are ya headed young man?" he quizzed?

Fredrick feeling a little less frightened said, "I'm going to try and find work in Spokane, Washington. My brothers live there," tucking the food into a big pocket on the inside of his coat and rebuttoning.

"By the way. You need to take that money outta your belt and hide it," the man advised. "A money belt's the f'rst place anyone'll look. And don't let me see where ya hide it," he cautioned as Fredrick began taking the money out searching for another hiding place. "I don't need no temptations beck'ning me."

The train began to slow and the black man stood quickly and said, "Come boy, we have ta jump off here. Make your way to the bush," Frederick's new friend cautioned, "and stay there until the train starts moving again. The bulls are tough in this section and would just as soon shoot as ask questions."

They inched their way forward in the dark car until they felt the fresh breeze on their faces. "Git ready to jump," he said. "Use me to push against. I'll shove ya out. When ya jump, roll over with your arms around your head and then lie still." Tucking his head as the man shoved, Fredrick rolled over and down a hill feeling the sharp rocks rip at his hands, then soil, firm, unyielding, hard. After a few minutes he heard shots and the train slowed down, but by then the train had moved into the station. He hoped the man had jumped too. He hoped the man was not shot. Shaking he stayed where he was until he felt the touch of the man on his arm. Looking up he saw the man smiling down at him. "Good work man," his friend praised.

They made their way toward the other side of the station where they would reboard the train. By the time they got there the train was moving at a good speed. Fredrick had seen the bulls still milling around as they neared so they were compelled to wait longer. Once clear they started running for the train, but his short legs were having to work really hard. He pumped his arms as he ran trying to gain more speed and propel himself forward enough to grab onto the side of the box car , the heavy iron bars at the bottom of the door just inches away from his fingers. Fredrick finally managed to grab the bar and swing his legs up. Gasping heavily for air, Fredrick crawled into the corner.

"Good, ya waited," his friend commented reminding him of his presence. He had been so intent on catching the train, he hadn't noticed when his friend had gotten on board. "If ya hadn't waited, you'd of been caught fer sure," he acknowleged. "That bull out there is honoree. He'd love ta catch som'ne strong like you. I'd not like ta see ya fall under the wheels of this train, a delibrat' accident. Ya must be careful about that," he warned.

It was late in the afternoon. They had been traveling for a long time. Fredrick woke when he felt the train slowing down. It felt like they were in the mountains, the air was much colder, the train seemed to be moving up hill. He pulled his flimsy coat tighter around himself

Suddenly Frederick's friend shook him. "Sorry boy we got ta git outta here now before the train slows anymore. This time git movin' fast as soon as ya can. Run for that stand of trees ya see out there," he said pointing in the distance.

They repeated their earlier exit from the train. Fredrick going first with a shove from his friend. This time he leaped, rolled, and quickly jumped to his feet moving out in a dead run just as his friend had told him. Looking back, Fredrick saw his friend close behind.

They waited and waited for the train to start moving. The train had been sitting for a longer time than the other stops so his friend moved up to get a better look. Coming back Fredrick noticed the man seemed troubled.

"Well son, it looks as though we've a big problem. They're taking the box cars off the train. Ya listen ta what I'm tellin' ye boy! We're goin' ta have ta catch the bar at the end of the last car and climb on top of the cars. We'll have ta make our way ta the center of a car that is not too visible on top. On the top of the cars there's wooden planks they call cat walks. Ya'll have ta lie down flat and put your hands around the wooden planks entwining your fingers in case ya fall asleep. We have ta ride the rest of the way on top of the box cars. Remember ya have ta run and grab that ladder and git on top as soon as possible so ya can't be seen."

When the train began to move, Fredrick started running trying to keep pace and at the same time move toward the last car. Getting hold of the ladder, he swung himself up holding tight. As soon as he could catch a bit of breath, he quickly climbed to the top and made his way to the middle having to jump the span between the cars. Fredrick stretched out flat on the wood planks clenching his hands as he had been directed. Finally he saw his friend coming. He sat down on the planks beside him. "I'll sit awhile and keep watch," he told Fredrick. You close your eyes and git a little rest."

They had been riding trains now for a day and a half. Fredrick was exhausted, he closed his eyes and was asleep before the train picked up speed. Coming into a tunnel, Fredrick woke with the sound and saw his friend had laid flat on the plank ahead of him. When they entered the tunnel, he could see why one would not be able to remain upright and keep his head. The smoke from the engines blew back over them. They coughed and sputtered and suffered, mostly in silence. They spent another day and half getting on and getting off when the train stopped to service.

They reached Spokane in the early hours of morning. It was damp and cold, threatening to rain. The fright train yards were at the edge of Spokane in an area called Hillyard. Fredrick and his friend had gotten off just before reaching the freight yard. They said their goodbyes and Fredrick thanked him for all his help, knowing if it had not been for this man he might not have made it here. Who knows what would have happened to him. Shot by the Honorees, crushed under the train, knocked out and money gone. "Thank you God," he breathed aloud remember the faith his mother had taught him.

Fredrick found a lavatory at the edge of one of the buildings. What he saw in the mirrow made him laugh out loud. Frederick's light skin was the same color as his dark friend. He madean attempt to get the smoke and grime off from himself. The workman's soap he found didwonders to melt the grease but it felt scratchy on his light skin.

35

Lisa goes to work

Summer came and money was short. Father had no outside job and it was hard to make the money the family needed on the small truck farm. Mercy had found a job in Spokane baby sitting.

Lisa had been invited to babysit or rather keep a five year old company. Her parents didn't want her to because she was only twelve, but she fussed and begged until she was finally allowed to go. The five year old's mother reasoned that she would always be there. It would be Lisa's job to keep him entertained. She would take him to the park and keep him out of the way of the grown-ups. She would also help keep things cleaned up in the kitchen. Lisa really liked keeping the white refrigerator and stove shiny. She had never had anything like it on the farm. On the farm they only had an ice box. The wood kitchen range only had a small band of white porcelain with chrome for trim. She worked for a chiropractic doctor and his wife. Another man lived in the house as well. He seemed to be younger than the doctor.

One day the doctor's wife decided they needed to purchase a business. This turned out to be a motel with about twenty individual cabins, a store that sold groceries, and a lunch room that served beer. Lisa found herself sharing a bedroom with the five year old boy and three prize bull dogs. Next door there was a dance hall and Lisa wished it would go away. It was almost impossible to get the boy asleep while the music played. Lisa learned especially not to like Bing Crosby since that was the kind of music she heard over and over and over again.

This became a learning experience for Lisa. She had always been taught to do whatever adults asked. Now not only must she watch the boy when she got home from school, but she had acquired the job of emptying the ashes from the twenty stoves in the cabins if they had been rented. When that was done she was to deliver the food to the customers in the dining room. Lisa was bashful as most farm girls are and this was difficult for her. When the doctor's wife realized how difficult this new business was, she gave Lisa another new job to do. When someone came in the middle of the night for a cabin or groceries, it was Lisa who was required to get up and take care of them. One night two men came in and decided to con Lisa. They ganged up on her. As Lisa began to count out the items and tally the groceries for one man, the other man carried groceries outside without paying for them. Lisa was scolded for being so careless. But the good Doctor reminded his wife of Lisa's age.

Now came the worst part for Lisa. The man staying with the doctor and his wife began annoying Lisa. One day when Lisa went to empty the ashes, Ben was in bed. As she came through the door, he threw off his covers and showed his stark naked body. Seeing this naked man frightened her and she began to run and run and run. Her face burned with embarrassment. The tears fell from her eyes hindering her vision. Suddenly, the old doctor coming home and seeing her visibly upset reached out and stopped her. He gently put his arm around her, but he knew this frightened child would not tell him what had happened. "Come Lisa," the doctor said still holding her, "it is time to set the dinner table." Lisa, wanting to get away from Ben,willingly went inside.

It was at this time Lisa wished she was that small first grader in Kootanai, Idaho with her brother Phil. She thought of the old store with its candy jars lining the shelf at just the right height for her to see all that delicious candy. Mother only brought candy for them on Christmas because she said it would make their teeth fall out. But Phil, being an inventive boy, helped Lisa dig money from under the wooden sidewalk. Reaching through the cracks of each board which was spaced about a quarter of an inch apart, they managed to find at least five pennies most times. That was good for about fifteen pieces of candy, enough to share with Mercy and Gus to keep them quiet about their escapade. If Phil wasn't able to dig out at least five pennies, he would loosen one end of a board and lift it up especially if there was a lot of pennies under it. Lisa knew that one should not walk on the edge of the sidewalk because Phil through the years had loosened so many boards that, if you weren't careful it would come up and slap you in the face. Well, Lisa reminded her self, shaking her head to bring herself to the present, she wasn't a first grader anymore that part of life was gone forever she now had to face this.

Lisa's mother came to town on Saturday and the doctor took her aside. Lisa was afraid she had been bad and he was telling on her. But instead, Mother sat down with her and explained that they really needed her to come home. They had more work than Mother could do alone. The truth of the matter was that the doctor felt Lisa was in danger and he wanted her protected. Lisa was happy to be back home and worked twice as hard as she had before she left.

Mother had a small business making cottage cheese and butter to peddle in Spokane. It was up to Lisa to knock on doors in the city of Spokane to peddle the cottage cheese, homemade butter, and vegetables in when in season. Lisa hated knocking on doors. She was so bashful. But she decided it was better than dealing with Ben ever again.

36

Fredrick gets a job

Fredrick had the address where he could find his brothers. It was a good thing he had a keen sense of direction because it was a long way from the Hillyard yards to their place. He started walking south knowing his brothers were on the southwest side of town. After walking about an hour, he turned west and continued walking the cold breeze helping to keep him alert, the damp air helping to cool his skin from the burning of the harsh soap he had used.

Fredrick stopped and looked around. He decided he must be getting close because he could see a bank of tall buildings a short distance ahead and a sign on the lamp post read fifth and Grand. He reached into his pocket and pulled out the paper on which the address was written. Fredrick decided if he went one more block south to sixth, he should be able to find the house number. This wasn't so easy he first thought. Walking first one way then another, he was cut off by buildings. Finally, he stopped to ask someone and they directed him up the hill. He was getting very tired. The long walk and the three days journey on the freight train had taken their toll on his young body. But mostly the fear that he would not find his brothers plagued him. He was a stranger in big city. He had no more money for food and no place to sleep.

When his last bit of confidence was almost gone, Fredrick came to a old house that appeared to be three stories tall, bigger than the farm houses in which he grew up. The number on the paper matched the number on the front of the building. He went up the stairs and timidly knocked on the door. He knew he looked like a beggar. He wondered if they would open the door and then close it again without giving him a chance to declare himself.

A young woman answered the door, a tow headed boy about two hung on her skirts. The woman looked at him curious apparently expecting someone else.

"Hello, I'm Fredrick. I just got off the freight train from north Dakota. I am looking for my brothers Chris and Jeff. Do they live here?" The words tumbled out in a heap. He wanted to reassure her before she had a chance to shut the door.

"Yes," she smiled. They have a room here. They should be along any minute. They work at the hospital and should be home soon." Putting her hand out she said, "My name is Mercy. Come in. You can wait in their room until they get home. You look a lot like Jeff," she observed.

Fredrick found a pair of pants that looked like they might fit. Jeff was shorter than him, but their legs were the about the same length. Where Jeff had a short upper body, Fredrick had a long body making him about five foot ten. Fredrick came out of the room and found Mercy, "Do you think I might use the bathroom and take a bath?"

Looking at him critically. His face was clean enough she thought and his hands, but he had rings of soot around his neck and his clothes were filthy. "Good idea. You look like you have been working in a coal mine." She laughed as she found him some towels and showed him the way to the bathroom.

Fredrick found the rest of the clothes he needed not knowing or caring who they belonged to. At least he would be clean before he laid on the bed, and the brothers had to appreciate that. After his bath Fredrick felt like a new person. He was still tired and his body was red and raw from the scrubbing and the effects of the soap he had used in the train yard, but he felt safe and confident again. Fredrick started to leave the bathroom and than heard her Mother's voice reminding him to clean after himself. He looked at the tub and was ashamed. Looking around he found some cleaner and scrubbed the grease from the tub and sink. He picked up the towels and took them with him. "What can I do with these?" he said going to find Mercy.

When Mercy saw the new Fredrick, she felt sorry for him. His face revealed a young boy. She began to visualize how awful it must have been for him to be all alone so young coming on the freight train with all those bums that could have hurt him.

He said his thanks and went back into his brother's room.

A short while later Mercy knocked on the door to their room. "You didn't have anything to eat yet, did you?"

Fredrick opened the door.

"I have made some sandwiches. Why don't you come, have something to eat with my little boy and me."

Fredrick came out of the bedroom glad of the invitatation. Even though he was bashful, he was far hungrier.

With lunch finished, he thanked Mercy and picked up his dirty dishes, putting them in the sink. He returned to the room and lay down on the bed. He slept soundly until he woke to his brothers' voices in a hot argument. That was his brothers thought Fredrick keeping his eyes closed and hoping to get a little more sleep. Chris had always tried to be the boss. The argument was over the clothes Fredrick had on, each was accusing the other of wearing them. As he crawled out from under the covers, his appearance stopped the argument.

"Tomorrow morning," Chris began giving Fredrick orders without even saying hello, "you go up to the Sacred Heart hospital. They have a soup line there for people that are hungry and out of work. We ate there the first few days before we got jobs. Be clean and polite," he added.

Jeff came over beside him. "It's alright. They have had the soup line since the stock market crash. We get our food on the job since we don't have a place to cook here." Jeff said trying to make Fredrick comfortable. Jeff was remembering how lost he had felt when he first got here. He had Chris with him, but Chris was harsh and not one to help anyone but himself.

The next day Fredrick stood in the long line. Most the people there looked as bad as he had when he first got off the freight train. As he stood timidly in the line, he saw a young sister dressed in her habit. The long black dress hung on her slender figure. They framed her kind looking face. Fredrick wondered why she was here. He had only seen a few nuns before in New Salem, but they had been very old.

The sister moved up beside him, taking him by the arm, she said, "Come with me." She led him into the building and down to the kitchen. Pulling out a chair in front of a table, she directed him to sit. Then she went over to the cook and told him to fix the young boy a decent breakfast. She picked up a glass of milk and some silverware from the tray close at hand and set them down before Fredrick and sat in a chair out next to him. "What is your name?" she asked.

"Fredrick," he responded politely wondering if he was in trouble for being in the line at his age.

"If you are old enough, perhaps I can find a job for you to do around here," she said. "You look strong and healthy. So what is your age?" she questioned catching him off guard.

"I will turn seventeen in April," Fredrick lied hopeful he might go home and tell Chris he had a job.

"Well, I think you can handle the job I have for you," as his food came. "When you have finished eating, I will take you up-stairs and show you what is needed."

Fredrick ate ravenously trying to use manners so as not to offend the sister, but it had been a long time since he had a hearty meal.

When he finished, he picked up his dirty dishes and looked at the sister with a question in his eyes.

Sister Barbara, the cook called her, commented on his good manners. She was pleased that he had been trained to pick up after himself. She knew he would be just the boy she needed in her ward. He would not have to be told what to do, he would see what needed to be done for himself. Smiling, she pointed to the sink with her head then headed to the door and waited for him to join her.

Reaching her ward floor, she led him to a room with brooms and cleaning materials. "Do you think you could learn to use these to clean the rooms?" she inquired turning to Fredrick.

She took him on a walk through the rooms showing what needed to be done in the way of cleaning. When the lunch trays come up from the kitchen, you will take them to the patients and collect the empty ones when they have finished. You will clean and mop the floors and clean the bathrooms in this ward only. You will eat at the employee lounge for free. Now," she said turning to him with her hands on her hips, her head cocked a little to the side, and a twinkle in her eyes, "what is your answer?"

"Yes Sister, I will be able to do that. I was in the CCC camp for about eighteen months before leaving North Dakota," Fredrick offered his experiences with excitement in his voice at the prospect of a job so soon, and meals as well. Chris and Jeff would be proud. "I can start today if you like."

Sister Barbra shook his hand and said, "Be here at six o'clock in the morning. I will meet you here on this floor and get you started."

Fredrick walked briskly back to the house where his brothers were rooming. He hoped he would be able to continue staying with them for awhile. Reaching the house he entered the hall and headed for his brother's room.

Mercy saw him and asked if he had eaten.

"Yes, thank you. Sister Barbara at the hospital gave me something to eat and a job starting tomorrow."

Mercy looked at the young boy. She hoped he would be able to hang on to the job. He looked so young and shy. Looking at him, she could see his excitement. "You are very lucky. There are so many people out of work and you have a job this soon. That is wonderful."

Fredrick went into the room and laid down on the bed to rest and wait for his brothers to return so he could tell them about the exciting news. Jeff would be pleased he knew.

Fredrick lay on the bed going over in his mind all that had taken place since he left home. He began to think of his mother and imagine that she had been helping him through all the tough spots. He knew she prayed for him and he wanted to believe that she prayed for him still. He wanted to believe that she had asked God to look down on him and guide him along the way.

He began to think of the perils of his trip to Spokane and the long walk from the freight yards to his brothers and now the Sacred Heart Sister who had helped him. It seemed to him as though he had been guided every step of the way. Even Mercy had been amazed at his good fortune. His mother had always said he lived a charmed life. *Thank you God for being near me,* he prayed.

37

Fredrick and Lisa meet

Lisa was now in high school. One of Mother's customers had a twelve year old girl who wanted a companion for her so Lisa was allowed to stay in town with them. She went to school at John Rogers High School with her favorite cousin Mindy.

*   *   *

Fredrick had been working at the hospital almost fifteen months. He had been invited to join his brothers in their room with just a little extra rent.

One day Tim, Mercy's brother-in-law, asked Fredrick if he wanted to ride across town to where Mercy's sister was working. "Jeff wants me to ask her if she will double date with me and my girl. Around here," Tim instructed, "if you want to take a girl out to somewhere other than an afternoon show, you have to have someone with you for a double date, or you have to have a chaperone.

"Well, I haven't seen anyone I would want to ask out yet," Fredrick told Tim.

"You haven't stuck your head outside your room enough to get aquatinted with any girls," Tim teased. "All you do is work and sleep."

"I have seen some girls alright, but they seem a little pushy," Fredrick said defensively. "Girls at home were a little shier and waited for a boy to make the first approach. Sure I would like to ride along and see a little more of the city."

"Well, come along," Tim said jerking his head toward the door. "She should be home from school by the time we get there."

"I thought you said she was working. How young is she anyhow?" Fredrick wanted to know.

"Oh, she's in high school. I don't know what grade. She works in a home as a companion to a young girl."

"Oh! Well she must not be that young then," Fredrick conceded. "I thought you were trying to get Jeff a young girl just because he's short," Fredrick explained.

"No, I wouldn't do that to Jeff. Besides, there are lots of short people around here. No one thinks anything about it."

Tim stopped in front of a very small yellow house. He got out and headed for the door. Fredrick followed him and stood quietly beside him, his blonde hair blowing in the breeze.

A tall extremely thin girl answered the door. Her bright vibrant blue eyes lit up when she saw her sister's brother-in-law Tim.

"Hi, Lisa," Tim greeted.

"Come in, Tim." Lisa said. She missed her sister and thought she might just be able to talk Tim into taking him over to see her.

"You remember Jeff. He rooms at your sister's house," Tim said getting right to the point. "I came to ask if you would go out with him this Friday. I need a couple to go with my girl and me on a date.

A strikingly handsome young man stood by Tim. He had blonde hair falling over his blue gray eyes. Lisa found his soft features and thick lips exciting. Dragging her eyes back to Tim, she inquired, "Do I know the friend you are wanting me to date?"

"You know him," Tim said. "He lives with his brother at your sister's place."

"Oh him," Lisa said a bit dissapointed. "He is a nice young man, but he is short. I am tall and my friends tease me all the time. What do you think they will say if they see me out with someone that can crawl under my arm?"

"I'm only asking you to go with us tonight. It will be fine you'll see. Jeff is a lot of fun."

"Oh! alright," Lisa relented only because she liked going dancing and it was a chance to get out and maybe see Mercy. "I'll go this one time."

After Tim had gotten Lisa to say yes he remembered to introduce Fredrick to her.

"Hello," she fumbled embarrassed by the way he made her feel.

Hearing Lisa say she would not go out with Jeff again after this one date and feeling he would not be intruding on his brother Fredrick asked, "How about going out with me next Saturday night?"

"Yes," Lisa smiled. "I will be free."

Lisa looked at Tim for approval and found him nodding his head so she agreed to go with Fredrick though she did not remember his name since she had been so flustered when they were introduced.

Getting back in the car with Tim, Fredrick asked, "What about you, Tim?" Fredrick asked turning to Tim. "Can we count on you to double date again?"

"Sure," answered Tim. "We will have to get Jeff another girl since he is part owner of the car."

Lisa went back in the house. Everyone was gone she was there alone. Joan and her daughter were out shopping and her husband had not come home from work yet. Lisa was beginning to worry she had not paid attention to the name of the boy with Tim. The rule of the house was that she had to introduce Joan to anyone she was to date.

Lisa was upset with herself for not being more attentive. She had not expected this handsome young man to ask her for a date. Her biggest concern at that moment, however was how to handle the problem of dating Jeff. He was such a nice fellow and she didn't want to hurt his feelings. But she was self-conscious of her height. And since she was so thin it made her height all the more noticeable.

Lisa spent a frustrating week trying to remember Tim's friend's name. She should have asked Jeff she thought but then she didn't want Jeff to wonder why she was asking about some-one else on their date.

How could she introduce him to Joan. She stewed and won-dered what to do.

Finally Friday night came. Lisa resigned herself to the pros-pect of not getting to go out with this exquisitely handsome man because she was too embarrassed to admit she didn't re-member his name.

Joan came in about four and informed Lisa that the family would be out as soon as her husband got home from work. "You lock up when you go out with your sister's brother-in-law," she said.

Whew. She thinks I have a date with Tim. She won't be here to find out it isn't true. Lisa thought guiltily.

The car pulled up just after Joan left. Fredrick got out and came to the door to escort Lisa to the car.

Lisa spent a bad time for the first part of the evening. Since she hadn't remembered his name, and no one in the car had occasion to call by his name, she felt uncomfortable talking to him. Finally, about halfway through the nigh, Jeff turned around and said, "Fredrick, you can have a little part of the car too if you help pay for it."

Lisa sat back and ran his name through her mind. Fredrick, Fredrick, Fredrick. What a nice name.

In the meantime, Fredrick was worried that Lisa didn't like him. She was quieter than he had remembered when they met last week.

Lisa went to visit her sister's on Sunday. As they stood looking out the upstairs window to the parking lot below, Lisa noticed Fredrick. She thought him very handsome young man with his blonde hair blowing in the wind. He brought his hand up to smooth back the stray hair. There was a light sprinkle so it stayed back from the damp-ness. Lisa watching Fredrick from the window, "He's very nice," she commented turning around to face her sister.

"Yes, he is," Mercy said. "A lot quieter than his brothers Chris and Jeff. Chris is always laying the law down to him. But he doesn't argue with him."

"Brothers!" Lisa exclaimed. "Tim didn't tell me he was Jeff's brother. That's embarrassing. I told Tim I wouldn't go out with Jeff again the night he came after me to make a double date. Fredrick was with him. He didn't tell me they were brothers. Oh, I am so embarrassed," Lisa said putting her face in her hands. "I told Tim I wouldn't go out again because Jeff is so short. That's when Fredrick asked me to go out with him. I hope they didn't tell Jeff."

Mercy was laughing. The more Lisa talked, the harder she laughed.

Lisa's conversation was tumbling out, she was repeating herself in her humiliation. "When Tim came to ask me to go with Jeff, he brought Fredrick along. I was so busy thinking about my height compared to Jeff's and the handsome man at my door that I forgot to pay attention to his name when Tim introduced us."

"Stop laughing Mercy, I had a really bad week trying to figure out how I would get Joan to let me go since I couldn't introduce her to him without a name. I am sure Fredrick thinks I am not a very good date because I spent the first half of the evening not talking to him."

Lisa left the front way trying to keep from running into Fredrick or Jeff as she made her way to the bus stop that would take her back to where she lived. Lisa tried to figure out in her mind if this new discovery would be a problem. She really liked Fredrick and didn't want to give up seeing him if he asked her out again. But how would she handle the Jeff problem. She didn't want Jeff's feelings hurt. Jeff had been with them on their date and he had been with another girl. He didn't seem like he was upset with her, maybe no one had repeated what she had said about his height.

It was Lisa's birthday. Joan planned a party. She loved to create interest and have fun so she invited the two young men who had dated Lisa, Fredrick and Lisa's girl friend's brother. The evening was tense for Lisa, but Joan was having fun. She decided the party needed to get moving in a way to provide competition between the two young men. "Hey, why don't we play post office," she decided. This game meant the boy had to take a girl into an adjoining room and put a stamp on her which in reality was a kiss.

Lisa ended up in the other room with her girl friend's brother. The evening came to an end, but Fredrick was not to be out-smarted by the other young man who seemed to be taken with Lisa. At the door saying goodbye he asked Lisa for another date.

Fredrick left in high spirits because she had agreed to go to an early afternoon show the following weekend. This mean they could go alone.

When it came time for their date, Fredrick found that his part of the partnership in the car was only the money he paid. He very seldom got any use of it unless he was on a double or triple date with the other two owners. This afternoon meant Lisa and he would have to walk to the show. At least Lisa was staying with her sister today so he didn't have to go all the way over to where she worked to pick her up. If that had been the case they would have had to take the bus, and then he would not have had enough money for the show.

Chris decided to be helpful to Fredrick so he got him credit in a store where he could buy clothes and a bicycle telling him he would be able to get to work easier. The next week Chris con-vinced Fredrick to pay part of the money on a two door sport looking car. Fredrick was so proud to be part owner in the car with Chris as well as the car with Jim and Jeff.

The following week he had a date with Lisa so he went to Chris, told him he would like his turn at using the car.

Chris told Fredrick he wouldn't be able to use the car this week because he already had plans and was using it. Fredrick was good natured about it and gave in but was disappointed because he couldn't take his girl in the car and once again they would have to walk.

The next week came and Chris again informed Fredrick he couldn't use the car. Fredrick was disturbed and in his quiet man-ner pointed out that his whole pay check was going for the two cars that he never got to use, the clothes which Chris always wore, the bicycle which Chris used all the time. Not only that but Chris had over bought on Frederick's name and left him to pay the bill.

Fredrick was so indebted that he had to go to a credit councilor to pay off his debts.

Chris being the same selfish boy he always had been did not show any guilt for what he had done. The last straw was when Chris was called up to the army, and instead of leaving the car Fredrick had been paying on, he drove it back to North Dakota and gave it to his dad who knew nothing about Fredrick owning part of the car since Chris had the title in his name.

Fredrick suffered the unfair problems he was left with in silence. He knew this was just the way Chris was and there was no changing him. Some day he knew Chris would get what was coming to him, but it wasn't going to be at the hands of his own brother.

38

So do you want the job?

It was early June. Lisa was almost out of school for the summer.

One day Lisa was reading the help wanted ads and ran across an ad for couple to work on a big farm. Across town Fredrick had seen the same ad.

Sunday afternoon, Fredrick showed up where Lisa lived. "I'd like you to take a ride with me."

She agreed and they headed out to the farming country. On the way he told her about the ad in the newspaper and she said she had seen it too. When they arrived Lisa sat in the car while Fredrick went in to see the farmer. The man was a bachelor and was getting old. He needed help with the farm chores and a women to help cook and clean.

Fredrick came back to the car in a short while later. As he stood there by the window of the car looking down at her with his blond unruly hair blowing into his eyes, She felt he was the most wonderful person she had ever known. She knew she loved him. Suddenly he reached in and took her hand. "Well, do you want the Job?" Fredrick asked abruptly.

She knew that people would say they were both too young, but they had been earning most of their own money for sometime.

Lisa smiled up at him. "This is strangest proposal I have ever heard about," she said her bright blue eyes snapping."

When she answered him with an ecstatic YES, Fredrick leaned down and gave her a shy kiss, then he turned and went back into the house to tell the farmer he would be back to work the next week.

As they drove back to Spokane, they began to plan how they would be able to get married this weekend and be able to work the next week as scheduled.

"Joan will be a witness for me. She likes you. I think Phil will sign for me. He and Annie live at the edge of Cour D Alene near Post Falls, Idaho," Lisa offered.

Getting back in town, Fredrick dropped Lisa off at her place. Breathlessly, she ran in to ask Joan if she would help her. She was so excited she could hardly explain what she was trying to tell her.

Joan had a mild stutter which she had managed to control by not speaking until she gathered her thoughts but it caused her to open her mouth several times before a sound was made especially when something excited her. "Wha wha what are you trying to say?" asked Joan.

"Please, Joan." Lisa begged. "Will you go to Idaho with Fredrick and me. We want to get married, but I need your help. If I can get my brother Phil to sign for us and you will be a witness, we can get married. And we already have a job on a farm, but we have to be married because it's for a couple." Lisa finally slowed down and waited for Joan to talk.

"Well I . . . ah . . . don't know. You are both so young. Have you asked your parents?" Joan quizzed.

"No!" Lisa cried shaking her head frantically and pacing. "I can't do that." Lisa sat down and put her head in her hands. "Oh Joan, they won't give me permission." Then Lisa looked at Joan, "But Phil can sign if he will and they will go along with it. He ran off and married as young as Fredrick. I have been working since I was twelve. And you know," she went on with a little more confidence, "they don't have money to buy clothes and food. I am sure it will be alright as long as we have a job."

Joan finally wore down and agreed to go along, but she would only be a witness if Phil would agree to sign.

Sunday morning came and to Lisa's dismay her parents picked this day to visit her. She loved to have her parents visit, but today was just not a good time. Lisa's parents spent about an hour visiting. The entire time Lisa felt uneasy. Finally they said they were picking up Grandpa and Grandma for church so Lisa bid them goodbye with a big hug and kiss. "Whew!!! Lisa sigh. "I thought they were going to spend the whole day and we would not get to go."

Fredrick arrived in an old Model A he had just bought. Joan and Lisa got in and they headed to Post Falls to see about Phil. Fredrick stopped in front of a small house set back amongst some green bushes that hid the fact the house was not only small but quite old. Lisa got out and swiftly ran to the door while Joan and Fredrick were still getting out. Lisa wanted to get in the house first to convince her brother of her need before the rest got inside. "Phil. Phil." she called as her sister-in-law rounded the corner. "I need Phil to help me," she said to Annie as Phil came in the room.

"Whoa!" Phil said taking her shoulder to slow her down. "What's up ?"

"I have a job, but it takes a couple. Fredrick and I need to be married and I need you to be a witness. Joan said she would if you would. You got married when you were Frederick's age," Lisa baited, "So I need you to help me now."

"Well, now what's the job?" Phil asked.

By this time Fredrick and Joan were in the house. Annie was getting everyone coffee and trying to slow things down.

"It's working on a farm in Ritzville for an elderly man," Fredrick put in. "The man needs help in the field and Lisa will do the house chores."

"Have you given this much thought?" Phil directed the question to Fredrick.

"Yes, we had been looking for a job so we could get married and this gives room and board as well."

"Well then, if you plan on doing it an how, I guess we had better get it done. Jobs aren't easy to come by now a days," Phil stood up and telling his wife he would be back soon and walked out to his car.

Fredrick, Lisa and Joan followed behind Phil's car to the Judge's office just a few miles from their house. Lisa got out cold sweat formed in the palms of her hands. She kept thinking that her parents would somehow find out and appear any minute.

The Judge opened the door, "Who is the couple to marry?"

Lisa and Fredrick stepped forward and acknowledged they were the couple.

"Do you have eleven dollars?" the Judge asked.

Lisa handed him the money thinking she was glad she was good at saving money.

The judge looked at them sternly, "How old are you?

Lisa and Fredrick had already decided to say they were older than they needed to be so there would be no need to prove it.

Lisa spoke up and said, "I am nineteen."

Fredrick followed with, "I'm twenty-two."

The old Judge asked the witnesses to step forward and witness to this and then he began the marriage vows. Lisa went through hers without a hitch. When it came time for Fredrick, Lisa had to punch him gently on the back to move him along to finish the vows. Whether Fredrick got cold feet or just forgot what he was suppose to say the little nudge got him to finish.

Fredrick and Lisa thanked Phil. Lisa kissed her brother and told him where they would be. "We are going to tell Mom and Dad what we have done," she said as they left Phil at his house.

They reached Joan's place and thanked her and let her out before heading for the farm of Lisa's parents.

The old dog came out to greet Lisa. He had been her constant companion as she was growing up and on some occasions had saved her life. She would always remember the time he pulled her from the river so she didn't drown. Lisa reached down and gave the old dog a hug and as she headed to the house the dog followed at her heels separating Fredrick from her by nudging his heel.

Fredrick came in and gave a cheerful hello to Lisa's mother. Her mother liked him. When he came with Lisa to visit, he would ask her to play the organ. He and Lisa would sing the songs from the hymnal. Today he wasn't sure she would be so pleased to see him. "Mom," he said, "Lisa and I just got married."

Mother looked up in shock, "Well, I'll just have to have it annulled," she said.

"But Mother," Fredrick said standing before her in a very quite but determined voice. "I think I can get another eleven dollars to remarry before you can get seventy five dollars to annul it."

Mother became quiet and Father came in from the sitting room. "Did you two say you got married?" Father spoke up.

"Yes," Fredrick answered. "This afternoon."

"Well," said Father. "I wish you had waited a couple of years, but it's done now. Mother," he said, "Guess we just have to make the best of it." He started to head back in the sitting room then turned, "By the way, do you realize it's Father's Day." He didn't act hurt. He knew, this daughter of his loved him.

"Well, no," Lisa said in her old impish manner going over to hug him, "but guess, you got another son."

Lisa's father always enjoyed this very impish-natured child. He turned his back so she wouldn't see his grin.

They planned to spend the night with Lisa's parents before going out to the farm in the morning. Lisa's mother other took steps to see to it that her girl would know what she needed to do as a wife. Mother ordered Lisa to get the wash tub in and prepare it for Frederick's bath. After Lisa got the tub and filled it with the water from the boiler on the stove, she got out the soap, wash rag, and towel. She laid everything by the tub then called Fredrick in to take his bath while she went into the front room intending to sit awhile as he took his bath.

"Lisa," Mother said, "as a wife you have to go in and wash Frederick's back and make sure his clothes are there and laid out ready for him to dress, and then clean up the area after he dumps the water."

"Oh!" exclaimed Lisa, she had never in her life been allowed in the room while the men bathed even by accident. "Are you sure he wants me to do that?" she questioned.

Mother sternly headed her to the kitchen where Fredrick was preparing to take a bath, "Yes, this is a wife's duty and tonight you will find another duty as a wife."

Lisa timidly entered the kitchen. "Fredrick," she called out, "Mother said I must come help you take a bath. It is my duty. If you don't want me to," she said hopefully, "I will go back out."

Fredrick looked up from where he stood in his underclothes, "Come Lisa and I will tell you what she thinks is your duty."

Lisa moved to his side with her head turned so she would not see his stripped down form, "Yes Fredrick," she said mortified for her parents to be witness to this scene.

"What did your mother tell you to do?" Fredrick asked.

"Mother said a wife's duties are to be sure your bath water is the right temperature and to wash your back, and lay out your clean clothes, and clean up after you." Lisa looked up at Fredrick with a questioning deep-blue eyes, eyes that at this moment were almost black, a sign fear.

Fredrick took her in his arms, "Don't fret honey. It's alright. As soon as you wash my back, you will feel more comfortable. Your mother is doing this to help you feel a little less fearful of tonight when we go to bed together. Your mother is right. You need to be less afraid of being undressed before me and seeing me undressed. We will have to become acquainted with each other when we go to our job tomorrow. The old man probably thinks we have been married a long time."

Lisa helped her mother get dinner. She had made sure to have Lisa's favorite baked squash, baked potatoes and creamed new potatoes with garden fresh peas and cream sauce in the potatoes. For dessert Mother made apple cream pie. Mother knew Lisa would have very little of this for a long time.

As dinner came to an end, Lisa cleared the table and brought the plates and the pie heaped with homemade whipped cream. "Fredrick, you will love Mother's apple cream pie. No one else ever makes it." The pie was made with crisp tart apples diced and put into her delicious custard pudding, then she topped it with rich whip cream.

"I will have a small piece," Fredrick smiled at Mother. "I seldom eat rich desert." Father sat at the end of the table taking it all in and enjoying how Mother's attitude had changed since afternoon when the kids had first came home.

After the dishes were washed, Lisa went out to help feed the chickens and the pigs, as well as her old dog Pal. She was taking extra time doing the few chores of this small farm all the while wondering what her mother had meant when she said she had other duties tonight as a wife. Lisa knew from girl friends the word sex, though it had not been discussed openly. Lisa had only heard women at the ladies club whispering . She wondered if there was something else no one had bothered to tell her. Fredrick spent the next hour teaching what her wifely duties were and the meaning of the mysterious word sex.

Finally Mother said, "We all have to be up early. I think we need to get to bed. You two have to be on your way to the job and we have to about the chores. I'll pack you a lunch to take in the morning."

Lisa quickly dressed in her long flannel gown and slid into the bed she and Mercy had shared. Fredrick crawled in beside her dressed in his shorts and a undershirt. His warm body moved close to her. Giving her a soft kiss on the mouth, he said goodnight, and putting his arm over her as though to protect her, soon was fast asleep.

Lisa lay still for a long time wondering what was suppose to happen that she had not been told about. Finally she fell asleep.

Mother and Father were already up when Lisa woke. She quickly slid out of bed and dress. She hurried out to help with breakfast and the morning chores.

Fredrick soon joined them in the kitchen where Mother had already fixed him a cup of coffee. "Come, Fredrick. Sit down and have some coffee. Breakfast will be ready soon," Mother coaxed. "The chores are done and Dad will be in soon."

There old car was loaded with all the things they owned which wasn't much. As they prepared to get in their car ready to head out on life's new experience, Father came over to give Lisa a hug. In the meantime Mother was hugging Fredrick. She seemed pleased to turn over her baby daughter to this young man who appeared to be quite a gentleman.

39

A new family begins

Fredrick and Lisa arrived at the big farm outside of Ritzvile, Washington. This was a huge area for wheat farms. Each farmer had many acres, which meant most houses were far apart. As luck would have it for this very young girl, a family lived close to the old man and this is where they picked up their mail. Lisa made friends right away and found she was not too lonely.

Lisa got up the first morning to find the house was in a sad state. It was much in need of cleaning. The bedding needed washing. The windows needed cleaning. The cupboards, the floors, the furniture . . . It was a good thing she was young and had energy she thought. It seemed the old man had bought new sheets and blankets, but the clean had been put on top of the dirty so when she began to take the sheets off to wash them she found about four layers of sheets. Lisa was not a stranger to the job of heating water to put in a wash tub and the need to wash by hand on a washboard.

She spent the morning scrubbing the sheets and hanging them on the line to dry. As she went around cleaning, she found the house was infested with bed bugs. Remembering Mother had sprayed the baseboards with a squirt can of what she thought was gas she went about getting rid of the bugs. She put a squirt of gas over the bed springs as well as the base boards. Soon she could see the bugs dropping from the ceiling and coming out from the baseboards and the beds. She swept them up and scrubbed the floors with the heavy lye soap that she had found in the cupboard.

Lisa washed the windows inside and out with vinegar. It is a good thing it was summer and Lisa had all the doors and windows open as she spread the gas around to get rid of the bed bugs or perhaps the place would have blown up or at least caught on fire.

By night the wind had blown all the fumes out and the bugs seemed to be under control, but it is probably a good thing the old man did not smoke or there might have been enough left to set it on fire. When Lisa visited her parents later, she found that she had used the wrong thing to get rid of the bugs. Mother had used kerosene in the manner Lisa had used gas.

The next morning Lisa made pancakes for breakfast, and as her mother had done, she made dollar pancakes so her young husband was required to take several in order to get enough to eat. "Why don't you take them all," the old gent said thinking to say it under his breath Fredrick heard but did not let on that he had .

Fredrick and the old man took turns with a team of four horses spring toothing a large field. While Fredrick made his round, the old gent rested under a shade tree. It took the old man longer to make his round. Fredrick used his time while the old man made his round to run to the house to help Lisa make a batch of bread. Fredrick had been the one left to make bread when his mother had died so he was good at it. Lisa had not been allowed to practice with the flour making bread, money for flour was scarce at her home so Mother had not dared waste the flour teaching. Each time Fredrick was relieved he would run back and help Lisa with the next step of bread making. While Fredrick was making a round Lisa put the bread in the oven to bake before it had risen the last time and that night Fredrick and Lisa had a bread burying ceremony at midnight.

The next day Fredrick once again helped Lisa to make the bread, but this time he made sure she understood that the bread had to double in the pan before being put in the oven. This batch of bread came out so good Fredrick came in and gave her a big hug and told her how great a job she had done.

The week end came and Fredrick and Lisa drove into Spokane

and went to see Joan. Fredrick asked Joan if it was possible for her to come and stay with them for a couple of weeks. The harvest crew would be there, and he was afraid Lisa would not be able to know how to cook that much food. He knew he would not be able to help her since he would be stuck in the field.

Joan agreed. The first day there she taught Lisa how to kill a chicken, dress it and fry it for dinner . Lisa had a bad time trying to kill the chicken. She didn't even like it when her cat killed mice when she was little at home.

"Lisa," called Joan, "you are teasing the chicken to death. Don't run after it," she said watching her chase the chicken around the yard. "It will be too tough to eat." Finally Joan helped her catch it and chopped off its head. Lisa knew how to scald it and take the feathers off so she finished the job.

It finally came the day for the harvest crew to come. Joan had worked hard to help Lisa know the things she had not known, like killing the chickens, and how much food needed to be cooked for that many people. Lisa knew how to cook. Joan knew this because when Lisa had first come to stay with them, she got up and prepared a farmer's breakfast every morning until Joan had made her quit because they were all gaining too much weight.

When Joan helped Lisa with the washing, she taught her how to tie the sheets to the line, then twisting them so they got the water out without hurting her wrist as it had before when she was wringing them.

Finally the harvest was done and Joan was taken back home. Lisa hated to see her go. It was lonely out here, but she kept herself busy fixing the house up. Lisa didn't have much money and the old Gent was tight with his money so Lisa got crepe paper and made curtains for the windows. A special angel must have looked out for Fredrick and Lisa because Lisa had surely made many opportunities to have a fire in the house.

As was stated before the old Gent was tight with his money and especially when it came to buying food to cook. He bought the staples like flour and lard but rarely any meat. Since Fredrick was used to eating meat at home and at the hospital, he decided to go out at night and get Jack rabbits.

This particular night the moon was out bright and though Lisa really didn't know much about driving Fredrick showed her enough to be able to drive around the fields that had been harvested while he sat on the hood of the car and shot the rabbits as the car scared them out from the stubble. This meant they had fried rabbit every Sunday for dinner, along with fresh homemade bread which Lisa had become very good at making. The neighbors had given them some vegetables when she went to get the mail.

One day Lisa took the Model A to the neighbors to get the mail. Fredrick had started it for her and left the gate open for her to go through as he went to the field. Lisa stopped at the farm house and got out going inside to pick up the mail. She noticed as she got out of the car that the farmer had reached in for some-thing, but she didn't wait to see what. Getting back in the car with the mail, she drove down the lane heading for home.

Someone had closed the gate after she left for the neighbors. She parked a good distance from the gate so she could leave room to open the gate. She got out of the car and headed for the gate. Looking up, she saw Fredrick running swiftly toward her, but it was too late, the car chugged into the closed gate. Fredrick had not told her she needed to take the car out of gear.

Lisa had never driven before except to get rabbits. Then Fredrick had been in control of starting and stopping the car. That night, working together, they repaired the gate.

The next week when Lisa went to get the mail, the farmer took her aside. "You are out getting Jack rabbits at night."

Lisa looked at him with fright in her eyes thinking they were doing something wrong but answered him with a yes anyway.

"Don't look so frightened." he said. "It's alright, except at this time of year they can become diseased. When you dress them down, if they have bubbles under the skin don't eat them."

It was getting late in the summer and the old Gent had still not paid them any wages yet. Fredrick went to him to ask for his pay, but the old Gent put him off saying he needed to get his money from the harvest first.

That weekend Lisa and Fredrick went to Spokane to see Joan. They told her about not getting paid and asked her what to do.

Joan road back with them. Sitting the old Gent down she said, "You will have to pay the kids now because they have to leave the job. Lisa is expecting a baby and will not be able to keep up with the work."

The old Gent fidgeted and argued about needing. Joan argued even harder. Finally he relented and gave Fredrick his pay.

The old gent stood watching them drive down the long lane and through the gate, holding tight to the ring of rope that held up his pants and looking as though he hated to see them go. Lisa felt a bit sad watching him just standing their, but they could not continue to work for him when they could not get their pay.

Fredrick was again in need of a job. He went to a place that sells jobs and paid them for a job on a dairy farm. There was a cabin to live in and all the milk you could drink. They had been on the job for about two weeks when the Lady who had hired him said the man whose place he took was on vacation and would be back next week. He was only on vacation. Fredrick was upset with her as well as the one who had sold him the job because they had not told him the job was only a vacation replacement, and they had charged him a big price for it. The money he earned barely covered the job finding fee.

Fredrick went back to Spokane and got a job with the St. Luke's Hospital as a vegetable man. He was responsible for preparing all the vegetables and cleaning chickens for the hospital meals for all the patients.

Fredrick and Lisa now lived in a house that had been made into two apartments on the main floor. Lisa's brother Phil and Audrey his wife and their son lived in one of the apartments. Lisa and Fredrick rented the three adjoining rooms. If they opened the doors between the two apartments in the lower half of the house it made it look bigger.

The landlady's daughter lived in the upstairs apartment. The heating and cooking was wood which cost quite a bit. One day Fredrick and Lisa came home from grocery shopping. Since he was especially hungry and wanted dinner in a hurry, Fredrick built a heavy fire.

Suddenly the landlady burst through the door as if no one paid rent for that part of the house. "Put that fire out instantly," she raged.

Fredrick who rarely showed his anger calmly stated, "That will be quite impossible Ma'am."

"Well the pipes in that stove will blow up and you will be paying for it," she bellowed.

Frederick's comment was, "You can't get blood out of a turnip."

"I can get beet juice out of a dead beat," She screeched.

"Well lady," Fredrick said moving her gradually toward the door by herding her like a collie dog might move a cow using only his presence and his nearness. "What are you doing in here anyway?"

The landlady continued screaming at Fredrick in an excitable tone. "The water has been turned off while we make adjustments to the water pipes in the stove, and it is still off."

"Well lady, if you needed to repair pipes in this stove, Why didn't you wait until we came home or stand by our door and let us know that we couldn't start a fire. The pipes looked perfectly alright to me."

"The water is still off because the pipes are still being connected," the landlady gushed.

"It's a mystery to me what other pipes might need to be fixed that the water should still be turned off. They are connected here in the stove, or I would have noticed before building a fire. These are the only pipes in the building that I know of."

"Guess you will just have to turn the water on because I am hungry and need to cook my dinner," he said flatly closing the door on her.

The landlady stomped away and apparently had her husband take care of the problem since she did not return that night.

The next day when Lisa and Annie prepared to wash clothes, they found that the hot water seemed to be running low. To their dismay the apartment upstairs had been added and the only stove heating it was Fredrick and Lisa's cook stove which meant they had to build the fire up again if they were to have any hot water.

Phil worked at the same hospital as Fredrick. They worked the same hours and walked home together using the train trestle to cut off many miles. When the boys got home and discovered the water was too cold for a bath Phil asked. "What have you girls been doing all day to use up the hot water?"

"We didn't use it," Lisa defended. "The landlady's daughter moved in upstairs and has used the hot water all day."

"You mean they hooked an apartment upstairs onto our pipes?" Phil quizzed standing up and heading for the door, "Come on, Fredrick. We need to settle this problem right now."

Phil, his 6 foot three frame headed for the landlord's house with Fredrick right behind.

Knocking on the door, her husband answered. "What's the idea of adding that apartment upstairs without telling us? And what's the idea of connecting their pipes to my sister and her husband's pipes to heat their water? They have used all the hot water," Phil growled hands on hips, eyebrows narrowed, body leaning forward almost into the landlord.

"Well, that is the way it has always been. Their apartment has always heated the water for yours," the landlord explained.

Fredrick cut in, "I didn't mind heating water for Phil. He's family. But I am not going to heat water for someone else who uses it all and leaves none for us."

"Well, that is the way its going to be," the landlady said smugly coming in during the discussion.

"I guess if that's the way it has to be okay, but we will not buy the wood to do it," Fredrick said turning to go.

"Come back here," the landlady called, "Just what do you mean you won't buy the wood? How do you expect to heat your water?"

"Guess we won't," Fredrick shot back over his shoulder as he kept walking leaving Phil to finish arguing with her.

"Well, you had better figure out how I am going to get hot water or plan on getting less rent," Phil ordered as he too walked back home.

The next day the girls got up early. After they fixed breakfast, they drew all the hot water off and put it in their two wash tubs and as the water reheated they took their baths and then let the fire go out.

When the two boys returned from work the next afternoon the landlord motioned them over to his place. "My daughter tells me there was no hot water today. Didn't your sister cook breakfast today?"

"We eat at the hospital," Fredrick interjected. "Lisa doesn't eat much so perhaps the heater in the front room was enough for her today. We haven't been in the house so I have no idea what she did. But I told you yesterday that I have no extra money to heat everybody's water."

Phil cut in, "If I go in and find out that my wife and child had no hot water today, you can plan on less rent."

"Well," said the landlord, "Perhaps I can buy a cord of wood to help heat the water."

Now Fredrick saw a way to make a little extra money. He had been getting wood from the lumber yard just for removing it. He had to put it in the backseat of his Model A but it was free so he didn't mind the labor.

"I already have obtained the right wood to fit the stove, and I don't intend to split a whole bunch of other wood," he informed. "So you can pay me for two cords of wood. That should take us through about two months, then we can refigure."

"I guess that will have to do young man."

Fredrick was pleased. The two cords of wood would give him a half month's rent, and the landlord was not out any cash because he wouldn't have to order a regular cord of wood.

*   *   *

When Phil and Annie moved to a logging camp in Idaho. Lisa and Fredrick didn't want to stay in the shared house. They moved to an apartment with one room and a little kitchenette. It had a twin bed designed for a bachelor. It was all they could afford at the time, but it was enough. The apartment was in a big brick faced building with about sixteen steps to the entrance.

Lisa was nearing time for her delivery. She began trying to sew the little gowns the baby would need. Lisa had no idea how big the baby would be so she decided to make gowns that would fit her doll.

Lisa's mother had a cousin who lived a short distance from where they lived. She was comfortable to be with and Lisa visited her often. As children growing up, this cousin had visited them on the farm regularly. They all called her Aunt Mabel. One day Aunt Mabel was visiting her. She looked at the pitiful sight of Lisa's attempt at making the baby clothes. Saying nothing, she went home and made gowns that would fit a baby.

Lisa had been sick in bed several days. Since her paralysis as a child, she often ached so she paid no attention to the pains that ran from her back to her legs.

Fredrick came in from work and found Lisa panting and moaning in pain. "Do you want to go to the hospital? he asked.

"No," Lisa said. "I think my rheumatism is flaring up again. I have been sick for several days."

Fredrick was not comfortable with this but said nothing to her. He ran to the landlord's to borrow a phone and call Aunt Mabel.

"I think you had better not take any chances," said Mabel. "Take her to the hospital right now. If she is not having labor pains, they will send her home. But after seeing her last week, my bet is she is in labor and just doesn't know it."

It was eleven thirty at night when Fredrick convinced Lisa to dress and go to the hospital. As soon as the nurse saw her, she put her in a wheelchair wasted no time getting her into a room and prepared. Fredrick decided they must think she is in labor when they showed him the way to the waiting room for fathers.

Lisa's back and legs hurt as bad as they had when she was a little girl. Lisa wished her mother was here giving her hot salt baths like she did when she was paralyzed. It always eased the pain in her legs.

The nurse finished the preparation and Lisa found herself on a hard gurney being wheeled down the hall. She was taken into a brightly lit room.

Since she had been sick with congestion in her lungs, the doctor told the nurse, "We must use gas not either or she will have trouble." The doctor instructed the nurse to give her a small amount of gas and then he began to move his hand over her tummy. "Physician birth," the doctor commented to the nurse and just like that Lisa's head began to ring. Then she was gone into a deep black gully. First someone seemed to be screaming and then there was quite.

Lisa woke in a room with white walls all around her. She was bound tightly through the middle of her abdomen. Fredrick sat in a chair beside the bed holding her hand. "Hi honey," he leaned over and gave her a kiss, "We have a darling little girl."

"When can I see her?" Lisa asked excitedly.

"The doctor said that you are not well. They will pump your milk to feed her, but she has to stay in the nursery until you go home so she won't get sick."

Lisa remained in the hospital ten days with a tight binding around her middle. She had been cut and sewn up so she was very uncomfortable. Since her paralysis, Lisa had not stayed in bed more that three or four hours at a time. She always had this fear that one day she would not be able to get up. The ten days dragged by. Lisa wanted to see her baby. Her sister came to visit and said baby had red hair. Someone else said she had black hair. Lisa began to fret because she realized she would never know what her little girl looked like when she was first born.

Finally, Lisa and the baby were released from the hospital. Lisa was so happy to hold her little girl. She could hardly wait to show her off so instead of going home, they stopped by her sister Mercy's before heading home to their small apartment.

Fredrick parked the car and came around to open the door for Lisa and helped her out with the baby. Lisa was terribly weak having been in bed so long, and the sickness before the baby had taken its toll. Fredrick reached out and picked up his new daughter. He cooed and smiled at her and then held her in one arm while he used the other to help Lisa up the steps.

He helped her into the small apartment at the head of the stairs and laid her down on the bed. Then he lay the baby in the buggy they had bought from Lisa's Uncle Gene.

Lisa was so exhausted she fell fast asleep instantly. When she woke after several hours, she sat up in bed rubbing her eyes trying to get her mind straightened out as to where she was.

"Hi Sleepyhead. Your awake," Fredrick teased coming over and sitting down beside her. "I think the baby will be hungry when she wakes. I have already changed her, but I didn't have anyway to feed her." Lisa found that Fredrick had taken care of the baby, changing her little cloth diapers and tucking her back in the buggy. Her little girl was fast asleep.

"Oh I'm so sorry. I didn't mean to fall asleep. Thank you for being such a good daddy," Lisa praised putting her hand on Frederick's arm letting him know how impressed she was that he was so efficient.

Phil and Annie came in from Idaho to see the baby. It was apparent Annie was about to deliver her second baby. As Phil and Annie and their little boy were preparing to go back to Phil and Lisa's parent's farm, Annie bent over in intense pain.

"Phil," Annie called holding her stomach. "I think it is time to take me to the hospital. It looks like these cousins will be about a month apart. Maybe just seeing their baby got me in the mood. I think by morning we will have a new baby of our own."

It looked to Lisa as though Phil was going to follow in his parents' path and their two babies would be as close in age as he and Gus were.

The next day Fredrick and Lisa took their baby girl over for Mercy to watch so they could go see how Annie was doing. Arriving at the hospital, they met Phil in the hall who informed them that Annie had indeed delivered a son last night shortly after he had gotten her to the hospital.

Phil took Fredrick aside and said, "How would you like to come to Idaho? My boss needs someone else to help in the woods?"

"I haven't worked in the woods. What could I do to help?" Fredrick wondered. "I was raised as a farmer."

"I haven't seen much that you can't do so far. I think he can find a use for you. I believe anything he can show you, you can do it."

"That sounds good, but I would have to be able to find a place to live," Fredrick said looking at his foot moving it around in thought.

"No problem," his brother-in-law countered. "The boss is going to send a truck in to the lumber yard. "We can buy the lumber to build us each a cabin on the grounds where he is logging. He said he would take the money for the lumber out of our first pay check."

Little Jane was now three months old, and Phil's baby, little Dave, was two months old when Fredrick and Phil picked up the lumber to build their cabins. It was a bright early spring day when they took the load of lumber out to build their cabin.

Fredrick had gotten ten dollars worth of material and within a short period of time had their cabin built. It was a simple room big enough for a double bed, a crib, a small table and chairs set and area to cook in. Fredrick had made a hole in the shelf in the kitchen area to put a dish pan so it would look like a sink though it didn't function as one.

The cabin made Lisa feel like she was special. Fredrick was always doing nice things to try and make life easier and better like the time he hooked a wire to the car battery and ran it through the window to the head of the bed so they could have light.

Lisa and Annie enjoyed their crude little cabins. They washed clothes in the river and carried water from a spring to cook with it. It was nice waking up in the woods with animal noises and the birds chirping in the trees.

This morning as Lisa and Annie were washing clothes in the river. It was a cold brisk early spring day. The babies were in their buggies covered well against the cold and little Gary was sitting in the baby swing hung in a tree near by. Suddenly the girls heard a loud bang. Wondering what had gone wrong, they decided to gather the children and walk up the lane to where they had heard the noise.

They found the men in the cold water trying to push the logs that had broken loose when the bridge collapsed back to shore. Knowing the boys would be cold and wet, they went back to their cabins to build up the fires so they would get warm and be able to dry out. While they were building their fires, they heard a commotion and a great deal of men's excited fearful voices.

Lisa watched the babies while Annie went back to see what was taking place. She found that Fredrick had almost drowned being caught between a group of logs. Two of the other loggers jumped in to unbury him. When Phil appeared at the entrance ready to cross the bridge that was no longer there in a truck loaded with logs, he set the brakes and jumped into the water. He was a strong swimmer and made it easily over to Fredrick. He began pulling him to shore while the others pushed at the logs getting him free.

Getting Fredrick to the cabin Phil said, "What in the world were you doing in that cold water with those logs anyway?"

"The crew boss asked me if I could swim and when I said yes, he ordered me to help get the logs pushed to shore. I guess he thought I was used to the cold coming from North Dakota," answered Fredrick teeth chattering.

"I'm going over to see Harold, the owner, and let him know what the guy did to you. They've got bigger and older men that could have done that job." Taking all of his 6 foot 3 muscular frame, Phil stomped up to the main building where the owner lived. "What you trying to do. Kill my sister's husband?" Phil yelled as he entered unannounced.

Harold, a short balding man in his late thirties came out of another room, "What's your problem there, Phil? You seem pretty upset."

"You bet," Phil yelled. "I'm upset. Your crew boss had my brother-in-law in the river and almost drowned him."

"What do you mean he was in the river?" Harold inquired?

"The bridge went out before I got my load down. It's a good thing it went out before I got my truck down there. They didn't have it built very well anyway. It would have given way and we would have lost the load and the truck as well."

"Why didn't they bring the truck down with the winch it might have been slower but safer to cable and pull one log to shore at a time," Harold wondered aloud looking at Phil.

"I guess they thought the logs would get away if they didn't get at them immediately," explained Phil.

"Well there's no falls close by so they could be gotten even if they did float down river a ways. It's crazy to think a man's cold body in the water can fight a heavy log let alone a bunch of logs," Harold was getting more upset as he mulled over the thoughtless act of his crew boss. "I can't believe he would take a chance on a man's life like that."

The next day it began to rain. Lisa moved the baby bed and other things to keep them from getting wet. When Phil came over to visit that night, he saw the pans skattered all around the floor catching water. Laughing he said, "What did you put on the roof Fredrick. tar paper or roofing?"

"Tar paper," Fredrick said looking sheepishly at his brother-in-law.

"Guess you have learned another lesson, huh Fredrick?"

The rain kept up for several days and the men were not able to work. Since the logs were not being hauled, Harold had no money to pay the wages. He did have a charge account at the local grocery store though so they took their wages in beans.

Friedrick, however, was not fond of beans, so he put on warm clothese and went fishing. That night Lisa, Anne, Phil, and Fredrick had a dinner of fresh caught fish along with the beans.

Fredrick decided that, before the work got scarce and winter set in with this cabin not up to harsh weather, he had better find a job that would put more than beans in the pot. The next time he went to Spokane, he learned of a job at Eastern State hospital, a mental institution. Because of his record of good work in the two hospitals in town, he was hired immediately. Fredrick went back to Idaho and told his boss in the logging camp that he had another job. He was sent on his way without being reimbursed for the lumber he had bought or his back wages he had due.

Arriving back in Spokane, they went to Lisa's parents' farm. They were both able to pick fruit that was in season while Lisa's mother watched Jane. Lisa had picked the rotating crops as a young girl and was very fast at it. As a team they managed to earn enough money to pay rent on a house near their new job and have enough money left to buy groceries for baby and Lisa. Fredrick would eat at the hospital.

The two-story house they moved into was furnished. Lisa spent her days caring for Little Jane. She had conversations with her, asking her a question and then answer it for her. Soon Jane had mastered some of the words and would repeat.

Lisa made big pots of soup for her and the baby with lots of vegetables. She only had a meat bone for flavor because her food budget was slim. Some times the elderly couple next door invited them over for lunch. The elderly man always dressed so proper, as though he had been a business man before retiring. They loved to sit by little Jane, not yet ten months old, and watch her clean up her plate of food. They always had a well balanced meal, sometimes it was fried chicken, mashed potatoes, vegetables, and a desert.

Jane always ate her portion politely. She had to have a wet napkin near her which she used to keep herself and the area around her plate clean. This habit entertained the elderly couple, and they bragged to everyone they saw about her ability to eat by herself at such a young age.

From practice and necessity, Lisa learned to sew and made all of Jane's dresses out of clothes that had worn out. Taking just the part that was still good and sewing by hand, Lisa made dresses then added a bit of ribbon to make them pretty. The dresses didn't last long so Lisa would remove the ribbon saving it for another dress.

One of the hardest parts of Fredrick's job was to attend dances once a month and dance with the patients that were not mentally dangerous. The main problem he had at these dances was that some of the patients were in the hospital because their hormones were not right and they were oversexed. Fredrick was a shy, quite young man. These girls would often try to dance too close to him. He would have to hold them at arms length to keep them from crawling his frame.

The other problem he had was that even though his father played for dances, and Fredrick had attended many, he was not a skilled dancer. When he voiced this problem to Lisa, she was more than willing to teach him. Lisa loved to dance and was glad of the opportunity Fredrick's job had presented to her. She enticed him to take her dancing whenever she could using his job as her argument.

A young couple with twin girls lived on a farm a short distance from the hospital. They had a few cows as well as other animals. The fellow worked with Fredrick at the hospital and knew Fredrick had been raised on a farm in North Dakota. One day the fellow got so sick that he had to be admitted to the hospital.

He went to Fredrick and asked, "Would you please take your family and go stay on the farm. I need someone to help my wife with the chores until I am well. I can't pay you but I can buy all the groceries."

This sounded like a good idea to Fredrick. He knew Lisa and Jane were only eating soup because the kettle was on the stove when he left and still there when he came home. He had tasted it and knew it was tasty and perhaps even healthy, but he felt bad that she had so little to eat.

Fredrick agreed. They packed up to stay with their friends to help them out.

It was early December of 1941. Fredrick, Lisa and Jane had been with their friends about a month. Finally, Steven was sent home from the hospital to finish recovering.

It was Lisa's habit to get up early and get herself and Jane washed and dressed before breakfast. This morning she had made breakfast, bathed Jane and had her sitting in the high chair ready to eat. Steven came in followed by their twin girls and his wife. Fredrick, having finished up the chores, was washing up.

Steven looked at Jane in her chair, turning to his wife he said, "Look how nice Jane looks clean and dressed. Why can't our girls dress before they come to the table?" His wife did not answer him, but it was apparent she did not like what he had said.

Lisa felt bad that her friend had been made to feel inadequate. She tried to give her a reassuring look and started to make some small talk when the radio announcer cut, "Pearl Harbor has just been bombed by Japan."

They all sat glued to their chairs listening to the report. President Roosevelt came on and announced that war had been declared by the United State against Japan. The United States was at war.